The Menhattan Project

Victoria Flores & Leslie Wilson

with Lisa Bonnice

The Menhattan Project
Prism Two Publishing

ISBN-13: 978-0692272053
ISBN-10: 0692272054

"Love is like a fart.

If you have to force it, it's probably shit"

--Anonymous

.

CONTENTS

PROLOGUE

Am I out of control or just out of my clothes? Lust has always been my favorite of the deadly sins but at this moment, greed prevails. I'm afraid I'll never have enough of this ... enough of him.

The sheets still feel cool underneath me despite the heat coursing through my body. The warmth radiates outward from wherever his mouth is working—licking, sucking, teasing my flesh like each pore is filled with nectar. He circles my left nipple with his pink tongue while his hands move like independent entities to my right breast and between my legs. He pinches the skin at my upper inner thigh and I gasp at the beautiful pain. He covers my open mouth with his and I close my eyes, letting the warmth return like a flood. He's eager now, sliding down my body and spreading me apart. I watch his face disappear between my legs. I want to tell him to turn around, let me play, let me take him in my mouth and suck while my hands slide up and down the smooth, long length of him. The thought sends a gush of heat through me and I think yes, having this man's cock in my mouth while he treats my clit like a tiny, perfect bead of ice cream is exactly what I want. I part my lips and inhale to say just this, but when I try to speak the only sound that comes out is buzzing. Buzzing, loud and intrusive, like a swarm of bees or a dentist's drill.

Or an alarm.

I silence it with undue force and a loud sigh. My body is slow to come out of the dream and I wish I were one of those people who can just roll over and pick up where she left off. My subconscious has never been that cooperative.

I open my right eye to the sun peeking through the blinds. The light's peaceful beauty is quickly shattered by a throbbing headache pulsing through my whole brain.

Copious empty wine bottles, half-empty glasses and an overfilled ash tray litter every surface of my studio apartment. I smack my lips and clear my throat, desperate for water.

"What day is it?" I mumble, collapsing back onto my pillow.

"Thursday?"

I shoot up to a seated position with dizzying quickness and wince at the sudden rush. *Oh, right—him.* The events of the previous night slowly come back to me: the drinking, the flirting, the kissing … the sex. Oh, the sex!

It wasn't a dream, it was a memory.

I am momentarily tickled by a jingle for some unknown product composing itself in my brain: "When the man in your head is the man in your bed, pray you don't wake looking like the living dead!" A leave-in conditioning treatment, maybe? Or better yet, makeup you can sleep in …

"Last night was fun," he says.

"It was," I agree, racking my brains for this fine specimen's name. Resisting the urge to ask him what exactly happened between us, I do a private victory dance in my head for coming up with at least one answer on my own: Eric. His name is Eric, of that I am sure. He looks like a cross between JFK and Jon Hamm. *Whatever went down last night, it was absolutely worth it.* Even if this man gets out of my bed and waltzes out of my life, it was worth it. The more I look at him, the more gorgeous he becomes. Perfect white teeth, hazel eyes, and beckoning from a half-thrown-back Egyptian cotton sheet, perfectly chiseled abs.

Well done, you.

He leans in to kiss me gingerly on the lips and asks if he can shower. His scruffy morning stubble grazing my cheek sends a tingle through my whole body.

"Of course, go ahead. Towels are in the closet just before the bathroom."

He casually eases himself out of bed. My gaze seems magnetically connected to his impeccable ass. It is spectacular. This man is a masterpiece.

When I hear the water turn on I snuggle back underneath the covers and welcome a warm rush of heat across my cheeks as the events of last night begin to unfold.

I'm not usually one to go out on a Wednesday— or on weekdays in general, really—especially if I already have a date for Thursday, which I do. But a group of my girlfriends swore a new club opening would be amazing. Though attendance would mean traipsing all the way from my apartment in Chelsea to downtown Tribeca, they convinced me the trip would be worthwhile. When they promised free drinks and a chance to meet the club's new owner, I reluctantly agreed.

While I got dressed for the evening, I couldn't shake my mother's voice nagging in my head: "You never know who you'll meet, Vivian. You've gotta force yourself to go out even when you don't want to … those are the nights that end up being extraordinary."

Yeah, okay Mom. It must be easy to dole out romantic advice after three marriages and a constant stream of potential suitors just waiting to take up residence as Husband Number Four. Plus, she's never left Texas or even lived in a big city. It's a lot different here, and some of the things you learn out there simply don't apply here.

Though I've dated and enjoyed a heavy rotation of boyfriends since moving to New York City and dropping the excess weight, it's been a few years since any of those liaisons have turned serious. Staying single has been my choice—I've always been the one to break it off when a guy gets too clingy or things seem like they're headed for "The Talk".

Okay, maybe not *always*. Maybe just since a bad break-up a few years ago. Since then, I've been comfortable dating aspiring musician or artist types who like to spend time with a girl without getting too attached. They get what they want and so do I.

Besides, unlike my best friend Lauren—who swears the trouble with dating in New York is that the men here are "impossible"—I've always felt we NYC ladies hold the cards when it comes to relationships. We're career-driven, ambitious and independent. We know what it takes to get ahead in life and we're not afraid to go for it. For a lot of us, that means putting serious relationships on the back burner because it's impossible to concentrate on getting ahead if you're distracted. Lately, though … well, lately the singles scene has been feeling a little stale. I'm exhausted, to be honest. Last night, it was all I could do not to let that deep-down fatigue take over and stay home.

Seeing Eric across the club was like a shot of adrenaline straight into my veins.

My girls and I had clustered around a sliver of empty space at the bar. We had no trouble getting the tender's attention, and I stood with my back to the bar, elbows hooked on the edge. I like to scan a room when I arrive. Where are the danger zones I want to avoid (bachelorette parties, college students)? Where's the entrance to the VIP room? Where's the DJ and how crowded is the dance floor?

I was busy making my assessments when our eyes met—no, *locked*. I looked away, grateful for the low lighting that covered the blush I felt on my cheeks. When I pushed myself off the bar to turn around and order a much-needed cocktail, there he was.

"Hi."

"Hi, yourself."

"I couldn't help but notice you from across the room. Cheesy, right?"

"Right."

"Well it's true. I'm Eric."

"Vivian."

The next ninety minutes passed in a blur of vodka-Diet Cokes and easy flirtation. Over the loud beat of the music, I was able to hear him say that he was a model (of course he was—anyone that gorgeous would have to be) and photographer from Canada who had just come to New York after living and working in Europe for a few years.

"I love New York," he shouted over the din, "Europe was great, but it's good to be in a place where more people speak English! It's a lot easier to communicate."

"*Usted no habla español?*" I asked him, showing off my mother's native tongue.

He smiled, showing dimples so deep I could lose myself in them forever. "*Hablo un poco de español,* just enough to find the local *biblioteca* and to cuss someone out, but that's about it." Good thing I didn't even try to impress him with my father's native Italian.

He was probably the most exciting and exotic man I'd ever met, and I hung on every word. No playing hard to get here! I actually laughed out loud at the prospect of sleeping with a guy who must be used to taking his work home with him—I'm sure his bedposts are weak from all the notches he's carved into them. I envision his bed frame, once strong and sturdy but now mere toothpicks, crumbling into a heap after one too many nicks—but I couldn't help feeling incredibly flattered that he'd been so bold in his approach.

The room was filled with spectacular women, and he could have had his pick of any of them. I still struggle sometimes to remember that, after a lot of hard work, I'm pretty spectacular myself, but come on! This guy was HOT! I had to really try to not keep asking myself, "Why me?" and ask, instead, "Why NOT me?"

Our chemistry was stronger than any highball concoction. All I wanted to do was kiss him, suck him, blow him. I didn't care if I never saw him again—I just wanted to have him. It had been years since I'd had a one-night stand. Years. But when Eric at last grabbed my arm and pulled me close to whisper in my ear about going somewhere to be alone, the invitation sounded like the sweetest music I'd ever heard.

"My place. Let's go," I'd said, silently thanking God that my apartment was clean.

My eyes pop open when he strides back into the bedroom to announce it's my turn to shower. A towel is wrapped around his waist and his wet hair is slicked back. I wonder briefly if all models look airbrushed in real life. I want to respond to him, say something easy and up-beat like "Great" or "Thanks," but I know if I open my mouth the only thing that will come out is "Get that ass over here and fuck me."

I scurry silently to the shower, managing a polite smile that I hope doesn't betray the extraordinarily raunchy thoughts racing through my head. My boss will be in meetings all morning, thankfully, so I take my time letting the hot water try to outdo the heat still buzzing through my body from our night of incredible sex, briefly mourning the fact that I'm washing off his scent. It wouldn't do to go to work reeking of man-sweat and love juices.

I reach an arm out of the shower and feel around inside the medicine cabinet over the sink for a bottle of aspirin. Bringing the bottle to my mouth like a shot glass, I let two pills rest on my tongue and swallow them back with a gulp of shower water. *As good as a bottle of Fiji in a pinch*, I tell myself, ignoring the awful taste of hot, city tap water.

I try to affect the same easy-breezy towel wrap Eric has clearly mastered. I get close enough and open the bathroom door, letting steam escape into the hall.

The blinds have been opened and sunlight floods the room. The bed is made, with pillows fluffed and the coverlet neatly folded across the foot. *Interesting.* The only problem with this perfect scene is the absence of Mr. Perfect himself, who has conveniently disappeared.

Damn.

But seriously, what did I expect? I told myself it wouldn't matter if I never saw him again after last night—after I had my way with that beautiful body. But the disappointment I feel comes from somewhere low in my gut, a place I can't control by sheer force of will. I let out a loud sigh.

"I went downstairs and got us some coffee. I hope that's okay," Eric says, reappearing from the galley kitchen.

"Oh, hi! I thought you left. Yeah, sure—I'd love some coffee."

I don't drink coffee. Never have. But this morning I sip that cup of nasty dark liquid like it's ambrosia from the gods.

He watches me get dressed for work. I know I look good, but in comparison to his cut and chiseled physique, I'm more than a little self conscious. I'm sure he's slept with thousands of gorgeous women. I make a point of putting on extra nice lingerie, the stuff I would normally never waste on work. Time enough for him to see my daily wear if I ever see him again. We make small talk until I'm ready.

"Come on, I'll help you get a cab," he says.

The ease with which he conducts himself makes me a little nervous. Are one-nighters with random women such a regular occurrence for him—does he know the drill so well—that he feels comfortable telling me where to go and what to do in my own apartment? Does he know the kind of sway he holds over women who've had the privilege of seeing him naked and playing with that perfect cock? How can he not?

Two people are already in the elevator when we board.

"Should we exchange numbers?" I whisper. I see the woman in front of us raise her eyebrows but I don't care. Did she *see* what walked in next to me? Like I'd let a little social propriety stop me from locking down those digits. *Pfft.*

He takes my phone from my hand and types in a series of numbers. I secretly hope he'll enter his last name, too, since that is still a mystery. He smiles and hands the phone back as his starts ringing. He ends the call without answering.

"I called my phone from yours so I have the number."

I see from a quick glance at my call log that this is true. A smile lights up my insides and I think it's possible that my eyes are leaking rays of sunshine. *Get a grip*, I tell myself.

I focus on my doorman. "Good morning, Eduardo" I smile.

"Good morning, Miss Vivian."

"Eduardo. Eric Ellis. Nice to meet you."

Ellis. Got it. Vivian Ellis. It has a nice ring to it. I shake my head to release this high-school level fantasy and marvel again at his confidence. I'm both impressed and slightly confused by Eric's comfort level. Before I can decide if this display is assertive or just really, really friendly, he's holding a cab door open for me.

"See you later, okay? I have a crazy day," he says. The way he looks at me makes me think he really means the "see you later" part. It sure doesn't feel like he's blowing me off, albeit in a charming way. I start to think that I actually might see my exquisite one-night-stand again. No objection here!

"Yeah, okay. Sure." I smile, making a point of twinkling my eyes at him. He's not the only one with sex appeal, ya know. I wonder how he'll spend that "crazy" day: *Spray tanning, teeth whitening and spin class? Whatever, I still had a great time.*

The door closes behind me and I turn my head to watch him walk away. My x-ray vision imagines that magnificent naked ass under his jeans, and the way his muscles flex as he moves. Without disrupting my view, I order the cabbie up Sixth Avenue and across 59th Street to Madison.

I close my eyes and feel that tingle again. Eric's body pressing into mine. Eric kissing every part of me an inch at a time. Eric's tongue nibbling my inner thighs, his hands spreading my legs further, his eyes taking me in and his whisper telling me how beautiful I am. Eric pleasuring me until I'm on the brink of the most explosive crygasm I can remember, then pulling his mouth away and sliding into me like we are two puzzle pieces coming together after a long separation. Eric—

"We're here, Miss."

I feel like I've been caught in the act by my mother or a priest or a stadium full of spectators. I pay the cabbie and don't wait for change.

Walking across the lobby in my office building, only one thought occupies my mind: *Vivian Fiori, you are FUCKED.*

CHAPTER 1:
YES, I HIT THAT!

One of the big perks of a life spent focused on career rather than relationships is that I've worked my way up the corporate ladder to a posh corner office. Aside from the city views and prestige afforded by this honor, advantages abound. Today, one of those advantages is a door to close.

I'm a V.P. at a small venture capital firm, Prodigy Partners. We provide seed capital to start up businesses across sectors such as entertainment, technology and food. As exciting as it may sound it isn't always what it's cracked up to be. At times, I wonder where some of the more ludicrous pitches come from. What are these people smoking?

My favorite was a client who came in with a home-made infomercial, pitching a chest hair styling kit. It was all I could do to watch it without laughing and wondering if we were being punked somehow. He sat there, proudly watching, as the announcer stated, in schmoozey voice-over tones, "Chest hair is making a come-back! No more waxing!" while the video showed an extremely hairy man being glopped, burned and painfully ripped.

The announcer continued, "Some men are blessed with attractive chest hair. But not everyone!" as the video displayed a photo of "blessed" hairy male chest, followed by photos of men who are "not blessed" with captions under each photo: Tight! Ugly! *Out of Control!!!*

"Your kit comes with styling gel, a mini-hair straightener and styling guide," he continued, voicing over photos of small tube of gel, a thumb-sized flat iron, and flimsy pamphlet. Then the video showed a man delicately straightening his chest hair with this tiny implement. The hysterical "After" photo showed the same guy with strange looking, straightened chest hair.

"But wait, there's more! Order now and get a complete set of chest hair shaving stencils," with photos of stencils: lightning bolt, super hero emblems, Bart Simpson, etc. "Order before midnight tonight and receive a free, second set of stencils for 'down there,'" which were shown as smaller, similar stencils. These pictures were followed by photos of smiling men giving the "thumbs up," with various images shaved into their chest and pubic hair.

My jaw hung open as the video ended and the client excitedly asked, "Well? What do you think? Great idea, huh?"

This is where diplomacy is hard. I don't want to hurt the guy's feelings, or discourage an entrepreneur—because, who knows, maybe his next idea will be the one that catches on—but, wow. It was extremely difficult to not say, "Dude, aside from being a pretty stupid idea, you didn't even bother to Photoshop the 'after' photos to remove the burn scars and razor nicks. If you're going to shave Z for Zorro in your chest, it shouldn't look like it was done with an actual sword."

After a good private laugh, we "respectfully"

passed—well, as respectfully as we could while fighting to keep straight faces.

I have better things to think about today, like reminiscing about last night. Sitting at my desk, I allow my imagination to indulge in another replay of last night's festivities. I Google image search the name Eric Ellis, and search Facebook to see if he has a profile. He does, but it's private so I can't see his posts. I can only see the photos that he has set to share publicly. His Instagram alone has over a hundred thousand followers! I collect some particularly tasty shots and compose an email to my girlfriends with embedded links to some of Eric's more famous campaigns.

My particular favorite is a Dolce & Gabbana underwear ad that pictures Eric sprawled across a velvet sofa, one arm thrown casually overhead, his gaze smoldering into the camera. His other arm graces the length of his torso, his thumb hooking the band of delectably tight boxer briefs and tugging it down ever-so-slightly. I love that I know what's in them. I don't let myself think about all the other women who can say that same thing.

Did this thirty-three-year-old former fatty just win the lottery? Truth is, I sometimes still feel like that pudgy girl the cute boys won't take a second look at. Those insecurities never fully go away—not when your formative years are spent permanently cementing them in place.

I wish I could go back in time and let my teenage self know that someday she was going to be capturing the lustful attention of such a perfect specimen as Eric Ellis, Dolce & Gabbana underwear model. Although young Vivian would have blushed at the idea, I know she would have desperately loved to know that there was hope for her, as she was fed yet another pizza for dinner by her college-football-coach-weekend-dad, or fast-food/processed crap by her too-busy-to-cook mom.

I would love to tell her that her dad was wrong, as he compared her body to the cheerleaders at the university, where he was a hero and a god to all those who worshiped at the altar of the end zone. "When are you gonna lose that chub?" he'd taunt, "I can't even see your ribs! You'll never find a man with that fat ass of yours!"

I'd tell her that it's perfectly normal to wish her dad would stop seeing her as a potential sex object for other men instead of his daughter; that it's okay to feel like he should be protective of her instead of leaving girly mags lying around all over the house for him and her brothers to drool and ogle over, and that it's no surprise that she carries around a protective layer of fat so no one looks at her that way.

I'd tell her that some those cheerleaders, several of whom flirted with and were rumored to have actually slept with him because it was considered a major coup to sleep with the head coach, are now miserable, fat cows who are nowhere near as fit and toned as she will eventually be. I'd tell her that all of those extra pounds turned out to be a valuable focusing tool in college. No dates meant plenty of time and energy to study and get those good grades that Dad pushed for and insisted upon.

I'd tell her that someday she would be hot, too, but because *she* chose to be (but I would probably leave out the fact that it's pretty much a necessity living in NYC to be spectacular—it's tougher to get a job because you're judged by your looks first, *then* your credentials. Only women who have already made it have the luxury of eating. No point in giving her a total mind-fuck while she's still stuffing her face with Fritos). I'd make sure she knows that all of her hard work of starving and working out and denying herself all of the sensual pleasures of comfort food would pay off in the form of an evening with a Greek God, Eric Ellis.

I felt like I had just won a major award. So, of course, I couldn't let this triumph go unnoticed.

Subject: HIT THAT.

My phone vibrates almost instantly.

"Lauren. You get my email?"

"Giiirl," she drawls, in her cocoa-coated Louisiana accent, "why the hell else would I be callin'?"

"Do you think it's too soon to Facebook him? I already found his profile. It's private, so I can't see anything good."

"Yes! You gotta play it cool, girl. Let *him* do it."

"What about Instagram? He can't possibly tell that I added him, for crissakes, with over a hundred thousand followers!"

"Play it cool!"

"What if I wait 'til three P.M. or something?"

"Oh, I see how it is. You got it bad, huh?"

"Laur … the sex. Look at him! *The sex.* And …"

I hope she will read my silence and spare me the drama of saying it aloud.

"And … ?"

No such luck.

"And the not sex. The not sex was good, too."

"Well you can tell me and Arianna all about the

not sex at the Standard tonight. Happy Hour champers, remember?"

How could I forget? Champagne with my girls was one of the great joys in life. I was beginning to feel bubbly already, between the anticipation of some cold champers—our pet name for our pet drink—and the memories of hot, HOT sex.

The problem was, after last night, the last thing I want to do is commit to another evening out with the girls, especially because I have a date tonight, too. I would rather go straight home after work, clean up the apartment, drop off my dry cleaning, strip down and get back in bed. I want to let my mind run wild on sheets that still smell like him.

"Be there by five thirty," I say. The sheets will still be there when I get home. And fuck the housework. It would still be there, too.

In an uncharacteristic maneuver, I continue Google searching and falking (Facebook stalking) Eric for the rest of the morning. I then go to Twitter, Instagram, Pinterest, and even YouTube, where I find a hilarious old video of him from the Nineties, where he's in this insane neon outfit and his hair's all spiked. I have to admit, though, that he was even hot in that getup. There's not much personal information to be had, aside from countless pictures of Eric in suits, Eric wearing a watch, Eric wearing a bathing suit and mercifully, Eric modeling the hell out of Dolce & Gabbana boxer briefs.

As the afternoon threatens to pass with glacial slowness, I take myself to the post office and the drug store. I even force myself to leave my phone in the office, despite the creeping sensation that I've misplaced a limb. But I know I can't risk taking it with me. I *know* I'll do something stupid with it. A smoothie from Jamba Juice feels especially refreshing, considering I've been running hot all day.

At last three o'clock arrives and I toss my head casually as I click the "+1 Add Friend" button. Of course no one is here to witness how cool I am about all this, how obviously no-big-deal it is to submit myself for potential rejection to the man-god I took home last night. But just in case I need to feel better about all this later, the head-toss helps as a reminder that what happens next is of little to no consequence—a reminder of how I won't suffer humiliations galore if he ignores my friend request, and how my inner fat girl won't feel used and stupid for thinking she stood a chance with someone so obviously out of her league.

Dear God! How can such a good time with a gorgeous man turn me into such a maudlin, self-pitying, pathetic loser? Damn it, I spent way too long working on getting this body model-friendly to start letting that old crap seep in through the cracks! Pep talk! Pep talk! You are hot, Vivian, you are a goddess! He's lucky to have you!

I check myself in the reflection of my office window and smile. Yes, I am a goddess! Fuck him if he doesn't realize it! I am a catch. I am a wet dream. I am …

… rudely pulled back to the real world when my intern Brittany startles me with a knock at the door, flailing her arms and fanning herself.

"What's wrong with you? Does my three fifteen smell or something? God, I hope not. I'm so hung-over," I whisper, rubbing my temples.

Shaking her head from side to side she says, "No,

he is *smooooking* hot and in the conference room. You'll thank me later. Roger and Dan are waiting for you in there as well."

I push myself up from the chair and let out a loud sigh. Great. Another smoking hot man to contend with. I don't know if I can take another one. I grab my Diet Coke and eye glasses and head towards the conference room.

I can hear Dan's obnoxious snort from the end of the hall. I am getting closer but my feet feel heavier than bricks at this moment.

One more hour. One more hour.

Through the glass I see a clean cut, well-suited gentleman from the back as I approach the conference room door.

Perfect posture I must say.

I open the door and walk over to shake his hand. As our eyes lock my knees buckle. I am frozen and struggle to put two words together.

"Hi. Nice to meet you. I'm Eric Ellis," he quickly says, saving me.

"Hello. Nice to meet you, as well. Vivian Ell … I mean Fiori," I reply with a faint, nervous giggle as one of my knees threatens to give out completely.

Is this really happening right now?

I take my seat directly across from him and no, I will not be thanking Brittany later.

For the next hour Eric pitches his fast-casual food concept of chain restaurants to us. His plan is to open a chain of eateries that serve foods like baked potatoes with healthy toppings. He's smooth—even the guys are cowed by his breathtaking presence—yet he's a little nervous. I wonder if it's because of me, or just performance anxiety. It's sort of adorable and I enjoy his discomfort, just a touch. He's not *completely* perfect, is he? There is a *little* vulnerability, anyway.

"It's my job to look like this," he explains, "and it's hard to find healthy and delicious food on the go. I know I'm not the only one who thinks so. Look at these statistics," he says, referring to his Power Point presentation about the obesity epidemic in this country and the lack of healthy fast food. He switches to a slide showing the rise in sales of organic foods. "People are hungry for change. And where there is hunger, let there be good, quality food ready for them."

Clever. Even if I hadn't just spent the night with him, I'd be interested in his pitch. He's done his homework, and has given us all the information we need. This is exactly the kind of thing I'd love to invest in, if the client seems capable of pulling it off. And he does.

Then it occurs to me. Did he do his research and find out who works here at this firm? Did he contrive a meeting with me last night? Was our meet-cute really a meet-slick?

Nah. How could he have possibly known where I'd be last night? I didn't even know where I'd be.

I keep having flashbacks from last night between the Power Point and the analytics. It's taking every fiber of my being to focus on his presentation and not his package. One minute he is clothed and the next minute he's naked. My head is playing tricks on me. I can't wait to get the hell out of here.

At the end of the meeting we say our goodbyes and, just like that, he is out of my life again as if we had never met. We both deserve the Oscar.

I gloss my lips, bronze my cheeks and fling my

new Bottega over my shoulder. I finally escape the office after being held hostage by my one night stand. The day is perfect, all sunshine and cool breezes, and I practically run to the hotel where I'm meeting the girls.

By the time I arrive at the Standard, I feel refreshed and oddly relaxed.

Until I pull out my phone and see a new Facebook notification.

I click the icon and there it is—a confirmation from Eric Ellis, my new work/sex buddy. I feel a thrill of joy mixed with reluctance to allow this guy so much power over my happiness.

I rush inside because I know Lauren and Arianna will help me cull through my Facebook albums to ensure every picture looks fabulous. Ensuring no chub past in sight. Then the real fun will begin: learning about my new crush. My one night stand, that keeps on giving.

Yes, there, I said it: crush. I might like to keep my distance, but I know when someone has gotten past my defenses and into my head. And Eric has. For now I plan to keep this tidbit to myself. I know the girls will pounce on the idea of me pursuing an actual relationship, but it's way too soon to start shopping for SUVs and a house in Westchester. *I have a crush. Isn't that lovely?*

Lauren is sitting at the bar, swigging a dark purple martini while barking into her phone. I guess she needed something strong tonight.

She raises a red lacquered fingernail and says, "Gimme a sec, girl." Into the phone, she continues: "I'll drop it off tonight but only if it's two thousand, cash. I told you! It's the best stuff so stop hounding me. No, it's better than last time. It's pure AAA raw. I ordered it just for you! Like I said, a hundred grams in each bag. No synthetic materials. Top grade shit."

Sitting there I admire her beauty. She has wide, dreamy, doe-like eyes and perfect pillow-top lips. I've met her parents when they came to visit her a few years ago and I could see how she lucked out in the genetics department. Her father has a gorgeous chocolate skin tone that makes you want to just take a bite out of him. Mixed with that of her elegant, alabaster-skinned French-Creole mother, Lauren's DNA gives her the best of both worlds. Her creamy, tawny skin reminds me of the inside of a Caramello bar.

We met at a fundraiser for off-Broadway at the Bubble Lounge shortly after I moved to the city. It's been bubble trouble for ten years now! She was a godsend to me when I was working to lose all the extra weight, so supportive and helpful. We dieted together and sweated our asses off at the gym and countless yoga classes. Both of us had to completely relearn how to eat, with my upbringing on pizza, pasta and cheesy tacos, and her being raised eating things like her mother's killer gumbo and other Cajun delights and her dad's delicious BBQ.

We were one another's "beauty buddies," because we both realized that the way we looked when we got to the Big Apple may have been okay for the rest of the country, but we looked like hippos roaming loose on the streets of New York City, in comparison to everyone else our age.

She came to the city on a scholarship from Juilliard. She had a few brief stints in *The Lion King* and *Porgy & Bess*. It kills me that, after years of struggling, she finally gave up on her dream of being the next Angela Bassett. Lauren Lancaster, formerly known as Lakisha Mae Brown, a name handed down by her father, much to her mother's chagrin. No one dares call her Lakisha.

Well, I do, but only when I want to get her undivided attention.

I love listening to her talk, with her deep Southern accent that she never bothered to lose, except on stage. She knows that it helps her stand out from the rest of the ladies in New Yawk. She gets a lot of attention with the Southern Belle stuff, and if she really wants to capture someone's notice, she mimics her mother's beautiful Creole accent.

Myself, I managed to lose the TexMex drawl. Even though I was born in the United States, I still picked up some of my mom's lovely Spanish lilt—I loved her mild accent so, as a child, I learned to ape some of her more interesting pronunciations, but I've lost that since moving away. Dad has no accent at all, even though his parents spoke Italian in the house as he was growing up—they only used their native tongue when they didn't want the kids to know what they were talking about. But now I just sound like an average American. Nothing remarkable about my voice.

One of the things I love about Lauren is her ability to easily slip in and out of mimicked accents, and her exaggerated vocal stylings. It truly is a skill, to do it well, and she does. But ultimately, the parts for a skinny, bi-racial actress on Broadway are few and far between, even if she is gorgeous and has the style and grace of her lovely mother. She eventually had to find another, more resourceful way of making ends meet.

She hangs up her phone and slams it down on the bar. I raise an eyebrow. If I didn't know better, I'd say it sounded like Lauren was in the midst of a major drug deal.

"How's the hair extension business?" I ask.

After her breakup with Mark, Lauren started the business to get back on her feet fast. Once a week she heads down to Chinatown to tap her main source. She's even picked up a little Mandarin in the process. Nothing gets by this little Southern gal, who says extensions are "liquid gold on the streets of Manhattan." Women pay up to $2,500 for a flawless set of hair.

"Seriously, Viv, catering to this high maintenance clientele is getting to me. These stylists think they're celebrities too, and I really don't give a shit if Eva Longoria needs a twenty-two-inch number two by tomorrow. I don't grow hair out of my ass!"

"Well, you did until we went to J Sisters." We both shudder at the memory of hot wax on our most delicate of areas, and the hair being viciously ripped away. Viva Brazil!

"Word. The best quality hair comes from Brazil, and they're also the best at yanking it out!"

"Can you imagine being their advertising agency and coming up with their slogans?"

"God, I know!" She laughs and croons into a pantomime microphone, in a phony announcer type voice, "At J Sisters, we give new meaning to the phrase 'snatch you bald-headed.'"

We scream with laughter at her double entendre, as the bartender finally comes by for my drink order—champagne, dahling.

"I see you have that damn roller bag full of hair

with you," I say, pointing to the carry-on neatly tucked beneath the bar. Lauren is often seen walking the streets of New York with her recently upgraded Louis Vuitton roller bag. She looks as if she's perpetually catching the Luxury Liner to the Hamptons. "Yes! They're all on to me. They text and call me at all hours of the night with these fucking hair emergencies! Best part? I ran into Beth on the street today and she asked where I was traveling to."

"Argh. Nosy Beth."

"So I said I was going to the Monaco Grand Prix with my friend Jack. I told her I had to catch my plane just to fuck with her. She knows Mark and I broke up and that I'm now peddling hair to pay my rent! I couldn't bear to get into the details so I threw my Tod's shades on, held my head up high and jumped in a cab."

"Damn, girl, I really need some champers now," I reply, as the bartender delivers my two-for-one drinks, "At happy hour prices no less!"

She quickly changes speeds.

"Arianna is late. Bitch is *always* late. I told her four thirty so she'd get here by five but now it's five thirty and still no sign of her."

"You know she never wants to risk sitting alone at the bar, plus she'll use the 'I couldn't get a cab' excuse," I say. I'm about to change the subject to talk about my crush when we feel a warm gust of air as the front door glides open to admit Arianna.

As usual, every male eye turns to stare at her. She is a vision—impossibly beautiful—a true Goddess. Arianna is a tall, very thin, very gorgeous Eastern European woman with blonde hair and piercing green eyes. She only wears couture and her signature scent,

Chanel 22. She's thirty-eight but doesn't look a day over thirty thanks to Dr. Loeb, "the Michelangelo of the Upper East Side." Tastefully nipped and tucked, Arianna's beauty will take your breath away, but there is more to it than just her physicality—she exudes an aura of otherworldly magnificence, almost as if an angelic chorus begins when she enters a room.

"Sorry, honeys, I got stuck at Hermes."

"Who gets stuck at Hermes?" Lauren asks. Her exasperation quickly softens. "Gawd you're such a pill."

"What? I couldn't decide which Birkin Bag I want Andrew to buy me. I eventually settled for the crocodile skin."

Lauren and I roll our eyes in sync. The croc skin Birkin is only the most expensive in their line.

Arianna exudes a matter-of-fact vibe of extreme wealth and only her closest friends know that she wasn't born to it. Her family moved to Brooklyn from Latvia in 1987 when she was twelve years old and they didn't have two dimes to rub together. She still has a touch of her accent, just enough to make her sound exotic.

Her father opened a chain of bodegas known for importing the best pickled meats and vegetables the Slavic world had to offer. What can I say? The man knows how to play to a niche crowd. The family flourished, as did Arianna's beauty, and her father considered her a valuable commodity, trying to broker a good marriage for her, Old World style.

She decided, as a youngster in America, that if anyone was going to capitalize on her exquisite beauty, it would be her. She first married at eighteen. He was an insurance salesman whose most valuable asset was his ability to move Arianna out of her parents' house and into a roomy flat on the Upper West Side. She divorced him at twenty-two and remarried shortly thereafter, to a star hedge fund analyst. They stayed married for ten years before Arianna started feeling the itch to upgrade again.

Her most recent marriage (and divorce) was to (and from) a Jewish billionaire media mogul she met at Nello's. He left her for his much younger yoga instructor. We all agreed it was grotesquely cliché, even if he did tell Arianna that it was because she refused to give him head. "I'm not putting that filthy thing in my mouth!" she declared, in her defense. It wasn't that he didn't bathe, she confided to us later, she won't blow anyone, "... not as long as waste products come out of those things!"

We don't talk about it, but we all know that this was the first time that anyone ever dumped Arianna and it shook her to the core. She's getting older now and I think she knows, deep down inside, that the competition is getting younger, and girls today are much more willing to do things she's not able to stomach. Thanks to the endless supply of porn online these days, the males of our species have been led to believe that we're all breathlessly waiting to take it up the butt and that we all love jizz in our eyes.

But if she's feeling insecure, you'd never know it. Now Arianna has the Tribeca loft, which she never uses, the 61st and Park co-op and the mansion in Sagapanock. Marriageable stock for Arianna has always meant tall, dark and has some. Arianna Murphy-Lambert-Goldstein is a strategic woman.

"So what have you girls been up to? Roaming Manhattan one dick at a time, I presume?"

"Fuck off," I growl.

"Tell her about the model!" Lauren says.

"He better come from money or you're screwed," Arianna offers sagely. "The more beautiful they are, the less money they have."

"I have no clue what kind of family he comes from, but he's a working model and entrepreneur. As a matter of fact, we may be investing in his new venture!" I hear myself bragging and wonder if one-upping Arianna might be a bonus to meeting Eric.

"Remember the last model you dated? The one you chose over the guy I set you up with?"

Arianna is talking about Steve. He was gorgeous, sexy, and smart enough to keep up with me at my wittiest. I was completely smitten. Though he had three roommates in a shared two-bedroom convertible, I decided to give him a chance. Every date was either at a falafel house or a Chinatown dive. After a few weeks, my stomach couldn't take it anymore. I suggested a few nicer places to eat; if I was going to invite this guy back to my place, we had to go somewhere that wouldn't strike me down with bowel explosiveness that could rival a weapon of mass destruction.

My plan seemed to be working. We were spending more and more time together, and he stayed at my apartment most nights. He started leaving random articles of clothing strewn about. I prayed he wasn't planning a stealth move-in and chalked it up to forgetfulness. Still, I sat him down to explain that I thought we should slow things down. I felt terrible but relieved when Steve said he understood. He was looking for something more and thought we should end things if we weren't moving forward.

I was blown away. Never had I felt more masculine than at that moment, especially when I asked if we could still have sex occasionally.

Steve wasn't amused. He left my apartment like a puppy with his tail between his legs, bag of clothing in hand. Poor Steve.

"Your friend was nice. I liked him. But like I've told you a million times, he wanted to settle down. Marriage—"

"Who gives a shit about marriage? Take it from me—it's an institution more overrated than the FDIC. Plus, Marco was a BBB! Billionaire Bald Boys are hard to come by."

"Yeah, but Viv's new guy might be a Guppy," Lauren says. She's on her second martini. With every round, her voice gets a little higher. On nights we really hit the town, she's reduced to a nearly unintelligible squeak by the time we get in a cab home.

"New to New York, huh?" Arianna says, sipping her champers. "There are perks to a Guppy, sure, but nothing trumps a Billionaire Bald Boy. Just when I think you gals finally get it, you show me how much you have left to learn …"

A man bumps into Arianna from behind despite plenty of space at the bar, causing her drink to slosh dangerously. She gives him a feisty snarl as she steadies her flute of rosé champagne. This ploy for her attention is met with a look that could level a pro wrestler.

"Do you mind?" she barks. "There's enough room for you to hover over somebody else!"

She turns back to us and, in unison, we whisper "Nudger," our term for men so timid, they need to stage a meet-cute just to get a conversation going. Our like-mindedness melts us into laughter that draws the attention of everyone at the bar.

"Well, I have news," Lauren says.

"WHAT?!" Arianna and I half-laugh, half-yell in unison.

"I'm moving to Miami!"

Arianna and I sober up fast.

"What? When? Why?"

"I'm done with New York. I can't take the rat race any more. The men, pimping out hair extensions, the horrible weather, robbing Peter to pay Paul ... I wanna hang out on the beach, meet myself a Latin luvvah and call it a day."

Lauren and I have been so close, right from the beginning when we were New York Newbies together, but after she left her fiancé and my four-year relationship crumbled, we began to rely on one another in a different way. Swapping war stories and sipping champers by the Soho House pool did more than forge the bonds of friendship: we became sisters. I feel her news like a punch to the gut.

"I can't believe it," I say. "I'm going to miss you so much."

I pull her into a hug that I hope says what I can't: *I love you and I miss you already, but I won't try to talk you out of this because we both know you'd never say something so earth-shattering unless you'd already thought it through.*

"I could never leave New York," Arianna snorts. "Hell, I try to avoid leaving the Upper East Side whenever possible. But I'll visit you, darling—I love Miami."

"Farewell, City of Sleeplessness, York revisited," Lauren announces to the bar in her most highbrow tone. "Farewell, Minnows and Lofties, Sharehouse Poseurs and Groupers."

Arianna and I practically double over with laughter, but I am struck by the pending loss of one of the few people on this planet who knows the secret language of MENhattan—the lexicon of terms we've coined over the years to talk about the men in our city, in our lives.

"I have an idea," I say, all seriousness now, because I cannot bear to talk any more about Lauren leaving me. To do so makes it too real.

"Don't even think about suggesting we all move to Miami," Arianna says.

"No, nothing like that. I was thinking … we should spread the word about these guys. Write a book, or create an app. Or a blog! A last hurrah before Lauren leaves. Something that captures and shares everything we've learned, the hard way, about men in New York."

"Yes! You could call it *The Good, the Bad and the Ugly!*" Lauren chimes in, "and you can add hashtags like #thegoodthebadandthebaldy!"

"Hashtags? What exactly are those? I see them everywhere, but I've never been sure what they're for." I'm a whiz at Facebook, but the rest of the social networking sites are still sort of a mystery to me. I don't have time to surf the net nonstop to learn all these new things.

"You'll figure it out as you go. They just help people find what they're looking for."

"What? Who has time for that? And what's the point?" Arianna asks. Lauren, on the other hand, looks excited.

"I do! I mean, it doesn't need to be *War and*

Peace. Just … women trying to get a piece," I say, smirking proudly at my pun. "Laur, don't you remember how long it took for our naïve asses to figure out the players in this game when we first moved here? Don't you want to help other women do the same? Think of all the time we could save them!"

"True," Lauren replies, "It would have been nice to have some sort of handbook. But you know that men would hate it, right? They'd come back with blogs of their own about us!"

"Screw that," Arianna says, "Men have plenty of voice about women, and have been saying nasty things about us since the printing press was invented."

"Before that, even. Genesis, anyone? We've been getting the blame for everything that's gone wrong since Eve bit that apple." Lauren says, catching onto the idea. "We could interview our friends. Real stories from real women about real guys. We wouldn't be man-bashing; we'd only be talking about the players. Nice guys will know we're not talking about them."

"Nice guys, huh?" I ask, "Boy, when was the last time any of us have dated one of those?"

"Hell, when was the last time any of us has *met* one of those?" Lauren asks.

"True. But you've gotta admit, bad boys are exciting. As long as they're bad in the right ways."

"Aye, there's the rub," Lauren says thoughtfully, showing off her Shakespearian training.

Arianna is silent, a sign that she's actually considering this. I'd love to stay and convince her, but a text comes through from my dinner date. Matthew Price, a forty-something self-professed "detergent king" is waiting for me across the street. I met him at one of Arianna's *soirées* and she has made it her personal business to make sure that we get together. He's not wealthy enough for her, even though he's loaded, but she wants one of her friends to bag him. It's our second date, and I haven't even kissed him yet. I knock back a Red Bull, re-gloss my lips and kiss my girls on their cheeks.

Arianna laughs as she picks up her cocktail napkin and wipes off my lip print from her face, then from Lauren's. "Kiss first, then gloss! And, by the way, Matthew is one of those 'nice guys.' Don't fuck this up."

"I won't. I promise."

"*Zai jian,*" Lauren says in Mandarin with a slight twang. "That means goodbye."

"This discussion isn't over," I say as I slide off the bar stool and straighten my dress. "MENhattan. Think about it."

Before either one can respond, I walk across the street to Valbella, but I overhear Arianna saying to Lauren, "If you're going to live in Miami, maybe it's time you start taking up Spanish."

CHAPTER 2:
GROUPERS & MINNOWS

Against my better judgment, I press Send. "What are you doing?!" Lauren asks, grabbing the phone from my hand.

"What? I just asked how he was doing. No big deal."

"No big deal my ass. It's Friday! You're not acting like yourself, girlfriend. And by that I mean you're acting kind of …"

"Kind of what?"

"Honest? Kind of desperate."

The silence hangs heavy between us. As independent women who pride ourselves on doing it all, all alone, the word "desperate" might as well be four letters. The worst part is, Lauren is right.

"So," she says, anxious to erase the awkwardness, "how did it go with Matthew?"

"Great. Really. I like him." I don't tell her that the news that she's moving pretty much ruined any chance the poor guy might have had of receiving my undivided attention. I spent the evening watching his mouth move as he talked, but not hearing a word, as I tried not to cry as her news sunk in. My best friend, my soul sister, was leaving.

It felt worse than being dumped by a man—she knows me better than anyone, better than I know myself, in some ways. She's the only one who can really call me on my shit, because she's the only one I really let in. We've gone through so much together over the years, helped each other through jobs and crises and, of course, men. We've even joked on many occasions that if only we were both attracted to women, we'd have it made because we'd be a perfect couple. And now, when she leaves, I'll be alone. My others friends are great—I love them all—but Lauren is special.

After I got home from my mediocre date with a guy who deserved better, I bawled like a baby. I wanted to get it all out so I didn't lay it on her today. I know this move is hard on her, too, and I don't want to make her feel any worse than she already does. I want to be supportive and look on the bright side—I'll have a place to crash now in Miami!

So I keep the conversation light. "He's nice. And successful. He looks good on paper, and he's nice looking enough, but I don't know how attracted I am to him. I'm just not feeling the chemistry." I let my voice trail off because we both know what I'm thinking. "Plus …"

"Plus, you're *way* into the Canadian."

We both laugh. I don't know if it's how head-over-heels I am about a guy I just met, or the fact that Eric's nickname as "The Canadian" is just so totally absurd. Either way, it feels good to laugh about it. Anything to not think about the task at hand—packing Lauren to move. She's really serious about this. So I have to laugh, or I'll cry.

"Don't tell Arianna," Lauren says. "She's already started planning your wedding to Matthew in St. Barth's, where she'll find husband number four among his friends."

We spend the next couple minutes in the friendly quiet we're used to. The only real interruption to our own thoughts is when Lauren taunts me with the things she's leaving behind for me—her cold weather gear, a heated blanket and a pair of gross UGGs.

Each of us is focused on packing as much as we can into the boxes in front of us without making them impossible to carry. New Yorkers are acutely aware of what it's like to lug heavy packages from Point A to Point B, so even though Lauren has a crew of movers coming in tomorrow, we try to make the loads easier to bear.

Tomorrow. I can't believe Lauren only told us she was moving yesterday. Part of me understands that she has to move swiftly if she's going to go through with this, but I can't help feeling a touch of whiplash at the incredible speed of the transition. All of the secret planning that went into this move … she claims she had to do it alone, because if Arianna and I interfered, she knows we would have convinced her to stay. She's right—I would have tried like hell. In a city notorious for its overcrowding, I can't help but feel like the streets will feel empty once she's gone.

"I've been thinking about the Menhattan Project," I say, swallowing back the lump in my throat.

"Isn't that the program that developed the first atomic bomb during World War II?"

"No, smarty pants, MEN-hattan and it sometimes feels like a war zone with all these a-bombs. You know, assholes?" I smile.

"Yes! Girl, they're blowing up everything from the Upper East Side to the Brooklyn Bridge!" She gets a little more serious and says, "It's a great idea, and you're the perfect person to do it. So catchy! Blogs are so trendy right now, too. And I mean, who's got more material than you?"

I gasp in fake indignation. "What are you saying, Laur? That I'm some kind of 'ho?"

"Absolutely," she says with a grin. "Takes one to know one. But seriously—you should do it. Start with the women you know and I guarantee they'll bring their friends in on it, too. Like *The Help* … just … without the beatings."

Only a black girl could get away with that kind of joke. I can't suppress a snort. "Dark humor much? How about … *Sisterhood of the Traveling Panties?*"

"Now you're gettin' it!" she laughs. "Start with Groupers, Dealfish and Minnows, then work toward the rest."

"Always the logical one," I say, and I mean it. "How am I supposed to do this without you?" I try to say this without an implied guilt trip in my voice, but I'm not very successful.

"Without me? Since when did the internet have a distance restriction? Stop moping and tell me what you know about Groupers."

I take a moment to gather my thoughts, which are instantly more numerous than I imagined they would be. When I stop to consider the staggering number of men I've met in this city …

I take a deep breath and begin.

"Groupers, Dealfish and Minnows can often be found in a school." Lauren nods. Her eyebrows knit together like I am delivering the nightly news. "Groupers are the centerpiece of the three because they provide the bankroll. A typical Grouper is easy to spot; he sits quietly at a table in the club—he always orders bottle service, thereby guaranteeing himself a good seat—and rarely leaves his throne. The Grouper works as a hedge fund manager, real estate mogul or dominates a weird niche in the tech industry after discovering a new algorithm or obscure invention. Though Groupers aren't particularly social, they are never alone."

"And why is that, Professor?" Lauren leads. "Wait. You should be writing this down." She digs out a blank legal pad and a pen from one of her already packed boxes and hands them to me. "Pray, continue."

"Well, the Grouper can rely on his Minnow to bring him a steady stream of beautiful women." I make three columns on the pad, one for each, and scribble down some notes under the heading, "GROUPER."

Next, I label a column for "MINNOW" and talk as I write, "The Minnow is also probably responsible for getting Mr. Grouper into whatever hot club he finds himself in—Minnows are good for making plans. They know everyone and let the world know it by fist-pumping and high-fiving their way through the velvet rope like Moses parting the Red Sea. Minnows exist to scoop up the Grouper's leftovers, be they women, cocktails or business deals. The Minnow feels entitled to a cut of the Grouper's success because he brokers the relationships that lead to profit."

I pause to rest my hand and laugh at how thoroughly my friends and I have dissected our experiences. All our lives we've been told there are plenty of fish in the sea—and there are. But we've taken the time to categorize all the species in that vast ocean so we know where we stand in the hierarchy of predators and prey. Navigating the waters of the NYC dating scene can be brutal. The only way to survive is to know what you're up against.

"Minnows are usually hot, or their attractiveness is bolstered by a good personality," I continue, both talking and scribbling. "They come with stripper names like Sebastian or Armand and somehow manage to be at every major event—club openings in New York one night, Cannes the next, the Monaco Grand Prix a week later. Minnows are always working on a movie deal or an iPad app—though ask for specifics and he'll quickly change the subject. And get too close to the Minnow's Grouper? Well that's a whole 'nother heap of trouble."

"Yeah, they don't like it if you start swimming upstream to spawn with bigger, stronger fish. Ooo, you have to call Catherine about her Grouper-Minnow story! It's the best one I've heard so far."

Again, Lauren is right. This story needs to go into the blog, and I make a note of that on the margin of the pad.

Catherine dated a really cute Minnow once, named Alain. He was affectionate and attentive, and attached at the hip to a Grouper named Marcel. He would only take Catherine out to restaurants or clubs if Marcel was coming. Otherwise it was cheap dates— movies and take-out, that kind of thing. Catherine was at the mercy of a Grouper, and that song and dance got old *fast*. When she finally ended it over the phone, Alain's response was, "No problem. Hey, got Marcel on the other line. We're going to Darby tonight. Ciao, ciao."

The double ciao from a Poughkeepsie native

whose real name (we later learned) was Albert? Catherine learned her lesson about Minnows.

"Dealfish, now that's a whole 'nother story," I say, starting another column on my pad. "Dealfish are the types who always wear sleek aviator sunglasses—even inside, and even at night. When you ask a Dealfish what he does for a living, he'll tell you about a pending business transaction in one of a dozen sectors: biotech, alternative fuels, merchandizing for a children's book series, merging conglomerates in the finance industry." I jot this list, furiously scribbling to keep up with my thoughts. "There's no limit to what the Dealfish dabbles in, but you'd be hard-pressed to find out if any of his deals ever close."

When my phone buzzes, I'm so distracted I don't register what I'm seeing for a few seconds. Then it hits me: this is the text I've been waiting for. I call Lauren over and slide my thumb across the screen to reveal this much-anticipated message.

Hey, Sexy! Not around this wknd but I'll call u next week for dinner.

Screw Dealfish. Suddenly I'm the one on the hook with a species we have yet to name. Angel fish, perhaps? He certainly is heavenly.

"Dinner," I say to Lauren, "dinner. That's good, right? Promising? That's a date, not just a booty call. You don't think it has anything to do with him needing investors for his healthy potato restaurant, do you?" I hate to think that about him, but come on. I didn't just roll off a potato truck. Just because he's gorgeous doesn't mean he can't be a schemer. I mean, for God's sake, my girls and I are going to create a *blog* about how shitty some men can be.

"Stop! It's promising," Lauren says, looking over

my shoulder. I know she is trying to balance out my extreme excitement with her reserved caution because one of us should have a level head. But I also know this text is a good thing. It's not vague or shady in any way and it has brought a mile-wide smile to my face.

"Champers?" I say. The rosé bubbly, which I brought over from last week's charity event swag bag, should be perfectly chilled by now, and I feel like I finally have something to celebrate.

Our conversation takes an easy turn back to Menhattan, especially after we've both downed a mug of champagne (Lauren's stemware has been packed for hours—obviously, she was not thinking clearly at the time).

"You need a whole section on poseurs," Lauren says. "As they're a particularly prevalent predator."

We both laugh at her alliteration and the sing-songy way her words come out.

"There's the Penny Pinching Poseur," I say, punching my own P's and flipping to a fresh page on the pad, starting a new list. This blog will definitely not be lacking for material! "The Sharehouse Poseur and the Portion Poseur. Am I missing any?"

"Probably. There are so many different kinds."

"Well, a gentleman will make sure you get home safely in a cab and pay the cab fare to take you there," I say. "But sometimes the so called 'gentleman' will reveal himself as one of the different kinds of poseur during the ride. The Penny Pincher asks to get dropped off first 'because his place is on the way' and 'accidentally' fails to give you any money for the extra-long trip."

"And we all know," Lauren adds, sagely, "that when someone is cheap with their money, they are cheap with their love. Generosity comes in all forms."

Lauren and I exchange a knowing look and I am sure we are both remembering my first encounter with a Penny Pincher. He was a forty-five-year-old banker. He pulled that stunt on our first date, but I blamed it on his nerves. That is, until our second date. When he slid out of the cab that night, I leaned over and said, "Really? You want to get dropped off first AND you're not giving me any money for the cab?" His response? "Well, I paid for dinner!"

I was shocked. So was the cabbie, who stopped screaming into his hands-free headset long enough to tell me "Zat man iz verrry, verry rude." Suffice it to say, I never saw the bastard again. I make a note on the pad, and underline it twice, to remind myself to include his sorry ass in a blog post.

"The Portion Poseur is easy to spot," Lauren chimes in—this game is infectious, and I keep scribbling as she talks. "You'll know you've got one the moment you sit down to dinner. It starts with water, when your date tells the waitress you'll both have 'New York's Finest' with a wink that means 'Aren't I just *soooo* clever?!' The best response is simply: 'I prefer sparkling.' If your date scoffs, you know you've got a P-squared on your hands."

"Tell me, Teach—are there other ways to detect a Portion Poseur?" I ask, pen poised in midair, ready for more.

"Yes, you start by pouring me more champers," she says. I notice that we've already polished off bottle number one, and pop open a second. Lauren's moving and bubbles don't travel well—or so we tell ourselves. Lauren clears her throat and continues, her voice a little squeakier, her accent a little stronger, and her delivery a little more comical.

"The next giveaway that you've snagged a Portion Poseur is if he mentions ordering 'family style.' If I wanted to serve myself, I'd eat at home. And if I wanted to share, potentially order things I don't like, and have someone else pick through my entrée, I'd ... well, I'd never want that. Run for the door if he pulls that move—better to eat alone than from a trough."

Lauren's phone rings, and I silently thank God. My hand is cramping from all of this writing. I'm used to using a keyboard, not a pen! We both scramble to find her phone hidden among the piles of stacked clothes and open boxes littering the apartment. I win after pushing over a stack of throw pillows practically as tall as I am. "Speak of the devil," I say. Lauren's eyes light up when she sees it's Catherine.

"Hey, girl! Viv is here, we're packing. You're on speaker."

"Packing—I can't believe it! Saw your Facebook status and had to call to find out if it's really true. Why didn't you tell me!?"

Catherine's Boston accent whines through the phone and makes me smile. She moved here years ago and, though she claims her sports team allegiances will never change, she's assimilated to New York life like a caged wildcat finally released into the savanna.

"Yup, heading south. I didn't tell anyone until it was too late for y'all to talk me out of it! Were your ears burning? We were just talking about you! Tell us about that Sharehouse Poseur you dated."

"Oh, gawwwd," she drawls, her voice tinny on the speaker. "Just when you think you've found the real deal—a great guy who also happens to have a place in the Hamptons—he turns into a Sharehouse Poseur. It's like … like …"

"Like Cinderella's carriage turning into a big, fat pumpkin?"

"Exactly! Except this carriage turned into a lying sack of shit!"

Catherine's voice is animated as she recounts the story, and I begin to wish that I had a voice recorder, because she talks so fast. It happened shortly after she moved "down south," as she calls it, from Boston to New York—but she won't specify how many years ago it was. "I was young and naive," she says, "and that's all you need to know about my age, then or now."

She'd had a few dates with a guy she really hit it off with and was thrilled when he invited her to his Hamptons house for a summer weekend. She packed all the sundresses, floppy hats and sexy wedges she had in a borrowed Vuitton and waited for the call that he was downstairs to pick her up.

Except the call she actually got was to tell her to meet him at Penn Station—and she better hurry since the 4:53 would be crowded. Though she was new to the city, Catherine had already learned that catching a cab to Penn in the four o' clock hour on a Friday is next to impossible. So despite the fact that she was dressed like a Kentucky Derby spectator, she raced through the streets to 32nd and 7th Avenue. Sweating, heart pounding, she told herself a little effort on the front end of their journey would make relaxation by a private pool all the sweeter.

The train was packed. Catherine and her Sharehouse Poseur wedged themselves in a corner with her bag tucked behind her legs. The three-hour trip was nightmarish—crowded and noisy and not at all the sophisticated cocktail-hour-in-transit she had been expecting. Nonetheless, dreams of ocean views and slushy margaritas kept her faith strong, and his cute, witty banter distracted her from the field of red flags unfurling right before her unseeing eyes.

When they finally arrived, Catherine and her guy were picked up from the station in Bridgehampton by one of his friends. He took them to an eight-bedroom house, as beautiful and spacious as Catherine imagined it would be. She kicked off her shoes and stretched out on their bed to relax and decompress from the long journey. About fifteen minutes later, her date's friend Sal rolled in. Then David showed up. Then Josh, Lee, and all their crews. Before Catherine knew what hit her, there were twenty people crammed into the once spacious-seeming property.

"Ah, yes, that was a hard lesson in the ways of the Sharehouse Poseur," she says. "He 'owns' a Hamptons mansion for $1500 ... only trouble is, he shares it with twenty of his friends and only has access one weekend a month! Hey, what's this all about, anyway? Why are you gals bringing up my sordid past?"

"Viv is starting a blog!" Lauren squeaks. I can practically see the champagne coursing through her veins.

"No shit! What's it about?"

"YOU!" we scream, in unison. "Well, us too," I explain, "and every other single woman in New York!"

We fill her in on the premise and she's almost more enthusiastic than we are.

"Call Shannon," she advises. "She was stuck with that Loftie for awhile."

"Arianna, too!" Lauren says.

"I have a better idea," I say. "C, give Shannon a call and ask if she can do early brunch tomorrow. The two of you can meet us and Arianna at Le Bilboquet. Sound good?" I make a mental note to pick up a digital voice recorder before we all meet.

"Fantastic. And it'll give me a chance to say goodbye …"

We all go a little quiet when the reality of Lauren's departure washes over us.

"Hey, no tears," Lauren says, even though she's blinking rapidly to hold them back. "Tomorrow at twelve-thirty. Le Bilboquet."

We say our goodbyes to Catherine and I realize it's time for us to say goodbye, as well. We've made a significant dent in the chaos littering Laur's apartment but I know she'll be up for hours more, sifting through her things and deciding what can go. I make a hasty exit after a hug too quick to lead to a maudlin display, and remind myself that I'm relieving her of most of her winter gear. She won't need it where she's going, and it'll be nice to have a few things that make me feel like she's still close by. Nothing like a free shopping spree between friends.

CHAPTER 3:
CASA DE PENIS ERECTUS

Known as much for its French bistro fare as its stereotypically standoffish (and handsome) wait staff, Le Bilboquet is an Upper East Side staple. Though the maître d' is ice cold to Catherine as she puts our names in for a table of five, he thaws instantly under Arianna's enchanting goddess smile. They exchange a few pleasantries *en français* and before long a corner table opens miraculously. We glide into our seats and settle into our coffees and sparkling waters.

"That is so not fair," Lauren pouts, "I spoke French to him last time I was here trying to get a table, but apparently Cajun French isn't good enough for *monsieur le serveur glorifié.*"

Arianna gives her the hairy eyeball, "Well, it would help if you didn't call him a glorified waiter."

"Even if that's what he is?" Lauren challenges.

"Good point," Arianna relents.

"So this is it, huh? Your last meal in NYC?" says Shannon, who is dripping with posh Om symbols and expensive crystal jewelry. She is convinced that she died a colorful and tragic Janis Joplinesque death of an overdose at Haight-Ashbury in a past life. But her mantra in this lifetime is "Abundance is mine," so she dresses like a wealthy postmodern hippie. Her comment to Lauren feels like she took the words right out of my head.

"Don't remind me that I'll be leaving all this food behind," Lauren says.

Arianna clears her throat.

"And you ladies, *of course*," Lauren adds. "But you can visit me—the Poulet Cajun from Bilbo? Not so much. The only other place I can get Cajun chicken this good is in my mama's kitchen."

We place our orders—or rather, Arianna rattles them off in French that seems to impress even our surly waiter. It always does. Lauren and C are having the Cajun chicken; though it's not typical brunch fare, the plate here is world-renowned. I take my usual— the arugula salad with chevre which has exactly four hundred and twenty calories. Dressing on the side. I hope that someone orders fries, because one French fry stolen from someone else's plate is officially calorie free.

Shannon, the New Age goddess who wears only organic, natural fabrics, surprises us by ordering steak tartar. "What?" she says in response to our raised brows. "I'm doing a protein thing." We continue to stare and she protests, "Hey! I'm not a vegetarian!"

"Yet!" Lauren and I cry, in unison. God, I'm gonna miss her. We are so alike.

I have no idea what Arianna orders in her rapid French but within minutes we are all sipping delicious Bellinis—the champagne and peach juice goes down a little too smoothly for this early in the day but this is, after all, a farewell party.

"To Lauren," Arianna says, raising her flute for a toast, and we all clink glasses. I know what it costs her to show any emotion, so I'm not surprised that she hasn't removed her sunglasses. I sniff—loudly and involuntarily—but resist streaking the crisp white napkin in my lap with black mascara.

"Ladies, ladies," Lauren says, "enough with the tears! I'm moving to Miami, not dying."

"But isn't leaving Manhattan the same thing?" Arianna shoots back, "My God, the men there wear flip-flops and shorts everywhere they go. The beaches are littered with homeless people and immigrants! You don't *move* to Miami, you visit!"

"Ha. Ha," Lauren says drily. "Coming from a first generation immigrant, that's rich."

Arianna shoots her a friendly sneer. "Touché," she says, raising her glass again to Lauren's barb.

Lauren continues, "I'll have you know Miami is lovely. I didn't just throw a dart at a map and decide to move where it landed. I have family and friends there, and I miss palm trees and the scent of sunscreen and orange blossoms. But discussing the merits of south Florida is not why we're gathered here this morning. Neither is crying over my departure," she says with a pointed gaze in my direction. "We're here to talk about Lofties."

A collective groan cascades from one of us to the next as I pull out my brand new recorder. The kid at the store told me that it's the best one they have. Its recordings can be saved on my computer as mp3 files, and it came with software that will help me to transcribe them easily. This is going to be so much better than taking notes because I don't want to miss a word of this meeting of the minds.

"What the hell is that for?" Shannon asks. I forgot that she didn't know yet about the blog, so we all fill her in. She's as excited as the rest of us, but she tells me, "You know, your iPhone has a recording app. You could have saved yourself some money."

Duh. I didn't even think of that. But, the transcribing software will come in handy, and using this little handheld device makes me feel like a cub reporter, and that's kind of fun.

"Whatever," I say, waving off her concern. "Let's talk about men!"

"I'll go first!" Catherine says. "A Lofty comes with all the bells and whistles that blind a woman at first."

Shannon nods her approval, and Catherine continues, "But an experienced dater will spot the warning signs. First and foremost, when you meet this guy, he will always—*always*—lead with his loft."

"*Casa de Penis Erectus*," Shannon says.

"Exactly," Catherine continues. "He'll bust out with some reason to mention his place, like, 'Oh, I went to Art Basel last month to buy some art for my new loft in Soho' and when you get there, you find out that he unintentionally bought some Mr. Brainwash when he was drunk and now fancies himself an art collector. Worse yet is when he says 'You should come to my next party … at MY LOFT.' If you make the grave error of attending said party, you'll find a hundred twenty-somethings running around and at least three of the Loftie's ugliest moocher friends."

When Catherine laughs, her green eyes sparkle. She's got hair extension to her ass and tits to her neck, and though she thinks of herself as a prude, you'd be hard-pressed to find anyone who believes her. She dresses "this close" to slutty. There is a fine line between that and "sexy" and she walks that line well. She's a closet freak, into god-knows-what, from what I can tell by where her stories *end*. What she's not telling us, by its implication, has us all intrigued and is the subject of lots of fun conjecture. Personally, I'm convinced she's into a little S&M. I can see her as a dominatrix—with a heart, of course.

Her attire is provocative to say the least, and even I can't keep from staring at her cleavage, it's so out there on display. Catherine will flirt with any male, anywhere, any time. A real estate broker in a town where the space you live in defines who you are as much as what you're worth, Catherine is a pro at closing tough deals with hardened business men. Happy hour usually finds her at the Peninsula or the St. Regis. She looks different every time we see her, but swears she isn't having work done. Rumor has it that Dr. Loeb cut her off recently, but there are plenty of other doctors who would love to have such a devoted client.

"I don't get these Lofties," she continues sharing her professional expertise. "As wealthy as they are, they never seem to have enough soda or ice to make a decent drink. The Lofty is like ... well, he's like an American tourist in a Bangkok brothel." She sips her drink and adds, "Don't ask me how I know what a Bangkok brothel is like—or how an American tourist would act in one."

She winks as we all laugh, intrigued now, and continues, "He slithers his way through the party, kissing cheeks and bobbing his head off the beat to Usher, wondering which girl will be his victim for the evening. He boasts about his latest solo around-the-world expedition. He telegraphs from a mile away that he's a player. He wants you to know; he *needs* you to know. Floor-to-ceiling windows are for men who want to see and be seen. So buckle up—you won't be the first or last woman to romp around in his T-shirt the morning after."

"At least try to get some good jewelry out of it before he calls it quits at three months," Arianna says. "Lord knows I've done a lot more for a lot less." I roll my eyes. This girl does not go down, so I don't know what on earth she *does* do, to get these men to fork over like they do. Enchanting beauty must be enough for some men.

"Yeah, and make sure he either lives alone or really owns the place," Shannon chimes.

We all turn to face her because we know she's about to recount one of a dozen horror stories from the not-too-distant past. Her stories are always full of crazy behavior and psychological insights. Shannon is a psych-majored ex-nurse, turned yoga instructor, who comes from money. Such a dichotomy, combined with life in New York City, makes for some interesting times.

She's used her wealth to indulge in having a free spirit, which often means she dates guys who are poor for a variety of reasons. Most are "in between" jobs and/or apartments. For someone as gorgeous, funny and exceptionally toned as Shannon, putting up with low-level guys isn't a necessity. Shannon preaches peace and true love, and considers it her personal destiny to find the soulful connection her parents share. They taught her to follow her heart, pick a profession that fills her with a sense of purpose, and pursue happiness always.

The result is that while Shannon might be inordinately mindful and centered, she has a terrible time distinguishing between a man with a job and a man without. It's not that she doesn't realize the guys she goes for are unemployed—she does. But she believes in their goodness and ability to prosper. She believes in their *potential*, she tells us, and she lives to analyze their motives and issues. She believes in "healing the aura" and says she can see their energy fields. She loves nothing more than to try to discover and work through "past life karma."

Waiting for potential to flourish usually keeps Shannon in dead-end relationships far beyond their expiration. She makes horrible choices when it comes to men and wonders why the twenty-two-year-old living on the third floor of her building—who she's been conveniently screwing—won't buy her dinner and only calls after midnight.

"And if he does own the place," she continues, "make sure he's not one of these serial sub-letters who rent it out for photo shoots or charity events. You could be packing your bags to crash on someone's sofa every time he cuts a deal. True story! Happened to me."

None of us is surprised, but we wince anyway. This kind of shit happens totally indiscriminately, not just to nutbag-magnet Shannon.

"I also caution you all about the Country House Trap," Shannon says.

"A well-known ploy of the Upstate Poseur," Lauren interrupts. "So-called because the fabulous estate he dangles in front of you like a carrot on a string is often more prison than princely abode."

"Mm-hm," I say around a mouthful of arugula. "Close cousin of the Sharehouse Poseur." I gesture for Shannon to resume the floor and she does. I'm so happy that I'm recording these gems, because I'm too busy eating to take notes.

"This guy invited me to his house in Chappaqua. He made it sound glamorous and Kennedy-esque— like the whole reason he left the city was to hob nob and live in a mansion on an English-style estate. Only problem is, when we finally arrived after two and half hours of brutal driving over the Tappan Zee—yes," she pauses, seeing our horrified faces, "stuck in traffic on the longest fucking bridge in New York State. I told him not to cut over into Jersey, but he just had to take the Parkway, because he insisted on taking the 'scenic route.' I couldn't even enjoy the skyline view from the bridge, it was so awful."

She shudders at the memory and continues "So he pulled us up to a *one-level ranch* house in need of mega repair, a serious cleaning and some *major* refurbishing." She sits back in her chair, in a huff, and tosses back the rest of her drink.

"I spent the whole weekend raking leaves, dodging spider webs and chatting with the landscapers in broken Spanglish. All the while, he kept saying, 'Don't you just love the fresh air?' I wanted to flatten him." She pounds the table and we all crack up. When someone as sweet as Shannon feels the call to violence, you know it's bad.

Hearing the venom in her voice reminds me how she earned her nickname, "Shannanigans." She threw a drink in the face of a guy in a bar once who called her fat, after she wouldn't dance with him. This girl is not above getting downright stupid when she has had one too many cocktails. She calls it her "Inner Amazon," but I call it her "Inner Drunk Crazy Bitch."

"But ..." Arianna leads, sure there's more to the

story and assuming, as I do, that it probably has something to do with "karma."

"But I gave him another chance," Shannon says.

"Uh huh," we all say, in unison, nodding at each other, knowingly.

She blushes a little, aware that we all question her naïveté. "Well he mentioned a place in Aspen! How could I not hang on for that? Besides, I felt like I had a real past life connection with this one."

Arianna winks at me and I raise my eyebrow back. Do we know our friends, or what? We all love Shannon, but sometimes her woowoo stuff just doesn't fly in NYC.

Shannon doesn't notice the wink, and plows on, "And I'll have you remember I got wise after the country house debacle. I called a good friend who lives out there—ski *and* yoga instructor, and let me tell you she lives the high life. Anyway, she helped me with some due diligence. We discovered 'his place' was really his aunt's condo in Carbondale, twenty minutes outside of Aspen. I called him on it and he caved. I told him I couldn't be with a liar. It goes against my spiritual beliefs to be anything but transparent."

"Poseurs are a tricky breed," Catherine adds. "They think our panties will hit the floor when we see all the flashy material stuff, but in the end the well dries up as soon as their true selves shine. I bet some of them are even good guys on the inside, but they're so busy covering it up in an effort to impress, we may never know."

Shannon dives in, "Yes! Everyone has the potential to be good. It's just a matter of how much baggage they're carrying around with them!"

I sense that Shannon is about to start getting a little too deep for casual, catty brunch talk, so I change the subject. "So for the sake of informative blogging," I say, "what are our Top Five Questions to Ask Before Going Away With a Guy?"

"Number one: Are we going to be the only couple in the house?" Lauren starts. I hold up one finger, to count it.

"Two: When were you last there?" Shannon adds, as I add a finger to the count. "Y'know, to make sure the indoor plumbing works and stuff." We all nod in emphatic agreement.

"Number three, but it should be number one: What will we be doing while we're there?" says glorious Arianna. "I don't pinch hit for landscapers."

Just the thought of Arianna doing any kind of manual labor dissolves us all into laughter. When I think Catherine's Bellini is in danger of shooting out her nose, I calm us all down with my own contribution, while adding a third and fourth finger to the count: "Four: What is the *exact address* of where we're going?"

"Yes!" Catherine shouts, a little too loudly, "That way, if you don't know, you can Google Map it before even leaving your house. Street view, ladies, street view!" We all nod in agreement. How did we ever survive without Google?

"And finally," Catherine continues, "number five: How are we getting there?"

"That's easy," Arianna replies, breezily, "The answer should always start with 'private': private car, private plane, even private train compartment. You name it, so long as I'm not mixed in with the steerage."

"Ahem," I clear my throat at her, "You are sitting with steerage now, and you have been steerage yourself at some point in your life. Remember?"

"In another lifetime, darling, and I have left behind any desire to mix with riff raff."

Arianna's snobbery is rewarded with a round of eye rolls from all of us, even though we all sort of agree with her, in a guilty kind of way. We all totally understand that desire.

The conversation begins to get off topic, and we stop talking about the blog and men. There are other things in life, you know! Before I know it, we've settled up with Bilbo but not without my usual survey of the bill. I've caught extra things added to checks—not just here, of course—one too many times to not risk looking like a cheapskate. I don't know whether it's deliberate or human error, but once again, I saved us ten bucks from an extra sparkling water we didn't order.

Now we are standing outside. The clock has just crawled past two, and through the window I see a pair of stilettoed feet dancing on a table, their owner fully aware that passersby can see up her short skirt; Bilbo's notorious reservations-only dance party on weekend afternoons is one of the rowdier scenes on the Upper East Side. The bass thumping and occasional whoops filtering outside contrast sharply with the sad, heavy silence hanging over our heads.

It's easy to see that we're trying to maintain the closeness of being seated around a small table. We don't want to leave each other because we don't want Lauren to leave New York. Yes, she's just a plane ride away, but we all know that once someone leaves the city, it's never the same again. Her reality will include palm trees and Cubans. Mine, well, mine will continue to be exactly the same as it's been for ten years. I am especially dreading the empty hole in my life she's about to leave in her wake. But one thing's certain about NYC: it never stops, no matter who leaves or how badly you wish for things to stay the same.

Eventually it's just the two of us huddled at the corner, making excuses to let available cabs go by. We stand there, talking, as if we hadn't just spent hours together. "What am I going to do without you? How am I ever going to figure out what's going on with Canada without you here?"

"Girl," she says, "haven't you read *He's Just Not That into You?*"

I give her a dirty look.

"Don't gimme that face! I know you have. I gave you a copy for your birthday the year it was published!"

"Oh, shut up." I punch her lightly in the arm, and flag down a cab. "One of us has to take the first step, and here's a taxi to show that now's as good a time as any. Call me when you get there?" I say, barely holding in the tears.

"Stop it!" she sobs, "you're gonna make me cry! I'll call as soon as I land." She grabs me in a tight hug, and I squeeze her back, careful not to smudge mascara on her shoulder. I make a mental note of how it feels to hug my best friend for what feels like the last time ever: soft, loving and gently scented by expensive hair products.

The movers had already come to load all of Lauren's things into a truck early that morning. She'll go home for a final walk through the apartment she's called home all these years. Then it's off to JFK with nothing but a carry-on and her iPad. That's how a New Yorker does it.

"You can always come back," I say, pulling away and wiping my tears with the back of my hand.

"And you can always visit," Lauren replies, doing the same. We both laugh as we look for something to wipe our hands on, and she pulls a tissue out of her purse.

"I will. I'll even buy a new bikini to wear on the beach. I love you."

"Love you too, girl. Now get in the cab so I can unglue myself from this corner."

We hug again for a long, long time, until the cabbie impatiently honks his horn for me to get a move on. Neither of us wants to go, but we do.

I get in the cab and know that my mood makes it seem dirtier and stinkier than it really is. I check my phone, having neglected it in favor of the fabulous company I've enjoyed the past couple hours. It vibrates as I pull it out of my bag.

"Hey, gorgeous, it's Matthew. Whatcha doin'? Wanna go to Raoul's and grab a bite?"

It's good to hear his voice, even if he's my Number Two choice in men. And, as good as the arugula salad at Bilboquet is, it's still just a salad. A girl's gotta eat. Well, at least look at the food.

"Sure. I'm already in a cab but I'm uptown. Meet you there in fifteen?"

When I step out of the cab on Prince Street, Matthew is there to offer me his hand. He's a gentleman, this one. I like that.

What I don't expect from this chivalrous fellow is what happens next: he pulls me into his arms and plants a heated kiss square on my mouth. I feel his tongue gently push against my teeth and I melt into him, his arms and his kiss, and allow his warmth to fill the emptiness I feel at Lauren's departure. I may not have fallen head-over-heels for Matthew, but he's here and he's holding me, in a great, comfy warm hug. I love a man who gives a good hug. Sometimes that's the only thing that matters.

CHAPTER 4:
BRIDGE & TUNNEL

I can't run fast enough. No matter how hard I pump my arms and churn my legs, I don't seem to be getting anywhere. To make matters worse, I am being chased by a pack of wolves. Everywhere I turn, there they are: staring with beady eyes, growling and snarling. Their hot breath curls around my face and it's hard to breathe. Soon I will feel their sharp teeth closing around my skin, powerful jaws ...

The dream feels eerily similar to the one I use to have quite often in my teenage years. I was the youngest of three and the only girl. My father was incredibly strict and wouldn't take anything less than straight A's, and he was a regular drill sergeant about it. All of his years as a college football coach taught him the importance of education because he saw a number of his favorite "dumb jock" athletes having nothing to fall back on when they didn't get signed to a major league team.

Studying was a twenty-four/seven job for me back then, and I lived on pizza and pop—pizza and beer, in college. By the time I graduated college I had a 4.0 with a summa cum lard ass, nickname courtesy of dear old Dad. He thought he was being funny. I thought he was being a dick.

In any case, the dream reminds me of the way I always felt back then—that, despite my best efforts, I was always on the verge of being swallowed up.

I feel my phone buzzing against the nightstand.

"What's wrong?" Lauren says to my groggy greeting. "You sound weird. Did I interrupt something? You didn't drink and scribe last night, did you?"

"No, no—nothing as terrible as drunk texting, no. Just woke up from a bad dream, that's all. I was taking a nap. How was your flight?"

"Easy. How was your date with Matthew? And why are you napping now? It's Sunday night."

"Exactly. Sunday afternoons are made for napping, especially after being out late last night. Matthew is nice. He's no Canadian, but he's an amazing kisser. Our day date turned into an all-day-into-the-night date. He wants to go out again on Thursday."

"Good. Arianna will be thrilled. So listen, I'm calling because I did some thinking on the plane ..."

I pause in my stretching because this could be it—this could be Lauren realizing she made a huge mistake and telling me she's coming home on the next flight out.

"I want to contribute to the blog."

I exhale audibly but hope she doesn't misinterpret my disappointment to her suggestion.

"What? No good?" she asks, and I can hear the embarrassment in her voice. "You're right, it's stupid. This is your thing ..."

"Chill, girl! It's a great idea! I would love to have you contribute. I'm just waking up here—cut a sister a break."

She's suddenly going a hundred miles an hour, and her contagious excitement gets me up and padding to the kitchen to hunt for breakfast. I find a Slim-Fast shake in the back of my refrigerator. I move that aside for now.

"I wrote something on the plane, once they let me turn my iPad on. That was a boring ass flight and I couldn't sleep, so I typed it out. I'm sending it now. Feel free to change it around but I think it's pretty badass if I do say so myself. And I do."

"Thanks, mama. Can't wait to read it. Call you after."

"X-O, girl."

"X-O."

I settle into my desk chair with something resembling a parfait: yogurt, organic granola and fresh strawberries I grabbed on a whim during my last Whole Foods run. Every time I walk in there I convince myself I'll emerge healthier, committed to supporting local farms, maybe even vegan. Instead, I walk out broke and loaded down with things like wheat grass that will grow mold before I ever bother to juice it into a super shot. Within an hour, I've forgotten my resolve and I glug a Diet Coke or get a whiff of Smith and Wollensky during lunch and it's all over—I can't pass up the smell of a good steakhouse. Must be the Texan in me. Then I spend the rest of the week eating a fistful of wilted organic greens three times a day to make up for the calories and the money spent on my new and improved healthy lifestyle.

The subject line to Lauren's email says it all: B&T.

There's no doubt in my mind that this entry is about her Bridge and Tunnel man. He was Lauren's favorite mistake. We all have stories about B&Ts— men who have to travel from New Jersey or Long

Island to get to Manhattan and who, apparently, live by wildly different rules than we residents do. I open the email and read:

> Oh, boy, Bridge and Tunnel—where do I begin? I guess at the beginning.
>
> The first few years living in Manhattan, I swore off B&T on the advice of my friends. "Don't go near *that*," they'd say, "*that*'s from New Jersey." Other times, I'd watch my girls end a conversation abruptly when a guy in a club revealed he was "over the bridge" or "under the tunnel" from Long Island. B&T boys were taboo—that I learned quickly. What I had to learn for myself is "why."
>
> It took me a little longer to figure out that the Hamptons were also part of Long Island, except guys from there were immune from the B&T curse.
>
> Anyway, I never quite knew why me and my girls were blowing off guys just because they didn't live in the city limits. We were snobs, I guess, and I went along with it because I was new and needed friends more than a guy in my bed. All I knew for sure was that I wanted a man who would treat me like a princess, STAT! Little old Lauren from Louisiana was ready for the royal experience.
>
> As I continued to live in New York, however, I met more and more B&Ts, and I was fed up with the dating "rules." This guy was hot as hell and I didn't care if his accent made it sound like he was trying to swallow back half of his words on their way out of his mouth. He was

dapper, a whiz on Wall Street. No expense was spared when we went out, but he never flashed his money around like some wannabe baller. Yeah, my B&T knew how to treat a woman. From the finest restaurants to the best clubs, jewelry gifted for no reason, drivers to take us around town ... Fuggettaboutit! He had it all. A happy hour martini would lead to a bottle of Cristal, then oops—"I'm in Miami, bitch!" He thought nothing of spontaneously boarding a plane for a weekend of beachside bar hopping.

Living life in the fast lane leaves no time to hit the ATM, so B&T guys carry around fat, silver money clips—monogrammed of course. B&T boys don't miss a beat when it comes to having the best of everything. One night I lost my phone at the club and was totally broken up about it. The next morning, a brand new B-berry was waiting for me with my doorman. Who does that? Bridge & Tunnel boys, that's who!

Their attention to detail gets applied to everything in their lives, especially restaurants. I saw a whole new side of New York: Rao's, Il Mulino, Il Cantoroni, Scalinatella, Strip House and countless others. Before I met my B&T, I thought Greek food was a chopped salad with feta and kalamata olives. Then he took me to Milos. He ordered everything from tzatziki to htipiti, skordalia to octopus with revythada, sardines and fresh fish. He insisted that I try everything, explaining that his taste was impeccable. And you know what? It was.

One night in the dead of winter, we were walking down Park Avenue and I couldn't hide the fact that I was freezing my ass off. I was in my "uniform": black mini dress, black boots and nude fishnets (they're classy, I swear). In my rush to meet B&T, I'd left my house wearing mismatched gloves and an old hat that kept blowing off. New Yorkers generally don't invest in nice hats and gloves because inevitably they get lost, stolen or ruined in one season.

Not a B&T, though. Never a B&T.

He turned to me in the middle of the street that night and proclaimed, "You need a fuh!"

"I'm listening," I said.

From then on, I had sheared mink coats with matching mink earmuffs, and chinchilla stoles. I reveled in the pampering. And why shouldn't I? You schlep to work every day, freezing to death and fighting for space on the train, engage in umbrella wars on the sidewalks, argue with taxi drivers, work with aggressive bitches who would happily push you into oncoming traffic. So who cares if someone wants to spoil you a bit?

My girls were not pleased. They refused to call my B&T by his name, only referring to him as "Brooklyn Boy." Were they jealous? Probably. My man may not have gone to an Ivy League school and he certainly wasn't born in the "right" zip code, but he knew how to treat a woman—in and out of the bedroom. Oh, yes, you can be sure I made it clear to my cattier friends that my B&T knew how to rock my world. The sex was off the charts—and to this day, it's still some of the best of my life.

The moral of the story? Don't stereotype! It wasn't until I hit thirty that I opened my eyes to dating different types of men with different backgrounds. It changed my life.

The other moral to this story? B&Ts have it all ... including lots of women. They're notorious players, as I learned the hard way. They want to live large and will do whatever it takes to feel like kings, whether that means a penthouse in the city or a four-story brownstone in Cobble Hill.

If you get lucky enough to get a Bridge & Tunnel boy, lock it down! If you can reform him of his player ways, you could be getting the royal treatment for life.

I immediately call Lauren but struggle to dial because I'm so excited.

"Girl, that was amazing! Funny and smart—*you* should be writing this thing!"

"Aww good—so you liked it? Remember Chris?" she says, and I know she's regretting how things ended.

"Yeah, he was a dollface. Only ..."

"Only he couldn't keep his dick in his pants?"

"There was that."

"But before that, I was crazy about him. Remember how great he was? And how bitchy Arianna and Closet Freak Catherine were about him? Man, they could not stand that boy!"

"Yup."

There's a long pause. I wonder briefly how many of our choices are shaped by our desire to avoid the judgmental cattiness of our friends. The prospect is depressing but I'm rescued by Lauren, who says, "You know he's married now."

"Ah, mama—you'll find the right one. He's out

there! Trust me!"

"Yeah," she says, her fiery confidence returning, "in Miami, bi-otch! I gotta go; the car's downstairs. Heading to Mynt tonight. Time for Laurenita to get her mojito on."

"Enjoy it! Call me later."

When I hang up it's like all the energy from our phone call disappears. I'm as melancholy as I was when I laid down hours ago. I haven't heard from Canada, and while I have a text from Matthew waiting for my reply, I don't feel like it. He wants to know if I ski. I assume an invitation to his place in Jackson Hole is coming, and I could probably use some time away.

However, I feel like I need to take things slow with this one. Not just because Matthew comes off as a good guy—maybe a keeper—but because in my heart of hearts, I can't commit to anything until I find out what Canada is all about. Who needs Jackson Hole when the Great White North can fill the only hole I'm worried about?

By the time I tidy up the apartment, drink that Slim-Fast, order take out for dinner and lay out my clothes for Monday morning, I'm wiped. I fall onto the sofa and check my phone out of habit.

You free Wed for dinner and a play session?

Holy shit. Canada. My mind is off and racing at the prospect of a "play session" and my stomach drops when I realize this guy can get me with nothing but a text message. It's not even a sext message, either. *Fuck, you are in deep, girl.*

I wait a respectable thirty seconds to reply. He confirms. Is it Wednesday yet? Because I am ready and waiting to eat, play, love. We'll be meeting at a bar near my place at eight o'clock. How convenient, I think sardonically. But what can I expect? I fucked this guy after knowing him for twenty minutes, and if I'm honest I would've done him sooner if there hadn't been so much traffic leaving the club. I'm not the type he's bringing to church.

I immediately text Lauren and her response says all that words can't: !!!!!!!!!!

My takeout, a 332 calorie turkey burger from Energy Kitchen, won't be here for thirty minutes and I figure I might as well work up an appetite. I slide into the sheets with Lily, the soft, silky, cylindrical companion who lives in my right side nightstand.

"Hello, old friend," I whisper.

I flip the switch to Speed Three—no time for idle chit-chat. I press her gently against my warm body and imagine my first night with Canada. His hands pull me into him and I feel his erection straining against his jeans. He traces a line of hot kisses down my neck until his mouth closes over my nipple and suddenly his hand tangles up in my hair and he pulls—just hard enough to make me arch my back so his teeth press into my flesh. I'm unzipping him now, and as soon as I free him from his boxer briefs the warm, wet tip of his penis joins his fingers at my clit and I'm coming, coming, coming …

I let Lily drop to the sheets. The aftershocks of my orgasm send ripples down my legs. I will lay here and enjoy the afterglow, catching my breath for another fifteen minutes until dinner arrives.

I've gotta eat before Round Two!

CHAPTER 5:
THE MENHATTAN PROJECT

Monday turns out to be a blustering, cold and rainy day. It's all I can do to make it through a day of work. This is the kind of day where anyone of right mind would curl up in bed with a book and a mug of hot chocolate. And when I see on my schedule that afternoon a meeting with the guys about Eric's restaurant venture, I know that I have to make up some excuse to get out of there.

If we had not already crossed the line into "personal relationship" territory, I would absolutely recommend that we do whatever we can to support Eric's project. It's a great idea, financially feasible, and he's done his homework. His pitch was good and I have no doubt that he has a fighting chance.

But …

Visions of future accusations and mayhem flood my head, and I know that I cannot be a part of this decision. I tell the guys I forgot about a dentist appointment, and beg off. "I trust you to make the right choice," I call out to them as I flee, chicken-shit, out the door and into the elevator.

I have to wait longer than usual for a cab, so I'm soaked to the bone when I get home. I strip off my wet things, pull on some yoga pants and a fluffy sweatshirt, and curl up on the sofa with my laptop. I might as well use this downtime to put my money where my mouth is and create this blog, even if I don't know a hashtag from a hash pipe. I have a lot to learn.

After spending a frustrating half hour trying to decide on which blogging site to use—I'm a complete newbie at this, so I have no idea which one is best—I finally decide that WordPress has the look I want the blog to have, and it seems pretty easy to use. But then when it's time to actually create the blog, I realize that I'm going to have to give some personal information. This will not do.

I wrestle with this in my head. On one hand, this blog has to be anonymous or I won't be able to be truly honest. On the other hand, anonymously dishing dirt about someone—even if I'm not naming names—is another chicken-shit thing to do, and that's twice in one day. Am I really that big a weenie, that I can't face confrontation?

Yes, I decide, yes, I am that big a weenie.

This whole phony name and concern about my identity being revealed has me wondering if this is a good idea. I know that I'm not breaking any laws, and I wouldn't get into any *really* serious trouble, but I'm going to be posting my secrets, and the stories my friends tell me. I want them to be comfortable talking to me. While I'm not usually a Nervous Nelly, I'm a little scared. So I make extra sure that there is no way anyone can track me back to the blog I'm about to unleash upon the city.

I can't use my real email address or name, so I create an anonymous account. I already use Gmail and I don't have time to learn a new email site, so I go there and create an account for menhattanproject@gmail.com. Once that's done, and I've verified it on the blog site, I create the blog at http://menhattanproject.wordpress.com.

Just seeing the words *The Menhattan Project* as the blog's header sends a thrill of excitement through me. I'm really doing it! I don't really have much of a creative outlet in my life, and this project has reminded me of how much I loved writing when I was younger. I always got good grades in English, and my college creative writing professors were very encouraging. In fact, one was downright dismayed when she learned that I was majoring in business.

"You have such a gift!" she said, but at the time I was too young and insecure to take the compliment at face value. I thought that she was just sucking up to the coach's kid. It helps to remember her words, now, when I'm faced with the daunting self-assigned task of being a voice for the women of my generation.

I create the "About" page with what I hope is tantalizing text:

> *Welcome to the Menhattan Project, a blog that romps through the streets and the sheets of the world's greatest city, Manhattan. Let's have a little girl talk, shall we? Ladies, chime in and share your stories! We're all in this together, right? #letsdish*

I have no idea if that hashtag is appropriate or what it's for, but everyone else is doing it, so I give it a whirl. I am #clueless.

Lauren's blog, which is already written and only needs a little bit of tweaking and anonymizing, is a perfect debut piece and gets posted first. I know this will make her happy, which is a bonus. I grin just imaging the look that I know will be on her face when she sees it. I already hate that she lives so far away and it's only been a day since she left. In reality, I probably wouldn't have seen her today anyway if she still lived here, but knowing that I couldn't if I wanted to really sucks. Combined with this weather, I have the potential to go gloomy, so posting her blog makes me feel like she's still here.

I look at the clock and see that it's still pretty early in the day. Creating the blog didn't take half as long as I thought it would, so I pull out my notes and recorder and start transcribing all of the tales my girls have shared with me for future blogs, and edit them into readable essays. What great stories and what great blog posts they'll make! I have so much fun with them, that I can't wait to post some more of them, but I can't post more than one blog a day. Can I?

Well, of course I *can*, but do I want to?

Nah, I don't want to get ahead of myself. I copy and paste several completed blog posts onto the WordPress site and save them as drafts. I don't have to post them, but at least now they're done and stored on the site for whenever I choose to make them go live. They're just waiting for clearance to take off.

As I'm playing around with the site's dashboard, I see that I can post blogs on whatever date I choose, so I change the date on Lauren's blog to one week ago, and post a couple more—I give Groupers, Minnows and Dealfish all their own posts, with their own phony dates, and create categories to sort them under, in case I create any follow-up blogs on those topics.

Once I have those four blogs posted, I give it a rest. This feels like a good start. I still have the all of the various Poseur blogs and a couple others saved as drafts, which I can post whenever I choose. Meantime, I'll gather more stories.

I look at the clock again when I notice that it's after dark and I need to turn some lights on. Hours have passed, and it only seemed like minutes! My foot has fallen asleep from sitting on it for so long, and my legs are stiff. I can actually hear myself crunching when I stand up and stretch. That is definitely enough for one day!

I send Lauren a text with the blog's address and wait for her response.

It doesn't take long. My phone rings and when I see her name on my caller ID, I answer it nonchalantly, "Thank you for calling The Menhattan Project. May I help you?"

I have to pull the phone from my ear, she's squealing so loudly, "GIRRRRRRRRRRRRRRL! I LOVE IT!!! You put my blog first! Oh, that means so much to me. I wasn't sure if you really liked it or if you were just being nice."

"Aw, honey, I thought it was great! Obviously. Did you read the rest of them?"

"Not yet. I was too excited. Give me a minute."

I wait, patiently, listening to her clicking and tapping away on her computer. She reads the other blogs, half out loud to herself, cackling, "I love it!" now and then. "You know, don't you, that putting a hashtag on the 'About' page doesn't make any sense, right?"

"No! I don't know what half of this shit means. I'm lucky I have time to keep up with Facebook. I just know you're supposed to hashtag everything you post online."

"Girl, that's just for Twitter, Facebook and

Pinterest, you know, sites like those where people use hashtags for searching. But it looks kinda cute there, like maybe you meant it that way, just to be funny. You do have a Twitter account for this, don't you?"

"No, do I need one?" My heart sinks. I've been avoiding Twitter because I just don't see the point, but I've definitely been feeling the pressure from my friends who do.

"Well, it would help when you post a blog to blast it out on Twitter with a hashtag Menhattan, or hashtag douchebag if you're writing about that kind of guy. That way people who want to read the subject you're writing about will find it, and the ones who follow hashtag Menhattan will know when you post a new blog."

"Ugh. Fine. I'll get a Twitter account."

"And Facebook. You gotta build a Facebook page for this."

"Oh, for God's sake. This is going to take a lot more time than I thought."

"Uh huh. Now lemme finish reading."

She's finally finished and gushes, "Oh my God, I didn't think you'd really do it! I love this idea and I'm so proud of you! I can say I know another celebrity!"

Panicked, I remind her, "NO! You can't tell anyone it's me! Besides, I'm hardly a celebrity and neither is the blog. I just posted these today so no one but you and I even know about it."

"Hashtag NotForLong!" she cries, "Don't worry. I won't tell anyone it's you, but I'm sure as hell gonna tell everyone I know about this blog! Every woman I know will be sending you their stories, I can already tell. There's just something about the energy of this thing. It feels so … right, somehow. I see big things ahead for you! Hashtag SuperStar!"

I laugh, "Now you're starting to sound like Shannon, with all of her psychic predictions."

"Eenie meenie, chili beanie, the spirits are about to speak," Lauren intones, in a spooky voice. "Girl, I gotta go. I'm sorry to hang up so soon, but you caught me just as I was walking out the door to get some groceries in this place. There are boxes everywhere, and there's nothing in my fridge except for a half eaten empanada and a cold cortadito, and some basic supplies that my cousin brought for me when she picked me up at the airport. I haven't eaten anything but fast food and a quick peanut butter and mayonnaise sandwich since I landed yesterday. I need something green!"

I remember that she used to eat those god-awful sounding sandwiches when we first met and I, as her diet buddy, had to talk her out of habitually consuming her favorite double-fat calorie overload. She refused to stop eating them until I agreed to try a bite, "… just so you'll truly appreciate what I'm giving up. The secret is using Miracle Whip, not just any old mayonnaise." The sandwich wasn't as bad as it sounded, I admitted—in fact it was pretty good—but I wasn't about to let myself get hooked on something so gloriously fattening.

"Be careful with those! Isn't that what killed Elvis?"

She laughs her goofy laugh and says in an exaggerated Southern drawl, "Nah, that was peanut butter and nanners." We both make disgusted noises, and she wraps up our call, saying, "Okay, hun, buh-bye. I'll talk to you sooooon, writer girl!"

We hang up, and I go back to my laptop to once

again admire my handiwork. I see a comment notification on the first blog already. My heart races. Already??? I click the comment link and see, posted by "Lakisha Mae," a comment that reads, "I LOVE THIS! Imma tell all my friends about this blog!" with a smiley face emoticon.

I love it, too. If nothing else, it makes me feel like my best friend never left.

CHAPTER 6:
MOMMY HAVE YOU SEEN MY BLANKIE?

After making double, triple, quadruple sure that there is nothing to do with the blog that can point to me, last night I sent out an email blast to all of my most hooked-in, scene-stealing, trend-setting friends about a certain blog I stumbled upon while looking for a new recipe for grouper. Only my closest friends, who are all sworn to secrecy, will be in on the joke, but it made me laugh.

"The blog's anonymous author is funny and smart," I wrote to them, "and shouldn't we all try to support a fellow female powerhouse trying to make sense of the men on our blessed island?"

The rallying cry landed on willing ears and this morning I was inundated with emails thanking me for the link. Watching my Google Analytics stats steadily climb was all the confirmation I needed that my girls had come through once again by forwarding the link to "The Menhattan Project" to every potentially interested woman on their contact lists. The excitement of having the blog take off helped pass the hours quickly—a feat I didn't think was possible as every hour seemed to stretch into infinity while I waited for Wednesday to arrive.

Even so, today feels like it's moving so slowly, time might actually be passing in reverse. I text my friend Meredith about margaritas at Dos Caminos Soho tonight. When it comes to Tequila on a Tuesday, I know I can count on Meredith. Her confirmation for 5:30 skinny margs is a bigger relief than I'd care to admit.

Meredith has been peddling pharmaceuticals for as long as I can remember. She always says showing up for work in Manhattan is half the job; the other half is a combination of constant smiling and ass kissing. She's the kind of woman who can roll into work on Friday after an all-nighter entertaining clients, knock down a sugar-free latte and a Red Bull, and face the day with more enthusiasm than a high school cheerleader at homecoming. "Pharma Fridays", as I call them, are an aspect of the job that would destroy some and break most—but not our Margarita Meredith.

Meredith recently moved out of the city to Long Island with her new husband and his two bratty kids. She has pale, alabaster skin and curly black hair; her light green eyes, which would look spooky on anyone else, complete her ethereal look. Still, the stresses of work and step-mothering two horribly mannered children have begun to take their toll. She's gained a little more weight than she likes to carry around and doesn't turn as many heads as she used to.

Long gone are the days of sex in the stairwell of Mount Sinai with some young, hot surgery resident. Even Meredith's typical outgoingness has taken a nosedive of late. She's becoming a woman who gives great advice but can't ever seem to follow it herself. Proof positive? While she's sweet and affectionate, Meredith exclusively attracts men with overbearing mothers—and her husband is no exception. She would have warned any one of us off such a "catch" if the shoe was on the other foot, but she didn't hesitate to cram her feet in and skip down the aisle.

Shannon, our favorite armchair guru/shrink thinks that Meredith needs to examine her own personality to see why these guys are attracted to her and why she puts up with them. Men marry women just like dear old Mom, and Shannon thinks Meredith is blind to why she's so magnetic to Momma's Boys.

But today I plan to put Meredith's experience with the dreaded Momma's Boy to good use. Lauren and I decided I'd "confide" that I know the anonymous author of the Menhattan Project blog— an ex-pat living in Paris I happened to meet on a business trip. I feel kind of bad about not telling her my secret, but too many people know about this already, and Meredith is too busy being a wife and mom to be as close knit as the rest of my friends who already know.

I'll tell her I'm doing recon as a favor to further the cause. I can't imagine any of my women friends— who consider talking a veritable Olympic sport— would pause too much to question my cover. Meredith is no exception.

She walks into Dos Caminos looking frazzled.

"I don't want to talk about it," she says in response to my concerned look. "It's just … stuff. Home stuff. Can't get into it now."

"At least not without a margarita," I say.

It doesn't take long for a Patron Silver

pomegranate margarita—no salt—to make its way in front of Meredith. It takes even less time for her to down half of it and start rattling off a litany of complaints about Joe, her husband, and Linda, his mother.

"He would still be sucking Linda's *tit*," she spits, "if only she'd let him! He can't go to the fucking bathroom without alerting her first. Mommy tells him where to live. Mommy tells him what to wear. Mommy tells him what to eat and, most offensively, who to date and marry. How I got enough of her approval to get Joe down the aisle I'll never know, but she's made it clear since the nuptials that *they* are blood and I am ... well ... not. I don't know if my husband has a single original idea in his entire brain. And don't get me wrong—we all love a man on good terms with his mother. But this? This is a bit much."

"Can I ... my friend ... put this in her blog if she changes the names to protect the innocent?" I hope she doesn't catch my little slip of the tongue. "Dating a Momma's Boy is a topic that a lot of women can relate to."

"Hell YEAH!" she says, gulping down the other half of her drink as I pull out my recorder. She looks surprised to see me so prepared to take down every word, but lets it go when brain freeze hits and she takes a breath, squeezing her eyes shut against the discomfort. Shaking it off, she continues after waving to the waiter to bring her another.

"A Momma's Boy will never back you up when it comes to disagreements with the mutha. It's always 'My mom said we should ...' and 'Linda thinks ...' Sure, at first you think it's sweet that they're such close friends, but don't fool yourself. You'll never come first. 'Joe,' you say, 'You don't have to call your mother to discuss which humidifier to buy. It's a humidifier. *Just. Pick. One.*' But of course he picks up the phone anyway."

When Meredith was single, she described an extreme Momma's Boy scenario that I've never forgotten. In fact, as she sits here droning on and on about Joe and Linda, I'm a little shocked that she didn't learn her lesson from that infamous MB. I ask her to tell me that story for the blog, and she's happy to oblige, once the waiter drops off her second margarita.

"We met when I was out with my friends one night. After our third date, he asked me back to his place. I figured it was harmless enough—where's the risk in a little smooching and cuddling, right?" I nod encouragingly. "I protected my honor in advance by mentioning I had to be up early for work. His response? 'Doesn't everyone have to work tomorrow?'"

Which Meredith thought was just adorable.

"So," she continues, after a long pull on her drink and another brain freeze wince, "When we got to his place, I noticed pictures of his mother all over the place. There were a few solo shots of just her, a few of him and her, and some of the whole family unit: Mom, MB, Dad. Everyone has pictures of their family, I thought. *Right?*"

Again, I nod, "Absolutely."

"He'd opened a bottle of good red wine and handed me a glass. We sat on the sofa, talking and drinking, eventually abandoning both in favor of kissing and some good old-fashioned heavy petting, which was great. Things were going very well.

Wrapped in each other's arms, we made our way toward the bedroom. And once I'm lying down, he pauses."

She gives me a look, warning me that something big is coming.

"'Come with me,' he says. 'There's something I want to show you. In the closet.'"

I can't wait to hear it—I love this story and she knows it—she's enjoying the fact that I'm on the edge of my seat. She continues, dramatically, "Alarm bells started to peal in my brain that very instant, but I held out hope that my date was just into a little kink. Nothing wrong with a little kink, right?"

"Yes! Right! Just tell me!"

"He took my hand with a sweet earnestness that made me believe that whatever stood in that closet would be fine—great, even." She gives me another deadpan look. "I was wrong."

After another pull on her margarita and another wave to the waiter for a third cocktail—she's going to be staggering out of here if she doesn't slow down—she finally continues.

"'I want you to meet ... *Blankie*,' he says, pulling a tattered cream-colored rag from the closet."

I blink in mock disbelief and smother a guffaw.

"Yeah. His fucking 'blankie!' I swear, it looked like it hadn't been washed since the Reagan administration. That didn't stop this pathetic urchin from pushing the thing into my face, saying 'breathe deep and smell my childhood.'"

We both laugh so hard our sides ache and people at the other tables start to stare. Wiping tears from her eyes, she picks up the recorder and slurs, directly into the mic, "Did you hear that? SMELL MY

FUCKING CHILDHOOD!"

We dissolve into helpless mirth and the waiter gives us the stinkeye as he delivers her third margarita. "Would you like to order a pitcher?" he asks, with more snark than necessary.

She waves him away and takes a big sip, catching her breath. "Needless to say, I was suddenly, inexplicably exhausted and had to go home immediately. I never saw him again."

She checks her makeup in a mirror she digs out of her purse, saying "So. Enough about me. What's new with you?" I start to give her the lowdown on Canada, about how it's driving me insane that I don't know if or when I'll ever see him, and wondering if I'm wasting my time with him, but she interrupts me to ask, "Haven't you ever read *He's Just Not That Into You?*"

"Seriously?" I shriek, "You too?"

"Well??? Have you?"

"Yes!" I insist, "But this is different. He's so ..."

"Honey, that's what we all say. Drop him. I don't care how good the sex is."

I catch her checking her watch when she thinks I'm not looking. It's pretty obvious that she is no longer into the conversation. Her mind is on other things and I let her off easy, especially because I don't like where this conversation is heading. "Do you have to go?" I ask.

"Yeah, I do." She pounds back the last of her margarita, and scarfs down some chips and guacamole before sliding out of her chair and grabbing her purse. "Sorry to run, dollface—gotta get home and feed those brats."

With a kiss on each cheek and a half-hearted

wave, she totters drunkenly out the door.

I shouldn't be surprised. Since Meredith got married and moved, she's been distracted. I don't hold it against her, especially after seeing how miserable she is trying to cope with Joe's family. All us gals share the notion that she'll be back in the city in a few years. Until then, we'll keep her seat warm.

Meantime, I got two good blogs out of our visit.

Walking home in the balmy evening air, a lovely switch from yesterday's weather, I feel a swarm of butterflies in my stomach when I realize that this time tomorrow, I'll be face to face with Canada. I haven't been this excited about a guy in a long time. Four years, actually, since Jeremy and I broke up—but who's counting?

I can't deny that the prospect of a real crush is a little terrifying. There's a certain catch-as-catch-can attitude that comes with having a crush. We convince ourselves it's safe to set down the safeguards we've been carrying around since the last time we had our hearts broken. We tell ourselves this time will be different.

Then maybe we should not fuck on the first date, says a voice in my head. Curiously, it sounds like my mother. But come on—even *she* would have slept with this one.

Chills run down my spine despite the night's warmth as I think of Jeremy: the Bigger Better Dealer. Realizing this would make yet another great blog, I pull out my voice recorder, surreptitiously speaking into the mic, hoping no one notices the crazy lady talking to herself without a Bluetooth in her ear.

The Bigger Better Dealer always has a weather

eye on the horizon, hoping to see the next big thing—or the next gorgeous, younger woman—coming his way. Unable to commit, he's a prime-time player, hell bent on stealing the best years of your life.

We met at a party the year after I moved to Manhattan and lost a ton of weight, about nine years ago. I was feeling really good about myself—newly thin, freshly in love with my new city—he was cute, young, and the textbook Alpha Male to my Alpha Female. The romance was a whirlwind infatuation that led to us moving in together—or rather, me moving into his place—just six months after we started dating.

We took luxurious trips and had romantic adventures. Our families met after the first year and got along great. It seemed like I'd finally found Prince Charming. I was just waiting for my glass slipper—in the form of a Graff diamond, of course.

After two years I began to wonder in earnest about a proposal. We never spoke about where our relationship was heading, and if I so much as skirted the issue, he'd literally break into a sweat. Then he'd get angry—wasn't I happy with the way things were? Why did I need to push him so hard? Didn't he make me happy?

By the end of our third year together, he'd only told me he loved me once without prompting from my end. I started to question if he really cared. The frequency of our conflicts increased as I pressed to find out what I think I already knew.

"I want to be loved completely," I said one day. "I want to be adored. I want someone who can't breathe without me—who can't live without me."

"Then you should go find that," he said.

I was crushed. He'd ripped my heart out with those six simple words, and confirmed what I'd known all along: we would never get married.

The feeling of rejection was soul-sucking and complete. Why couldn't he see that I didn't want just *any* man to adore and love me—I wanted *him*. But the hard lesson I learned was that you can't force a man to love you the way you want to be loved. All he can do is love you the best way he knows how. Sometimes it's not enough.

Part of me was afraid to leave him all those years. I thought if I could just be a little more perfect, he'd change his mind and put a ring on my finger. Without my realizing it, my self-esteem had dwindled to a barely-flickering flame, and I started to gain weight—a sure barometer that things weren't going very well.

At the end, I was tired—no, exhausted—of feeling inadequate. I was a strong woman in the finance world. I had put myself through business school and had always taken life by the horns. I carved my niche in a city where I hadn't known a single soul before stepping foot off the plane at JFK. What had happened to me? What had happened to my power? He made me feel like that isolated little fat girl that nobody picked on their team. Unwanted. But now I was the fat girl again, because of him!

The last year was the hardest. I needed an out. I didn't have the strength to end it on my own; my personal happiness didn't seem like enough of an excuse. I started praying for him to cheat on me so I'd have a good reason to leave.

On our four-year anniversary, I told him he would have to produce a ring or I was out.

Soon after we went on a trip to Punta Del Este. When I came home as unengaged as ever, I was Punta Deppreste. I couldn't believe he would sacrifice our life together over a principle. And I really couldn't believe I was about to do just that.

I sat him down and told him I was leaving. In fact, I'd be out by Friday. He swore up and down he didn't know he was on a timeline and begged me not to go.

I laughed and cruelly said, "Four years of my life is not a timeline, it's a waste of time!" Looking back, I think I must have sounded downright maniacal. "What did you possibly think was going to happen?" I said.

I left with the clothes on my back and two suitcases. That's all I needed; the rest I could improvise. I was working, had a great salary and had just struck a huge bonus. I was on top of the world, albeit from a friend's sofa.

The BBD and I went back and forth for a bit, hashing and rehashing all that had led to our demise. At the end of the day, we both knew he'd never change, and neither would I. Eventually he did a lot to help me adjust to being single again. Regardless of how things ended, we loved one another and I think he felt bad about the way it all went down. He helped me find a new apartment, which was the first real step to getting my bearings in what had become an entirely new world. It's not that so much had changed in those four years—it's that I had.

I am about to let the sullenness of this solitary walk take over and I'm already planning the conciliatory glass of wine I'll drink when I reach my apartment in two blocks' time. That's before I'm grabbed abruptly at the top of both arms.

"Guuuuurl, what is happeninnn?!" my friend Gil drawls. "Dayum, you look goooood. Who you bangin' these days that you look so glowin'?"

Gil is one of the girls. He's a gorgeous Latino, very funny and *very* gay. Just my type. Most of my gay friends lead quiet, relatively normal lives, but who doesn't love a screaming queen?

He lives in both Dallas and New York, and I haven't seen much of him since his new lover got transferred to Texas with American Airlines.

"You look sexy per usual," I say, genuinely thankful that Gil has unknowingly broken the depressing spell about to settle on my shoulders. "How's the honey?"

"Ugh, I just looove him. He's damn ahh-may-zing. I'm just glad an old gurl like me finally got lucky, okrrrrr?" he screeches.

"I'm so happy for you! You definitely deserve it, bitch. God knows we all do, okrrrrr?" I say, happy to be laughing.

Why is it that every time straight girls get together with gay men, everyone turns into a black girl from the 'hood? *Okrrrrr?!*

We chat about the blog and I can't help but reveal my connection to Menhattan. I don't mean to, but it slips out in conversation. Blame the booze. But for all the rumored sexual promiscuity in the gay community, Gil is a lockbox when it comes to secrets. He hints that including a queer perspective could expand my readership to his entire demographic.

"And guuuurl," he says, "do I have a doozie for you. You got a hot minute? Let's grab a cock-a-tail somewhere. Imma 'bout to blow your mind up."

As we walk arm-in-arm to Il Bastardo on Seventh Avenue, I feel my steps lighten. We sit at the bar and order matching mandarin Cosmos.

"I love it here," Gil says.

I can see why. The bartender is a dead ringer for Josh Duhamel and the fitness factor of the other men at the tables is off the charts. Although it's been years since I've dropped all the chub, I still feel like Precious amid all these model-esque figures. "Okay," I say, shaking off my self-consciousness, "let's hear it, bitch!" I whip out my recorder and Gil squeals with glee that he's being interviewed. "Gurl, you're like a salsafied, female Anderson Cooper!"

Gil tells me that back when he was a flight attendant, a co-worker set him up on a blind date. The co-worker claimed that the mystery man had seen Gil out at club Splash ("Puddles, child," Gil says, "mere puddles.") and asked for an introduction. Since finding a worthy male partner in NYC is more difficult than finding a worthy article of clothing at a Barney's Warehouse sale, Gil asked for every possible detail. Jeff described Brandon as tall, very cute, and very ginger.

Gil was pleased. Visions of a cutie with ghost-white skin and a pristine, chiseled smile with freckles artfully sprinkled over his cheeks popped into his head. He told Jeff to give Brandon his number.

"This was the mid-nineties, gurl, before cell phones," Gil says. To both of us, it seems like a lifetime ago.

He didn't hear from Brandon that first week and asked Jeff about him the next time they worked together. Apparently Brandon told Jeff he called several times but got a busy tone. Gil didn't believe it but let it go.

Eventually, the connection was made and the two men spoke on the phone. Brandon's voice was sexy and smooth. Gil could only imagine what he looked like in person.

"I was friskier than a cat at its nip," Gil tells me. "I insisted we meet soon but tried not to sound desperate. We planned our date for that Friday. Needless to say, I did what every good gay man does before a hot date. I got a mani, pedi, shopped for a new outfit and took a wire brush to my ass."

When seven o'clock came and the door buzzed, Gil went to meet his date with heated anticipation. Brandon was everything he'd imagined.

"He smiled back at me and we chatted for a minute, but I could tell he was feeling unsettled. He was shifting from foot to foot—and cheek to cheek, I saw—bobbing his head like a man strung out. Was he high, I wondered? Nah—didn't seem tweeky enough. Eventually he asked to use the restroom and excused himself. I showed him the way and busied myself pouring our drinks. Though I had every intention to wait, I started sipping my vodka tonic when the minutes ticked by. Five minutes ... ten ... fifteen.

Twenty minutes passed, gurl. Hand to God."

"I finally mustered up the courage to knock on the door and ask if he was okay. He responded nervously that all was well. I heard the toilet flush. I figured that was the end of whatever episode was happening behind that door. I went to turn some music on, resolved to handle this little faux pas with grace. That's when I heard it ..."

"Heard what?" I ask, and realize I am literally on the edge of my seat.

"The second flush."

"No!" I gasp.

"*Yes*. I heard feet scurrying and the sudden crash of porcelain on tile. I made my way back down the hall to find water seeping out from underneath the door. *Uh-uh*, I thought to myself. *Surely this man 'cleaned the kitchen' before coming over*. I couldn't have been more wrong, gurl. And when I saw my Turkish cotton towels pressed against the door, I downright de-MAN-ded to be let in. He hesitated, but what choice did he have? The door swung open and there he stood, shame faced, his loafers soaked to the leather. The toilet was filled practically to the brim with paper. But my eyes were drawn away from that desecrated porcelain throne to a god-de-dam *abomination* on the floor. And I do mean a-BOMB-ination ..." Gil pauses to let this sink in. I nearly choke on the image forming in my mind.

"It wasn't ..." I say, hoping against all hope that I'm wrong.

"It WAS, gurl," Gil says, leaning in conspiratorially. "That diva got shit all over my floor!"

"No!" I say again, and I really can't believe this is

real. Dating in New York is more of a health hazard than any of us thought, apparently.

"He apologized profusely and was obviously completely embarrassed. I didn't know what to do until I remembered that I had a pair of bedazzled rubber gloves with the feathers at the ends, given to me as a gag gift. Perfect for cleaning up this decidedly not funny moment. I hated having to throw them away, but they were a casualty of Shit Storm Brandon."

Gil sighs, and I know he's actually thinking about those gloves, missing them and despondent about their ruination. "I told him not to worry, shit happens … I just never thought I'd mean that literally. We cleaned up the mess using every available absorbent object in my apartment. In fact, we used so many towels that Brandon offered to run down to the store and buy more. I should have gone with him to pick out the color—anything but moss green, I prayed. Twenty minutes later, I knew he was gone for good. All I was left with was a diluted cocktail and someone else's dirty underwear wedged behind my toilet."

"Gil, that is … *horrifying*," I say, and of course I mean it.

"A couple months later, I spotted Brandon at a local club." A sheepish grin spreads across his face as he relays the night's events:

"I wasn't sure who was more embarrassed, him or me! Once I saw him I bolted for the door. He came running after me apologizing and telling me how he panicked and couldn't face me. He promised he would make it up to me and wouldn't you know?"

"He never called?"

"He never called."

"Bad dates do not discriminate," Gil says. "That man pulled a Ho-dini!"

"A Houdini, like the magician? Because he disappeared?"

"No, gurl," he interrupts, "I said that queen pulled a HO-DINI."

We both howl with laughter at the sheer comedy of the whole situation. I know this is the perfect time to show off the sexy pictures of Mr. Canada I have on my phone.

"I've seen him! Damn gurl he's *foine*!" Gil says. For a moment I dread he's about to tell me Mr. Canada is a fixture on the gay club circuit. "Not at bars, obviously, but in ads. He's gorge. Go, gurrrrl!"

Phew!

"I'm seeing him tomorrow, so I gotta scram home to get my forty winks. Mwa, mwa." We air-kiss each other's cheeks. He picks up my recorder and shrieks into the microphone, "Buh-bye, MEN-hattan!"

"I think I'll hang out here a bit," Gil says with a wink, handing the recorder back to me.

I toss it into my bag, grab my sweater and go, and again send up a small prayer that this city always seems to throw you the lifelines you need exactly when you need them. For all its madness, I wouldn't hang my hat anywhere else.

CHAPTER 7:
OY VEY!

I come home from work the next day to find a welcome email from Lauren in my inbox. Skimming through its contents, I can tell I will enjoy the next ten minutes all the more with a glass of red wine. I pour it, stemware in hand and iPad in lap.

SUBJECT: Penguins

To all my Jewess sisters out there, this is for you.

Remember when your parents said, "Why can't you just find a nice Jewish doctor or lawyer and settle down?"

Well, Mom and Dad, I'll tell you why.

Unless Wonderboy is taking over his parents' law firm or medical practice, or he's the most talented surgeon that's ever squirted Botox, he'll be broke until he's in his forties and work sixteen-hour days until you've forgotten what it's like to see him on a day-to-day basis. When he finally starts bringing home the bacon (kosher turkey bacon, of course), you either won't want him or he won't want you. He'll move on to a younger woman impressed by his wealth and forgiving of his sexual ineptitude. With the state of interest rates on student loans what they are, your ex's new young thing will have to tolerate him if she wants to eat.

The good news? There's hope. In New York, that hope comes in the form of a man I like to call "the Penguin."

Most Penguins have lost their hair due to increased testosterone levels, which means that cue ball comes with an aggressive sense of ambition and extreme success. He's dressed to impress his fellow real estate developers, bankers and entrepreneurs. These are the men who make real deals—not to be confused with Dealfish, who fall woefully short of their Penguin overlords.

As my good friend—let's call him "Craig"—says of himself and his Penguin brethren: "I may be short and bald, but I stand tall on my wallet."

Craig is a wealthy Jewish real estate developer. "Wealthy" is a significant understatement. He loves to play the field but never promises what he can't deliver—not in business, and not in the bedroom. He wears custom suits and Brioni shoes. "If I'm going to look good, you better believe I want my girl to look good, too," he says, slicing into a Wagyu steak. We are at one of the finest restaurants in town, where Craig is a regular. He hasn't waited for a table here in years, he tells me. "What can I say? I take care of the girls out front and they take care of me." Craig wasn't shy about slipping folded-up bills into the hostess's hand when we arrived, even though there wasn't a wait. It's safe to say that Craig is a man who knows how to get what he wants.

"Women love a man they can have fun with," he huffs, "and that usually requires a bankroll. What are a handbag and some red-soled shoes for a woman's contentment? It is what it is."

The oracle has spoken.

If you're looking to study the Penguin in his natural habitat, there's no better place and time than Power Lunch hour on 57th and Park. Penguins galore! You'll see them waddle around, rushing to fill their bellies like their black-and-white-feathered friends in *March of the Penguins*. Lunch may be a time to indulge, but it's also time for a meeting. Penguins never miss a chance to make a deal.

The Power Lunch is particularly key for the Penguin, as one can simultaneously negotiate sales, drink to new partnerships and sate a never-ending appetite for red meat. L'chaim!

Scope out Cipriani's, Michael's, or Fred's at Barneys. Those rows of black town cars in midtown don't mean the UN is in session. No, my friends—merely lunchtime on Park Avenue. Hotties everywhere!

The Penguin's hotness has less to do with chiseled abs and more to do with the chiseled ice sculpture of you as a Greek goddess he'll have commissioned for the birthday party he throws you at the James Hotel's private rooftop bar. Penguins have worked for their wealth; most of them started from nothing and have skyrocketed to positions where they make things happen here in the city. They usually have two cell phones going at once and find it hard to have a conversation without checking one or both—at least during the day. At night, these men are yours. They live by the mantra "work hard, play hard"—which means you'll have a great time with these good-hearted, fun guys.

Penguins don't have time to cheat on you—not usually, anyway. All they really care about is work, excellent food and great sex. If you can handle being on your own during operational business hours but like to party hard—in style—once the sun goes down, you might be just what a Penguin is looking for.

See that gorgeous, leggy blond walking down the street with a short, well-dressed baldy?

Now you know why.

Penguins are most successful with women they scoop up after the unsuspecting doe has just split with a broke hottie. It's like taking candy from a baby. She's weak, lonely, broke from supporting the scrub and in major financial straits. She can't believe her good fortune—or the enormity of his.

If you're not Jewish (aka, a "shiksa") and a Penguin asks if you'd convert, say yes! Jesus was Jewish after all—why shouldn't you be? Plus, being Jewish gains you instant access to the best part of being Jewish: the holidays! There's a Jewish holiday practically every month, and you'll have to be home to supervise the caterers for each and every dinner you host as a result.

Plus, you can rest assured that your liaison won't last forever. Unlike their beaked counterparts, human Penguins don't mate for life. Keep it light and enjoy the ride. If you're at a place in your life where getting involved with a "baldy" won't put a crimp in your marital plans, relax and enjoy! You're about to get the royal treatment.

Craig has some additional tips:

"Typically, Jewish men won't marry a non-Jewish girl if they don't have any kids. Since they want any progeny to be raised Jewish and Judaism recognizes the mother's religious as determinant of the children's ... well, you get the idea. However," he adds with a mischievous grin, "if a Jewish man already has children and he's looking for a second wife, he probably doesn't care quite so much about her membership in the Tribe. They don't have to appease their families anymore and can marry at will."

It's perfect! I love that Lauren is such a good writer that I don't have to do anything to it before I post the blog and blast another email to my friends, telling them to *share!!!* With that out of the way, I can get ready for Canada.

I've been through three wardrobe changes already and now, as I stare at the end result and dab on a final coat of lip gloss, I wonder why I've bothered. If the night goes as planned, this hard-fought ensemble will end up in a heap on floor.

"Fuck it," I say to myself. I settle at last on jeans,

a cute top and sample sale Loubis. Yes, I try never to pay full price for anything and luxury footwear is no exception. Despite what premium cable would have you believe, Manhattan women aren't out every week buying $1200 shoes—even those of us with fabulous jobs. That Bottega bag the girls can't get enough of? Online discount site! Sure, they're still expensive, but not as expensive as the boutiques here in town. The truth is, plenty of successful women still live practically paycheck to paycheck, trek up to fifth-floor walkups and clip coupons from the Sunday papers. I consider myself pretty well ahead of the game, but even I can't pass up designer deals.

I walk the few blocks to the restaurant Mr. Canada and I decided on via email and sit at the bar. I'm a few minutes early—intentionally, I might add—and order a glass of champers, only ninety one calories, to sip while I wait.

Ten minutes later, Eric strolls in and takes the bar stool next to me as if we've met here this way a million times before. I am again struck by the easy way he takes command of a room—even a room full of strangers.

Eric rests one foot on the wrung at the bottom of his seat and time stops as he leans in for what feels like the longest kiss of my life. His lips are softer than I remember and his breath tastes like spearmint. I see fireworks behind my eyes and my heart literally skips a beat. Somewhere in the back of my mind I think what a cliché that is, but my mind also pipes up that most clichés are true anyway so it's fine, just fine to stay here in this fairytale moment for as long as it will last.

"It's so nice to see you again," he says, his lips

brushing against the skin below my left ear. "You look beautiful. And sexy."

The same practical part of my brain that won't seem to shut up about clichés is screaming *Fuck yeah, I look sexy! You think this is easy? You think the gym at six A.M. is a good time?! I've only been hot for, like, ten years!* But instead I glance down for a coy moment and when I make eye contact again, I say, "I bet you say that to all the girls." I suddenly realize how insecure that makes me sound, even if it is probably true. I quickly recover, "But thank you. You look pretty good yourself."

"Good" is the understatement of the century when it comes to Eric and his appearance. This guy, I swear, got better-looking since last week! How can one person have this much charisma, this much appeal, magnetism and charm? My brain struggles to wrap itself around the concept but quits in favor of another fireworks display when Eric puts his hand on my lower back and kisses me again, more deeply than before.

I think I'm in danger of passing out from a combination of champers and pure ecstasy when the hostess comes over and tells us our table is ready. Before I can blink, Eric has thrown a twenty on the bar and is offering his hand to help me slide off the high bar stool. He doesn't step back, though, so I welcome the opportunity to press my body against his. I can feel he's as delighted by our reunion as I am. I only hope it's for the same reason.

If it weren't for the table between us, we would be touching each other uncontrollably all through dinner. As it is, I'm starting to think nearby patrons can feel the heat radiating from between my legs.

Watching Eric's lips move as we talk about everything under the sun—work and family (mostly his), traveling the world, our careers, favorite movies and most loathed restaurants.

"I love good food," he says, gazing around at the dishes being served to the neighboring tables, "That's one of the best things about traveling as much as I do. I'm a huge foodie and would love to be the next Travel Channel star, like Andrew Zimmern. I watch the Food Network religiously and love to cook the kinds of cuisine I get to try all over the world. That's actually what inspired my healthy fast-casual concept."

Great. I've spent my adult years staying away from food and counting friggin' calories to stay thin. A damn foodie? Just my luck!

I pray he doesn't want to talk about his restaurant funding because I'm still somewhat uncomfortable with the compromising position in which he has placed me.

"I do have to say we did a fantastic job not letting anyone in on our little secret," he says, winking.

Annnnd here we go.

"I was completely floored when I saw you! Pretending that we hadn't just … ahem … spent the night together was the hardest thing I've ever done." I wonder again, briefly, if he knew in advance about me and arranged our pre-meeting meeting. I push that thought away because I don't want to think about the implication. "The guys love your idea. They want you to come back for some follow up meetings!"

"That's great! I am invested one hundred percent to this but let's not talk about work."

Smartly done. Is he serious, or is he playing me?

As he changes the subject and continues to talk about his travels my mind goes straight to the gutter. I think of those lips fluttering on my inner thighs and at the soft flesh enveloping my clit. I give an involuntary shudder.

"You okay?" He pauses mid-sentence, interrupting a story about a photo shoot in Japan during which his native hosts took him out for "Italian food": ramen noodles with catsup.

"I'm … I might … I might be having a few salacious thoughts at the moment. But please, go on. Japan. Noodles, Catsup."

"So it's not just me?"

"Clearly, not."

We take a moment to stare into one another's eyes and I can tell we're both letting our fantasies play out in the silence.

"Dessert, or more champagne?" the waitress asks. I realize that nearly three hours have passed when I feel like I've only been sitting here for fifteen minutes. We've made each other laugh, told interesting stories, toyed with each other's fingers across the white expanse of good cotton tablecloth. Because every moment has been setting me on fire, time has smoldered to something meaningless between us.

Move along, bitch, can't you see we're mind-fucking?!

She drops the menu cards at a gesture from Eric; his stare has never left mine. His voice is soft when he says, "My friends are having this … party. Do you want to stop by?"

Though I'm flattered that he wants me to meet his friends, I'm fairly confident my legs will stop working if the tingling up and down the back of my body gets any more extreme. I need relief from this longing, this whole-body wanting.

"I think we both know the party is back at my apartment," I say, matching his tone.

"Check, please," he says, at last breaking the gaze we've held for a deliciously long time. I feel light-headed, as if I've just been released from a long-lasting spell.

Our clothes can't come off fast enough. Except those sample sale Loubis.

"I like," he says, pulling back from where he's laid me down on the bed. He takes the shoes off one at a time, but puts them on again after sliding me out of my jeans. He props my right ankle on his shoulder and nips at the inside of my leg. Our eyes lock again and stay locked as he sucks on his finger then slips it inside me. This close to exploding already, I can't help letting my lids close halfway but I'm suddenly filled with a hunger for the sight of him and I force myself to open them, to see him seeing me. The raw hunger—the pure lust—in his eyes sends me over the edge and I start coming while he croons, "That's it. I wanna watch you come."

He's wrapped my legs around him now and I know I'm falling hard for this man because I feel beautiful, absolutely stunning with him on top of me. He covers my neck and breasts with kisses, pausing to suck and tease my nipples. I reach inside those boxer briefs—the ones I've seen in pictures and which look about seventeen billion times better in person—and take the length of him in both hands, stroking up and down. I feel his groan against my neck and know we are both ready, more than ready, for what's next.

Eric leans his elbows on the bed so our faces are close. Here I am again, already penetrated by his gaze, so it feels like I am being completed when he slides into me. After a few thrusts I can't help retreating into the bright, fiery scene behind my eyelids. I'm coming again, instantly, endlessly, and soon the whole world is just one big explosion of color and light.

CHAPTER 8:
LUBBY MY LOUBIS

"Has anyone ever told you that you look like a young Demi Moore?"

I turn my head on the pillow so when I laugh—demurely—my morning breath doesn't blow right in Eric's face. Model looks or no, that's just not attractive.

"Only guys who are trying to get lucky. So you're a little late. But for the record, are we talkin' St. Elmo's Fire or Striptease?"

"Oh, I … I was actually thinking G.I. Jane," he says with mock seriousness. I fake indignation and slap his arm lightly. I can tell from the way he runs a hand across my torso that he was thinking Striptease all along. It feels like we are the only two people in the universe at this moment. That is, until my inner monologue takes over.

What? Are you a chubby chaser? Stop Vivian. Stop. When are you going to stop bashing yourself? Yes, you are hot. Yes, you are hot.

"Last night was fun. I like hanging out with you," he says.

I ignore the "just pals" sound of that and say, careful to match his casual word choice, "I like spending time with you, too," I don't want to miss the chance to get lost in those eyes so I angle my face in such a way that my breath wafts somewhere below his chin.

"What are you doing this weekend?"

"Hadn't thought about it. Why? Are you asking me out?"

"I thought we could check out this church in Harlem I go to sometimes."

Church??? "Sounds interesting. Sunday?"

"Yup. I can swing by around nine A.M. and we can head up there together."

"Amazing."

Amazing? Now I know I'm smitten. I can't remember the last time I was up in Harlem, if ever, not to mention church! But somehow I've just enthusiastically agreed to get my ass to the Great Not-So-White North of NYC—at nine in the fucking morning, no less. When people say love makes you crazy, they are not kidding.

"Do you have to be at work soon?"

"I have about thirty minutes to spare," I say.

Without uttering another word, he dips his head to the curve of my neck and proceeds to kiss me all over, letting his lips slide over my body connecting points of heat he makes with his lips. Just when the tingle I feel vibrating over my skin reaches a sonic frequency, he slips himself inside me ...

"Vivian? Vivian, are you listening?" Dan asks. He's standing in the doorway to my office, where he's caught me, once again, in breathless reverie. I hope it doesn't show on my face.

"Oh, yeah. Sorry. I was ... thinking about something else. What were you saying?"

I confirm our meetings for next week and answer

a few questions before rushing him out the door. Can't he see I have personal matters to attend to?

The day goes by quickly because I spend all my free time fantasizing about last night. At a quarter to five I pack up and go, double-checking I have everything I need before leaving to meet Arianna at Del Frisco's.

When I walk in the door of the famed steakhouse, Arianna is already holding court at the bar—surrounded by no less than six adoring men. I check my coat and grab a few jelly beans from the bowl at the entrance. At only five calories each, I have three. I'm feeling indulgent. I'm starving, and by the looks of things, we'll be a cocktail or two in before we sit down.

"Hey, V! V, come say hello to a few friends," Arianna coos.

Friends? If "friends" suddenly means "anonymous guys who pay for my drinks," then yes—I am about to meet a whole gaggle of new besties.

"This is Tim. He's a Managing Director at Goldman. And this is James."

"John," he corrects.

"Close enough. He runs DeerFund Capital in Stamford," she finishes.

"Hi," I say with a general wave. "Hi, everyone." I smile and take Arianna's elbow for a little aside. "Can we eat something soon? Alone? I really want to catch up, just us."

"Of course, of course—I already put our name down. Boys are good for free cocktails but I wouldn't actually dine with any of these people."

I think she's said this just a little too loudly, but if

any of the men present heard, they haven't taken offense. Or they have, but Arianna's beauty is too overpowering to let their egos get in the way of getting her number.

This is typical Arianna. She is well-known at Del's. In fact, she met her second husband here; when they parted, she made his banishment from the iconic restaurant part of their settlement. I settle into the stool made available to Arianna's left; someone hoping for chivalry points, I assume. I graciously accept a cocktail from Number Four (Or is it Two? They keep moving around so I can't keep track) and allow the conversation around me to drift into a murmur as I retreat into my memories of last night. Eventually I'm drawn back to the present by Arianna's musical farewells to her new admirers. When we sit down, her palm is full of business cards.

"No, no, no," she says, flipping through the first three. I see the stock mid-weight white paper and laser-printed block text—a telltale sign that these calling cards belong to men too quotidian for the great Arianna. But she lingers over a sleek black card and runs her finger over what I assume is letterpress printing. "But maybe, probably, yes," she pronounces. I don't catch the company or corporate title the card boasts, but whatever it is can be summarily described as "really important position that's led to the accumulation of extreme wealth." It looks like the lucky guy's name is Something Van der Sohn. "So how's the blog coming?" she says, switching topics as if she isn't a master of all things seduction.

"Good. Great, actually. My anonymity is still intact, which is a good thing I think. If people connect me to the blog, they might connect my friends and ... well, the guys my friends have been with. I want to keep all of us protected, y'know?"

"Very smart. We don't need all the Penguins getting even more swagger in their stubby little steps, do we?"

"We do not," I laugh. Arianna's cavalier attitude comes with an easy grace I admire. Sometimes I don't know if it comes from being jaded or believing in true love. Either way, it seems to give her power. "So the next topic I want to blog about is men and their wardrobes. You know, deciphering the man beneath, that kind of thing."

"Did you call Lisa?" Arianna asks.

Lisa is a mini-Arianna. She's currently married to her first husband, who is old, fat and very rich. Lisa only lunches at Michael's (where Penguins roam in their natural habitat), so when she invites us, we never pass up the chance. Lisa is perpetually running late from a Pilates or Zumba class—or whatever the latest Upper East Side stay-young-forever craze happens to be at the moment.

We take pleasure in referring to her as the girl with the million-dollar smile: she doesn't smile at men with less than a million dollars. She's a thirty- (possibly forty-) something fashionista with impeccable taste and a reputation for shameless name-dropping. Then again, it's not hard to dress like you walked off a Badgley Mischka runway with a 20k-per-month "luxury goods" budget, right? But that's Lisa: a regal ex-model whose diet consists of air and SmartWater. Her motto is simple: "You can never be too tall, too rich, too thin, or have too many handbags or pairs of shoes."

She and Arianna have a competitive frenemy

type relationship, always one-upping one another with the best shoes, bags, homes and high-society invitations. They are proof positive that women dress for women, not for men, and the rest of us are enthralled by their friendly rivalry.

Arianna texts Lisa to meet us and we order another round of cocktails from the waitress so we can all order dinner together. In the meantime, Arianna clears her throat as if she's about to deliver an oratorio at the Metropolitan Opera, so I quickly pull out my recorder and place it on the table between us. She begins:

"Clothing is crucial. It's the single most important aspect of a man's presence. Say what you will about 'loving what's on the inside'—you'll never find out what's under the hood if the ride don't look shiny in the showroom."

"Where do you come up with this shit?" I ask, shaking my head. Of course, she's right.

"It's beyond unattractive for a man to look like a disheveled slob. Grow up. Pull it together. Accept that a basketball jersey and board shorts stopped being 'a thing' when you stepped out of a dorm room for the last time. A well-dressed man wouldn't date a woman who walked around like she hadn't showered for days, or one whose best article of clothing was from the sales bin at Old Navy. Why should a woman tolerate that level of bullshit in a man?

I don't know if I agree that it's "bullshit,"—I've dated some nice guys who dress casually and I own a thing or two from the Old Navy sale bin—but I know what she's saying, so I let her go on. "My pet peeve is a man who wears a suit off the rack that doesn't fit. It's one thing if it fits off the rack," and in an undertone she adds, "I've heard wonderful things about the Brooks Brothers outlet. All the pants are finished. Who'd have thought?"

She resumes a more upright posture and checks her peripheral vision to make sure no one's heard her endorsing an outlet. "Anyway, poorly fitting suits scream 'middle management.' It's off-putting."

I'm reminded of a date I had once with a guy from one of those online dating sites, and I make a mental note to include this in the blog. The guy showed up in jorts and mandals (jean shorts—heaven forbid you should ever bear witness to this travesty from the early nineties—and scuffed up man-sandals, usually Birkenstocks or Adidas slip-ons). Of course my winner was committing the most egregious fashion crime possible: mandals with socks. Unless you're a Colorado tree hugger whose most refined formal wear is cargo pants without an elastic waist, you shouldn't even own mandals. Don't get me started on Tevas. The only time I want to be strapped into footwear is when we're talking silk ribbons on Loubis. For men, there's never an excuse.

"There are other fashion sins," Arianna continues, snapping me out of my thoughts. "I tend to forgive bleans—black, tight skinny jeans," she explains to the recorder, fully aware that she's being quoted, "when they're painted on a hot European guy whose accent makes up for the faux pas below. And there's the standard chino-blue-button-down-over-Hanes-tee-shirt combination. We can't forget that."

"Certainly not," I say. "It's the Leave it to Beaver 2.0 look."

"At least you know who the guy is when he wears that," Arianna says. "Midlevel sales, practically ninety nine percent of the time. And even though all men can be taught, it's best to avoid this particular look. They've worn and washed those pants so many times, there's a white rim at the bottom of their cuffs. You'll never convince them to take that shit off. Chinos Guy drinks light beer, still loves Dave Matthews and scurries home to a shoebox walk-up each night. Of course, there is that one percent—the elusive Southern Blue Blood. He's wearing this outfit because he doesn't know better. But he'll respond well to a strong hand, if you know what I mean," she adds conspiratorially.

You've gotta hand it to Arianna—she knows what she's talking about. Next she talks at length about the significance of how men dress when they go out in packs. You can always tell when a group of men are undateable because, according to Arianna, they all start to dress alike. Same jeans, same sneakers, same white button-down with identical rolled-up sleeves. Originality means a man can still make room in his life for new things; if he's a drone, there's a high probability his bachelor ways will be tough to break.

"Hi, dolls!" Lisa chirps. "Thanks for the invite! Life has been so crazy I've barely seen you two. I've been babysitting alllll week." She sits down in an elegant heap. This is what Rich Mommy Barbie must look like.

"You know it's not babysitting when they're your children, right?" I say.

"Ugh, to me it is," she sniffs. "Their nanny took a week off for vacation. Can you imagine the nerve? A whole *week*?" Lisa shakes her head, with wide-eyed disbelief. "So, what are you girls chatting about?"

"Men and their clothes, our loves and hates," I

say.

"Off. The. Rack," Lisa deadpans. "Hate, hate, hate! A telltale OTR sign? When his pants gather below the knee like curtains." We all laugh, and I explain that I'm helping a friend with the blog, with a quick, furtive wink at Arianna begging her to not rat me out. She winks back, obviously happy to be in on a secret to which Lisa is not privy.

"What a brilliant idea! I have lots to say on the subject." Lisa goes on, "This winning look is often found on your typical short, stocky type. He has to buy a large size but doesn't pay to have his clothes tailored. Of course, tall guys can't sneak OTR past me, either; when his cuff hits above his heel—and God forbid you see sock or worse ..."

Here she trails off while looking at each of us knowingly in turn. Our blank expressions shock her. "What? You don't know the greatest disgrace an already-shamed OTR dresser can experience? Exposed skin." She shudders and clutches at her heart. "It means he can't afford to send his laundry out and ... ran out of socks."

I notice Arianna's new "friends" listening from a nearby table and catch at least one round face redden.

Lisa continues in a voice that carries. She knows she has an audience now, and if there's one thing to be said about Lisa, it's that she loves an audience, especially if Arianna is among them.

"Shoes are huge. Probably the most important element of a man's attire from a woman's perspective. Men should always have their shoes shined and cleaned. I hate a scuff or a worn-down heel. If you can't take care of your shoes, how the hell can I expect you to take care of anything else? And besides, if he doesn't care about his shoes, you can be sure he won't be buying you any."

"Lubby my Loubis!" I say. Privately, I consider what a night of great sex can do for a girl's mood.

"Don't forget to watch for watches," Lisa says, "or should I say timepieces? I like something unique, not your run-of-the-mill luxury brands. Hublot and Blancpain, Louis Moinet Magistralis, Patek Philipe, Chopard—who a man carries on his wrist is a wonderful indication of his attention to detail, his style sensibility, and most importantly—his love for beautiful things. You see a Seiko? I say go." Lisa laughs at her own joke and I catch myself smiling, too. Beautiful and clever—these are my friends.

"Of course, there are exceptions to some degree," Arianna offers. "A sexy, much younger man can get away with the occasional Tag or Bulova, but he has to be really hot."

She and Lisa clink a silent toast to the truth in this.

"A man can throw you off, though," Lisa says. "Some of them have all the accoutrements but nothing in the bank. I'd rather have a very well put-together, modestly clothed man with a big bank roll than a flashy dresser with zero at the teller." Arianna signals to our waiter for another bottle of champers. Putting down her flute and folding her hands, Lisa looks like she's suddenly all business. "So what's going on with the Detergent King and the Canadian?"

"I guess Arianna told you?"

"Of course she told me! We're trying to get you married over here, but from what I understand you're making the wrong decision. A model, Viv? We've all been down that road. Have you learned nothing from the rest of us? Besides that restaurant idea of his will take years to turn a profit, if it ever does! Restaurants are notoriously difficult to get off the ground, especially here. You can't turn a corner without seeing some new eatery, which closes in six months."

"I know, I know! But you guys don't know anything about him. And he's a successful model, not some wannabe. Sure, Matthew is marriage material, but ..."

"So? Marry Matthew ..." Arianna begins.

Lisa finishes for her, "... and keep the model on the side! That's certainly what I'd do."

"Yes, yes, I know you would," I nod. After a brief pause, I tell them that Eric wants to take me to church.

"WHAT?!" the girls yell in unison.

"You heard me. Church. Gospel church. In Harlem. At nine in the fucking morning on a Sunday. What am I supposed to wear?"

"How are we supposed to know?" Lisa asks. "I worship at Bergdorf's."

The girls counseled that if I was going on a spiritual Mecca to Harlem with Eric, I owed it to myself to spend some quality time with Matthew. I text him about dinner on Friday.

Sure. How abt I cook for you at my place?

This was exactly what I was trying to avoid! I want to take it slow with Matthew, and I know going to his place will put me in a position I'm not ready for. Or am I?

Sounds good, I text back. Fuck it—time to throw caution to the wind. I'm a grown-ass woman. I can handle this. I can handle anything.

CHAPTER 9:
I AIN'T SAYIN' SHE'S
A GOLD DIGGER

"Holy shit, are you reading this?" I bark into the phone.

Lauren and I are both reading the latest article on dating in the *New York Post*. The author of the article—who, for the record, chose not to post a picture with her byline—claims there's statistical evidence that women are leaving Manhattan after a "certain age" because they can't find love. Even with three thousand miles between us, I sense Lauren's discomfort. As much as we both know the truth about why she left New York, we don't talk about it.

We continue to read and the article theorizes that the fault doesn't lie with Manhattan or its denizens; no, women are actually just choosing the wrong partners. The author's evidence? An anonymous blog whose vast experience and die-hard New Yorker attitude is making plain the who's-who of the dating scene.

"Not since *Sex and the City* have New York women had such a loud voice. Sure, there's Lena Dunham's *Girls* on HBO, but the *Menhattan Project* is for NYC's more ... ahem ... seasoned singles," the article states.

I'm thrilled and terrified. "Thank God, they don't know who I am," I say. "I don't need this kind of publicity in my life. If work finds out they will flip!"

"Who cares?" Lauren says, clearly grateful for a new line of discussion. "You could be the face of single Manhattan girls the island over!"

"Lauren, I don't need *all* my dirty laundry airing on a line over Park Avenue!" I say. "And speaking of which, I'm seeing Matthew tonight."

"I'm glad to hear it, girl. Get to know him a little better and you might just surprise yourself."

"I know, I know—I have to give him a chance. And he's divorced already, which means he isn't afraid of commitment. At least ... he *wasn't* afraid of it at one point."

"Sound logic in my book. How's Arianna? I called her last week but she couldn't talk—said she was busy doing something. Of course she didn't say what ..."

"Probably counting money from her divorce, that bitch!"

We both laugh. It feels good to let loose, but it makes me miss Lauren all the more.

"I'm going over to her apartment after we hang up," I say. "She has some old clothes and shoes she wants to give me. Which you know just means they're from last season. My happy ass is heading over there STAT."

"Save me something!"

"Duh. Clearly. Okay, I gotta run. Mwah, mwah."

I head over to Arianna's plush 61st Street co-op. I love visiting Arianna at home. It's a real grown-up's apartment: grown-up furniture, grown-up wall treatments, grown-up art. She has a Colombian housekeeper she loves, who's been with Arianna since her first marriage. Consuela would give her left arm for Arianna, and Arianna would do the same for Consuela. When I see them interact with one another, it reminds me that underneath Arianna's hard exterior is a truly soft heart. I can't blame her for keeping that vulnerability to herself. In this day and age—and in this city—you can't wear too much armor.

Consuela lets me in and winks, "You got here just in time. She's already given me so many clothes I'll never wear them all. I love when she cleans her closets."

"I know! I hope you left me some good stuff."

"Oh, she has some beautiful things set aside for you, things I'd never fit into. We'll be the best-dressed women in town, thanks to her!"

Arianna enters in time to hear our conversation and says, "My greatest joy is sharing my good fortune with the women I love." Just as I feel a bubble of warmth rise up at the sight of my kind-spirited friend, she barks, "What the fuck are you wearing? You look like a civil servant! I hope you're not planning on seeing Matthew like that."

There's the girl I know and love.

"Geez, unlike you I've been at work all day!" I can't help feeling just a little defensive. I look adorable. Corporate adorable, but still. "I'm going home to change once you load me up with goodies."

"Good. *Good Lord.* Come here, take a look at these. You're a size seven, right?"

"Yes!" I squeal. I can't contain my excitement. I'll take all the critique in the world from a woman about to give me entre to a private sample sale of all the greats: YSL, Choos, Prada, Manolos—you name

it, Arianna has it. And is about to give it to me *for free*.
"You sure?" I ask, politely restraining myself from
scooping it all up in my arms while shouting "Mine!
Allll mine!!!"

"Yes, of course I'm sure. And here are the
clothes."

"Wow! SHUT THE HELL UP! Are you
serious?! Will they fit me?"

"Yes!" Arianna can't hide the smile behind her
steely exterior. She loves indulging her friends, and
she knows I can't get enough of this stuff. "You're
doing me a favor. Look at this closet! I can barely see
anything in there."

"Thank you so much, Ari. This is amazing. You
know I would never spend this much on shoes."

"Yeah, I know, you cheapo! You take Maxxinista
to a whole new level."

I laugh but it's true. My strict never-pay-full-price
policy keeps me looking elegant for work and
fashionable in the evenings, but no one is mistaking
me for a runway model. These clothes are beautiful.
Arianna is giving me entire outfits pulled straight
from the pages of glossy fashion mags. Some of these
pieces still have the price tags on them. The
hopelessly practical part of my brain considers
returning them all for cash, or selling them on eBay,
but I know that would be awful and I dismiss the
thought after just one guilty second. I rub the clothes
against my cheek. I feel like a princess.

"You know," Arianna says too casually–her tone
puts me on high alert, "you could have all this and
more with Matthew. He's crazy about you! And *rich*."

"Can you let it go for just a second? Jesus!"

"Fine. But I should reveal that I have an ulterior

motive for inviting you over here."

"I knew it! That whole do-it-out-of-the-kindness-of-your-heart thing was just an act!"

"Whatever," she says drily.

"Fine," I say, suspecting I've been just a tad harsh. "What's this about?"

"Well ..." Arianna takes a deep breath. It's rare that the woman hesitates to say or do anything, especially around me or her other close friends. "I want to contribute to the blog, too."

I see that this was a big deal for Arianna to ask, even though on some level she must know I would never deny her. The woman hates asking for anything.

"Of course! What about?"

Her relief is palpable.

"Well, I'm sick of men throwing around the Gold Digger title like it's nothing."

I can't hide my confusion. "Arianna ... aren't you ... I mean, you're a Gold Digger, right? Or no— I'm sorry—isn't your preferred term 'Finance Fucker'?"

"I know, I know—and yes! But not every greedy little bitch can claim the title. Men shouldn't go around bestowing the moniker willy-nilly on every girl they meet."

"So you want to write about the men or the women?"

"Both. I want to warn the men about the kind of woman to avoid and reassure the women that it's okay to want a stable financial life. Being taken care of isn't wrong—but it is an art form. It's not about being a mooch, it's about being fair."

"You don't think women know that already?"

"Not all of them, or we wouldn't have such a bad

name! Hear me out," she says, rushing over to a chic side table in the hall. "I wrote some things down last night."

"Impressive. I like that you gave this some thought." It's true—I really am impressed.

"Well you let Lauren write something," Arianna pouts. "And besides, if you're going to offer expert advice on this topic, you have to consult the ultimate expert, no?"

Arianna hands me a stack of gorgeous stationery, each sheet covered front and back with her scribbled handwriting. Arianna hates her Blackberry, so I'm not surprised that all the work she's done is recorded by hand. I begin to read:

> The ever-ubiquitous Gold Digger. If I had a dollar for every time my girlfriends and I have been called this … well, let's just say I could afford to bankroll a few GDs of my own. Still, I'm sure men would find another label for us if they didn't use that tired old term. New York is filled with gorgeous, smart, educated, witty women. Who are they supposed to be dating? The cable guy? The taxi cab driver? The offensively-smelling gentleman behind the bodega counter? In the movies, such an odd pairing would ride off into the sunset, happy to live forever together on love alone.
>
> But this is real life, people. Women want to be with someone they can talk to, someone they have something in common with and frankly, someone who can show them new things. A better life? Maybe. But not always, since most successful businesswomen already have great

lives and more-than-sufficient incomes. Still, they want an equal. A partner. Someone to share their lives with who won't depend on them to pick up every tab. But don't get me wrong—I don't fault the girl making $35,000 a year at *Vogue* for wanting to be spoiled as well!

That being said, there are a few types of girls that ruin the fun for the rest of us. The first, and perhaps most offensive, is the Blood Sucker whose initials, BS, can appropriately double for another fitting term. Blood Suckers don't have a real eight-to-five to speak of. They often have mysterious pasts and questionable living arrangements that involve the brother of a cousin of a "real chill dude" they met on the subway.

You won't be able to pin down these girls' histories: where they're from, where they went to school. In fact, how these girls get by in life is completely beyond me. Their idea of a buffet-style dinner is consuming an entire bowl of wasabi peas, roasted peanuts and mystery crackers at a dive bar. Fine dining? The free bread and olive oil they inhale whilst waiting for some poor schlub to buy them a drink or meal.

But don't underestimate this wide-eyed barfly; she's sharp. And fast. And she knows what it takes to survive.

The Blood Sucker is looking for a big pay-out. They go from one guy's apartment to the next, taking anything that's free. If a guy invites her to dinner, she'll even bring two or three of her broke-ass friends. If she can't make it work with him, maybe one of her friends will have the magic touch that buys them all a free ride.

She knows where all the two-for-one happy hour specials are around town, wears the same boots year after year (replacing the heels every season or worse, filling in scuffs with a black Sharpie), and are generally soul-sucking vampires who slowly drain the life from those around them—men and women alike.

I have a message for the Blood Suckers: *You know who you are. Stop mooching off your friends. Get a real job, and don't expect the universe to pick up your tab. You're probably reading this blog on a chained-down MacBook in the Apple store. Pathetic. Men like women who are INDEPENDENT. Your ability to function in the world is SEXY—unlike your caked on eyeliner and strung-out "styling."*

The Blood Sucker is the complete antithesis of the Professional Girlfriend. This veteran of the dating game has never worked a day in her life and doesn't have any close girlfriends. "Women just don't like me," she'll claim. And when she does, gentlemen, take my advice: RUN.

The ProGF has one job and one job only: to date and live with VERY wealthy men. She starts young, probably in her mid-twenties, and each new conquest is progressively richer. She wears nothing but designer clothes and is never seen without her "boyfriend." She's rarely in the city; instead, she's always traveling to some exotic location or accompanying her latest catch on a business trip. You'll know the ProGF when you see her: drop-dead gorgeous, educated at the School of Hard Knocks, seemingly hypnotic power over anything with a penis. Money is her number-one motivator. Period.

This woman is dangerous and will do anything to keep her prize—until she's done with him, of course.

I have to wonder if Arianna isn't basing the ProGF on her own modus operandi, but she has a lot of close girlfriends and women love her—once they get to know her, that is. Otherwise, she fits that description to a T. I look up at Arianna when I've finished and realize my mouth is slightly agape—this shit was good! Who knew my friends were so prolific? "Where's the rest?" I ask.

I see a sparkle in her eyes. "How did you know?"

"There *has* to be more," I say. "A lot more. This is great!"

"Well," she says, a devilish grin playing across her lips, "I wanted to see what you thought of this first. But the next section I have planned is about the Retired Player. You know my feelings about the RP—he's my favorite type of gentleman."

I stop her, mid-stream, and ask if she's written this down. When she shakes her head, "no," I pull out my recorder and she smiles, loving the attention and continues once I press the Record button.

"He's fifty-plus, either looking to settle down or have fun with a sophisticated woman who's as good around a table of business associates as she is in the bedroom. The Retired Player likes a versatile woman who knows who she is. Of course, he likes to spoil that woman with gifts and trips, but the boon of spending his days with a beautiful companion is worthwhile.

"I've had many sugar daddies in my time. Some

older, some younger. All were memorable. My theory is that if all men learned of the aphrodisiac power of shopping, the world would be a better place. You know the N-word is my biggest turn-off." Arianna makes a huffing sound that expresses complete exasperation to a T. "'No.' Ugh. Just thinking about it sends shivers down my spine."

"I say, take the free drinks and anything else he offers. You're young and beautiful, and neither will last forever. When it's gone, you'll wish you had said yes to every opportunity."

There's no stopping Arianna now—she's on a roll. I sneak a look at my watch and decide I can still get home in time to freshen up for my date if I manage to leave here in the next fifteen minutes. I can't fault Arianna for being passionate on this subject. If she had ever decided to bring her powers to bear on global politics, I'm pretty sure the Middle East Conflict would be a thing of the past.

"You have to remember that a few thousand dollars to a business tycoon in NYC is just a drop in the bucket. The term 'Gold Digger' has destroyed perfectly good courtships—and the cat and mouse game in general. But the chase is an important part of the process for a man! He wants to shake his tail feathers, as it were—feel like he's impressing someone.

"But now, if a guy wants to order takeout when his girl wants to be taken out, suddenly she's a Gold Digger! Because of this, I prefer the term 'Precious Metal Hottie' to 'Gold Digger'. Is it my fault if I won't talk to anyone without a black Amex? Money is the leading cause of divorce in this country. Eliminate it early on if you can! I mean look at me; my parents were so poor, they got married for the rice! I've been poor and I've been rich. Trust me—richer is better."

When Arianna pauses for breath, I jump in and tell her how great all this is, how I can't wait to hear the rest, and how I have to hop in a cab if I want to get to Matthew in time. She assures me that she'll write out the rest of what she has to say on the subject.

We pack all my "new" clothes and shoes into an oversized Tumi. "Keep it!" Arianna says of the bag. "I can't believe I even had a Tumi in my closet." I try to keep my jaw from dropping all the way to the floor—my best luggage is American Tourister.

All the way home, I try to think of a way to thank her for her generosity, and quickly realize the best method might be giving Matthew a fighting chance at my heart.

CHAPTER 10:
LAFITE ROTHSCHILD

I stop at a local liquor store before heading to Matthew's place. Naturally I can't arrive without champers.

"Hey, Sun," I say to the gentleman behind the counter. It occurs to me that not everyone can boast of a first-name-basis relationship with their local wine merchant. What can I say? I like what I like!

"Hey, V—chilled champagne in the back," Sun says.

I grab my usual, 495 calories in an entire bottle, and enjoy how refreshing the cool glass feels in my hands as I bring it to the register. I notice the two women in front of me holding the same bottle. They are talking about men. I can't quell a snicker. It's the story of our lives.

"He's definitely a Minnow. Def-def," says one.

"You think? I thought maybe he could be a Sharehouse Poseur," says the other.

Holy shit! Women are really reading this! The Menhattan Project is catching on!

I'm not sure what to feel. I'm excited, of course—even the most amateurish writer strives to have her work read by the masses. But I can't ignore the apprehension I feel tingling at the back of my throat at the prospect of having put so much personal information out there for the wide world to see. Yes, I've kept my identity anonymous. But with the right detective work, could I be found out?

I have to put all thoughts of the blog on the back burner. I have dinner to attend to.

I walk into Matthew's sprawling loft on Mercer Street. The elevator opens to 3,500 square feet of perfectly decorated open space. A terrace wraps around the apartment's exterior, affording panoramic views of the city. I have never seen anything like this before, and I've been in some seriously swank apartments in my day.

I guess detergent is a booming—or should I say bubbling?—business these days. Matthew has let it slip that he invented some new formula for which Proctor & Gamble bought the patent. His natural humility kept him from revealing the price tag for such a thing, but from the looks of this apartment, it must have been a not-so-small fortune. On top of that, Matthew's first wife was an heiress to an oil dynasty. I, on the other hand, am heiress to a mound of dirt in West Texas—maybe a locker full of stained, sweaty football gear.

"Hi, gorgeous," he says as soon as I step off the elevator.

"Hi, honey. Wow. I think you should go bigger," I say, gesturing to the massive space before us.

"I hope you like beef," he says, slipping his arm around my waist and pulling me to him. We kiss, and I can taste peaty scotch on his breath. This is a man who enjoys a finger or two of the finest ambers, and the lingering sharpness feels warm on my tongue. "I'm making Kobe steaks with spring vegetables from this great CSA upstate. And there's chocolate truffle cake for dessert." He sees the look of awe on my face. "For the record, I didn't make the cake."

Looks like I won't be eating the rest of the weekend from sound of that menu.

"That all sounds incredible and delicious."

"You're incredible and delicious," he purrs.

Shit. He's already starting. The push-pull match has officially begun. His mouth closes over mine again and I curse again in my head, more loudly this time, because I feel that weak tingling at the back of my knees that lets me know I might want Matthew more than I'm willing to admit.

"I brought some champagne," I offer. Maybe that's what I need to clear my head. *Great thinking, Viv. Bubbles to get you thinking straight. Good luck with that.*

"Let's do it," he says.

The evening progresses easily. We are relaxed together, but our flirtations feel new and exciting. I nibble grapes and a few candied walnuts at the kitchen island where Matthew has directed me to sit. He's refused my assistance which is just as well, really, so I sit prettily and sip champers. He looks so cute chopping and dicing, sautéing and flipping pans. Every now and then he swings around for a kiss, like he can't stand the counter between us. The smells filling the air make my mouth water, and strains of Louis Armstrong dapple the silences between us when they fall.

This guy knows what he's doing.

We drink amazing wine with dinner as he talks about his children and how he longs to find love again. He is not embarrassed by his heart—a quality I admire. He is honest and truthful, compassionate and funny.

Shit. Let this be the booze and food.

Matthew gets uncomfortable whenever I ask about his ex-wife. He isn't very forthcoming with that aspect of his life. Is there some secret that he isn't telling me? For all intents and purposes Angela seems perfect. Gorgeous, intelligent and very wealthy. He often mentions she is a great mother to his two young children but when I ask why they divorced, he only responds with, "We grew apart."

Although he is still quite fond of her, I would be very interested to know if she is still quite fond of him.

"What time is it?" I ask after letting a last bite of chocolate cake melt on my tongue.

"Only midnight."

"I should go. My trainer comes at nine …"

"On a Saturday morning?"

"Yeah, he likes to kick my ass early. The bastard," I laugh.

"Well I can walk you out, get you a cab."

"Thanks, Matt. It was a perfect evening."

He walks me toward the elevator and right before he pushes the button, he puts both hands around my waist and spins me to face him, gently pushing my back up against the wall. His kiss is passionate, sexy. Very hot. Our tongues intertwine as his hands slip in opposite directions: one to the crest of my lower back, the other tangling in the hair at the nape of my neck. He kisses my neck and my ear, sucking gently on the lobe. He can't get enough of me in his hands or in his mouth, and before I know what's happening he's unbuttoned my blouse halfway to my waist and has moved his hot mouth down the line of my collarbone to my breasts. The tingling is stronger now, breathing heavier, and maybe that's why I don't resist as he picks me up in arms that are stronger than I expected and carries me to the sofa, where he starts to remove my clothes in earnest.

"Wait," I whisper, "I can't do this."

"Why?" he asks, his breaths short and quick.

"Because. Because it's too soon. I want to take this slow."

"We can take this as slow as you want," he says, but he doesn't stop unbuttoning my pants.

"Stop! I have to go," I say. My forcefulness has taken him by surprise; he's not a bad guy and he obviously doesn't think of himself as someone who would force a woman to do anything she doesn't want to. But he can sense that I do want to—that I *did* want to. What he can't detect is the comparison my mind has been making all night: Matthew versus Eric. Eric versus Matthew. They stack up against one another in a dozen different ways, neither man pulling ahead as the victor. But I can't deny that what I feel when my body is pressed against Eric's—the way the tingling isn't just a sensation but a *fire* in my body when he's around. And that tells me I shouldn't be here with Matthew. At least not yet.

"Wait, don't go," he says, recovering himself.

I grab my purse and sprint to the elevator, which comes mercifully fast as I push the button again and again. The door closes and I breathe a sigh of relief. My heart doesn't stop racing until I'm out of the building and into a cab—a cab I practically hip-checked a young Asian couple aside to get.

"Sorry!" I yell as I slam the door on their

indignant glares.

As the cabbie peels off, I look up at Matthew's sprawling verandah and see him standing there, staring down at me, shaking his head.

???, his text reads.

The poor guy must think I'm a complete psycho. Was I screwing up a good thing all over again? Matthew is total marriage material and is clearly crazy about me, but the chemistry doesn't compare to the off-the-charts magic I feel around Eric. If Eric wasn't in the picture, this would be a no-brainer and I'd be upstairs right now, naked, with Matthew.

Does romance *need* to be electric? Sure, I tell myself, absolutely. But does it need to be a thousand-watt megabulb? Could I be happy with a run-of-the-mill sixty-watt, a perfectly sufficient strength for a lifetime of sensible reading in bed?

My mother would say something like, "As long as he treats you right, the chemistry will come." *Pfft.* Great advice from a serial divorcée.

I walk into my apartment and despite being hot and bothered, I sit on the sofa and turn on the TV to the local news station. The sound is off, but I watch the images accompanying a story about a newly viral anonymous blog. "If you know the identity of the Menhattan blogger," a caption reads, "please contact NY1 at the number below."

Fuck, Viv—you've done it now.

How can this possibly be such a big deal? How on earth did this catch on so quickly? I knew my friends and their friends were having fun with it, and it was getting a little print coverage, but come on! I turn up the sound to hear the story continue, "experts" conjecturing about the identity of the blog's author. One "forensic examiner" claimed the writer must be a man—perhaps a gay man—because of the blog's style and straightforward language. On the opposite side of the split-screen, a second suit claimed the author had to be a woman, because a man wouldn't be so bitchy and jaded.

Bitchy and jaded? Has this idiot seen what it's like out there? Since when does the truth come off as bitchy and jaded?

At least their confusion assures me of one thing: no one's blown my cover. Yet.

***

The next morning, I meet Closet Freak Catherine and Rich Mommy Barbie Lisa for lunch.

"There has to be something wrong with me, right?" I ask. I've relayed the Matthew quandary in all its horrifying detail.

"When it comes to being serious about someone, sex is too important to fuck around with, if you'll pardon the pun. When I was with … oh, whatsisname … I used to stare at the ceiling during sex and think about all the crap I had to do the next day," says Catherine. "*Thrust*—call my sister. *Thrust*—buy ingredients for casserole. *Thrust*—pay the electric bill. I was very productive in that relationship. He was perfect in every other way: smart, successful, attractive. I needed a lot more naughty than he was able to give me. It was difficult to end it based on a lack of spark, but that's what happened."

Many women are in the same situation, I know. They marry the "good provider" with little regard for their physical needs as women.

"I had a choice," Lisa says, "to marry for love or a better life. I chose the latter."

In the end though, are you truly happy?

Lisa's husband is about twenty years her senior. He is wealthy to say the very, very least; there's nothing they can't buy or otherwise obtain. When she first started dating Michael, Lisa seemed happy. Not for nothing, she said the sex was great—that it was nice to be with "a generous lover who knew what he was doing." We all figured she'd managed to find that elusive balance between the best of both worlds: security and love, all wrapped up in one. We truly believed her, too. Years later, we come to find out it was all an act. She loves him, she says, but doesn't love to bang him. Apparently what's good in your twenties isn't so cute anymore once you're in your thirties or forties—and he's in his fifties and sixties.

"Everything bothers me about him now. The way he shuffles his feet. The way he chews his food. I have to pretend to want to hear about his day when all I care about is if he made enough money in the market because my youngest just got into the 92nd Street Y," she deadpans. "I hear the same stories again and again, like talking to an old person. *Because I AM talking to an old person.* Three bottles of Lafite Rothschild are never enough. I need the entire vineyard! You can't have good sex—let alone great sex—with someone who reminds you of your grandpa."

Catherine steps in once Lisa becomes so flustered she's reduced to anxiously tapping her foot and gulping her wine. "It's rare that a woman who marries for money can truly be happy for long. If you marry for money, that's all you get." Lisa nods. Her expression is a mixture of sadness and *I told you so*—clearly, this is a talk she's had with herself more than once.

"You have to figure out what kind of earning partner you need to have and support the family you want. If it's a billion, so be it. If it's $150,000 a year with two weeks paid vacay, that's fine, too. But living here? One or both of you has to be pulling in some serious chunk change if you want to live comfortably."

I remember calling Lisa at eleven A.M. one day not too long ago. I asked if she wanted to meet me at Physique 57 for a class.

"No, love, just popped a bottle! It's happy hour somewhere, right?"

"Yeah, if you live across the Atlantic. Are you serious?"

"You know I only drink when I'm alone or with somebody," she laughs. "I'm celebrating, honey bunny. Having a brunch party!"

"Celebrating what?"

"You remember, Christopher got in the 92nd Street Y."

I didn't say anything at the time because I didn't entirely trust myself to keep the judgment out of my voice. *So now that's a reason to start boozing before noon?* But I know my friend is unhappy, so I tried to change the subject. Before I could navigate us to something safe—work, maybe, or the weather—Lisa started gushing about her new boyfriend.

"So you're getting divorced?" I ask.

"No, silly," she slurs, "I'm still married. I just need to get laid!" She laughs a hysterical kind of laugh.

Sad thing is, I remember back in the day when she used to say Michael was a great lover—even with the huge belly hanging over his penis. He was always focused on her satisfaction. She loved it—or so she claimed.

Despite the fact that we're all digging into our lunch fare, Lisa lets us know Michael is pushing for anal sex—no pun intended.

"I don't even want straight sex with him anymore. Why on earth would I give him the up the butt upgrade? Bare minimum, it better be his birthday, Christmas or a solar eclipse," she says.

Catherine almost chokes on her egg white omelet. "Remember Andrew, that guy who only wanted to do anal with me?"

How could we forget? One afternoon, after a hardcore sex session the night before (that included sampling from the *poo-poo* platter, of course), Catherine felt her lower gut gurgling and brewing on her way to yoga. She thought she would hold it in until she got home. But as she moved into the Warrior One pose, she realized she had Number Two running down her leg. Mortified, she cut the class short, grabbed her mat and hoofed it home. She knew something was wrong and made an appointment with her doctor the next morning. He told her there could be permanent damage to her sphincter—and that she should be careful with any "back door activities" in the future.

That was the end of that. Not only did she have to live through a humiliating lecture from her doctor, she had to dump Anal Andy before she started getting the permanent dumps. Only God knows where he is now. Probably a successful gay relationship. When I suggest this, Lisa and Catherine squeal in perfect unison: "Caaaaaalvin!!!"

Shannanigans Shannon dated Calvin and, though she liked him, she always thought there was something a little "off" about him. They liked to do all the same things—shopping, going to art galleries, taking dance classes.

"I think I have to break up with Cal," she said to us one afternoon.

"Why? He's gorgeous!" I said. The sentiment was repeated around the table. Calvin was gorgeous, cut like a paper doll.

"I know, I know … it's just … he never wants to have sex. He just wants to cuddle. Frankly, it's weirding me out. He even pushes my hand away if I try to touch him *down there*," she said, lowering her voice.

That was it—another one bites the dust for Shannon. A year went by and she dated a couple nice guys and the usual suspect losers. Then she ran into Calvin at a masquerade ball at the New York Public Library. The electricity was magnetic; despite the fact that both of them were there with other dates, they couldn't take their eyes off one another the entire night. He texted her the next morning, something about wishing he had been at the ball with her last night, that she looked beautiful, that he was thinking of her.

Oh yeah, and what would you have done then? she texted. *Cuddled me to climax?*

No, he replied. *I'd tie you to the bed, leave your mask on and fuck your brains out.*

Really? Is that a promise?

Get over here. Now. You know I love how you look in

the morning.

Shannon told us that she briefly contemplated if she had made a mistake inviting Calvin back into her bed. Maybe her date last night had made him jealous—and maybe that's all it took for a man to realize what he'd lost. But, she didn't have much planned for the morning: coffee, the *Post*, laundry, the gym. She could squeeze in a fuckfest with a prime male specimen.

She jumped in the shower and casually walked the three blocks to Calvin's apartment in the Metropolitan Tower. The doorman escorted her to the elevator and pressed the button for the twenty-ninth floor. Calvin opened the door when Shannon's hand was still hovering over the knocker. He'd been waiting for her.

He pulled her inside, slammed the door and threw Shannon on the kitchen counter. There was no time for masks or ties; they had sex for hours with more passion than either had ever felt before. She was in love again. The pheromones were flying high. There was no coming down from this cloud.

Calvin and Shannon were inseparable for the next two months. The doormen at the Metropolitan Tower knew her on sight; they added her to Calvin's list of allowed guests. She loved hearing "May I get the door for you, Ms. Shannon? May I get that package for you? Ms. Shannon, the car is waiting." She liked waking up to stunning views of the park and sipping champagne while soaking in Calvin's monster Jacuzzi. Sure, they had reverted to some of their old cuddling habits, but when they did have sex it was superb.

What could possibly go wrong?

Now, Shannon is a part-time nurse. She works at a few clinics around town between yoga gigs, to get her "helping others" fix. One Saturday, she had been assigned to work a double but the unit was well staffed and she was allowed to leave early. She was supposed to see Calvin after work anyway, so she decided to surprise him early with a bottle of wine and a pint of fresh strawberries from the farmer's market she passed on her way to the train.

The doorman at the Tower let her up as usual, with just a nod and some polite chat as he called the elevator.

So Calvin had no warning when Shannon silently swung the door open and entered the apartment. He didn't hear her, but she heard ... something.

"GIVE IT TO ME!" she heard someone grunt.

Was that Calvin? No, it couldn't be; the voice was all wrong. Shannon slipped out of her shoes and fluffed her hair; Calvin must be watching porn. Perfect. No need for him to love himself alone when she'd gotten off work early—and was ready to get off.

"YEAH, BITCH, TAKE IT!"

Shannon's heart was in her stomach. She was excited but weirdly apprehensive. She took a deep breath and opened the door to the master bedroom. There she found Calvin, pounding a six-foot-tall supermodel with flowing ebony locks. In fact, that hair was so long and so luscious, Shannon thought for a moment she had found Calvin fucking another woman.

But that thought quickly evaporated when Shannon realized she was staring into a familiar face—one she'd seen on Hilfiger ads all over the city. Hilfiger *for men*, that is.

All over the city, guys are living on the down-low. The red flags were flying high on this one, but Shannon had ignored them. Beware the Double Dipper; he's one of the most dangerous players.

Shannon had called me, hysterical. "I need a fucking AIDS test!" she said.

I tried to calm her down. The woman was downright inconsolable.

"Fuck, Viv, I should have known!" she wailed. "He always had hemorrhoids and diarrhea. He told me he had irritable bowel syndrome! I'm such an idiot!"

"That doesn't mean someone's gay," I said. "Don't be so hard on yourself."

"And he always had these cysts in his ass. I'm a nurse so he'd ask me to excise them. I just blew it off as a genetic disorder or something."

"Damn, girl, that view of the park must have been something!"

"This isn't funny."

"I know. I'm just kidding! I just want you to see that you couldn't have seen this coming. Don't blame yourself. One day—"

"No. One day we will *not* laugh about this."

It was a hard-fought lesson for Shannon, but it's one worth learning. Sometimes it really is bi-now, gay later. I wonder briefly, while recalling her story, if she'll let me blog about it.

Catherine, Lisa and I finish up lunch and split the bill—we don't fuss around about treating each other anymore. We're too old for that.

"By the way, I think Lauren's coming back into town next month," I say. "Let's all do something?"

"Absolutely," says Catherine. "Maybe go to The

Box or something? You can invite this Mr. Canada we've all heard so much about."

"I'm seeing him tomorrow," I say, unable to hide my pride.

"So I've heard. Harlem, is it?" says Lisa. She gives a knowing smirk. "Good luck."

We exchange air kisses and head our separate ways.

Later that night I get a text from Eric. I can't remember the last time I've been so smitten, and the evidence is in the way I forgive him for not texting or calling unless it's to firm up our plans. He sure knows how to keep the mystery alive—I'll give him that.

Swing by at 9 to pick you up, k?

Yeah, see you then.

I can't wait to see you.

:-)

Does that emoticon say all I hope it does? "I can't wait to see you either and oh, yeah, I'm about to pull out my vibrator because you make me so fucking horny it feels like my vagina is melting down my thighs?"

It'll have to do. They say a picture is worth a thousand words, after all.

CHAPTER 11:
WUT UP?

"Hi," I say, absolutely unable to control my ear-to-ear grin.

"Hi. God, I missed you."

He says all the right things. Flattered, I ask, "You did?"

"I did. Let's go!"

We are both bubbling with energy that frankly surprises me at this hour on a Sunday. Being around Eric invigorates me; I'm buzzing like I've just downed two triple-shot Americanos in the space of a few seconds.

As we settle into a nearly empty train car and start chatting, I learn that Eric was raised on a farm with two siblings—he's the middle child. "I was pretty lucky to grow up in a happy family. My parents are still together, after forty years. They keep asking me when I'm going to settle down and tie the knot, but right now I'm too busy to think about it. I suppose when the right person comes along, I'll know."

He gives me a winning smile. Does that mean he thinks I might be that person? Or what? What does that smile mean?

He follows up with a quick comment that he

hasn't been in a serious relationship in ten years. I'm dying to ask about that smile but for some reason I feel like I can't. Like it's none of my business. I don't like feeling like this, like I'm second banana in this relationship, if you can call it that. It's a rotten feeling, knowing that I like him more than he likes me—or, rather, *not* knowing if he likes me as much as I like him.

"Soooo," he says, "what's your story? Tell me everything."

"Not much to tell," I say. "Born and raised in Texas. Went to business school in Dallas and have been in New York ever since."

"Are you close to your family?"

It's a question that always gives me pause, and this instance is no exception. Although I am close with my mother—a mostly Americanized Mexican Texan, I have a complicated relationship with my father, a second generation New York Italian. They met when he was on a football scholarship at the same university in north Texas where he now coaches. She worked at the campus bookstore.

Theirs was a passionate romance at first. He was a gorgeous specimen back in the day, built like a bull with a face like Pacino, and she was a ripe young Latina beauty. But after marriage and kids got to be an inconvenience for him with so many willing co-eds around, their marriage dissolved into not-so-funny recreations of scenes from I Love Lucy: Mom would scream at him in long and complex streams of Spanish, like Ricky Ricardo would when he was angry with Lucy but, unlike Lucy, Dad understood the language and knew that she was saying some pretty horrible things to him—things he certainly deserved to hear.

And that's just the surface stuff. It doesn't even begin to touch the fact that he really screwed my mom over when he left her with no warning—left her broke, after cleaning out their bank account and leaving with his new girlfriend. He was "that guy," the one who pretty much forgot to take care of his starter family, beyond obligatory weekend visitations, once he walked out the door. That kind of douchebaggery is really hard to forgive. I don't think I could even blog about guys like him without sounding bitter and issue-riddled.

Essentially, he and I are estranged. I call home on special occasions but the distance between us is so wide and so deep that we never move beyond stiff pleasantries. We speak, but we don't talk. His iron fist with regard to my grades, comments about my weight and disrespect for women has left me self-conscious and scarred.

While I don't necessarily like to talk about it, I am not ashamed of the way things are with my family, so it surprises me when I hear the lie come out of my mouth: "Yes, very close. I'm close with everyone."

He sees me squirm and drops the subject, but I hope that he's curious and has made a mental note to press me for details at a later time. I hate to admit it, but I really do wish he'd ask more about what makes me tick.

When the time comes, I'll explain my feelings about "daddy issues"—which has become a buzz-phrase for any woman with a less-than-perfect relationship to her father. It's no better with "mommy issues" or other familiar baggage; somehow, once you come clean about a normal childhood (one that isn't cribbed from an old *Leave it to Beaver* script), it always comes back to bite you. Arguing with your new boyfriend about his tendency to leave dirty dishes everywhere but the inside of the dishwasher? Must be your daddy issues. Can't get along with a mega-bitch at work? Mommy issues.

If I admit to my history, I'm afraid it will be used against me. I'd rather gloss over it all for now—at least until there's some trust here I can depend on. So I make light conversation about them, "They were quite a mixed pair—he's Italian and she's Mexican, so that makes me sort of a taco pizza."

He laughs, so I'm encouraged to continue riffing. "We used to have horrible dinners, like rigatoni and guacamole, and manicotti made with tortillas."

Eric, the foodie, looks mock horrified, and I add, "Hey, at least she never used salsa as spaghetti sauce!"

"Well, they made a beautiful daughter together," he says, brushing my hair back and kissing my cheek. I silently thank God for genetics. I did inherit my mom's perma-tan skin tone and Dad's ancestors' tendency to be curvy and voluptuous. Now if only I could stay thin like Mom, without living as she does on over the counter skinny pills, cigarettes and Diet Coke.

I am saved by the bell when the train jolts to a stop at our station. Eric rattles on a bit about how much he loves this church, this neighborhood. "I accidently found this place when I first moved to New York. I got off at the wrong train station, and spent the day wandering. I'd always heard that Harlem is dangerous, but I was pleasantly surprised to find that it's no worse than any other neighborhood as long as you stay out of the rough pockets. You won't believe the way they sing at this church. I don't go for the God stuff, I go for the gospel music."

He's so fucking cute, I can hardly stand it. I want to bite him. Hard. Only the threat of serious post-mortem judgment from the Man upstairs keeps me from suggesting we escape to a private nook for a quickie when we arrive.

The venue is magnificent. People rush to claim seats, and Eric ushers me into a pew while I take in my surroundings. Stained glass and high rafters, the smell of old paper and a confusing jumble of perfumes. A blaze of clarifying heat cuts through it all as Eric grabs my face and kisses me chastely enough for church, but with enough feeling to make me tingle.

Suddenly we are on our feet in a great wave of moving bodies. There is a tall, round black woman in a gorgeous floral-print frock whose swaying body acts as a metronome for all of us as we rock back and forth amid praise, praise, praise. There is an electric energy in the room. Spirit pulses in my veins. Thirty minutes into the service, Eric and I are both clapping and shouting "Amen" totally unabashedly, safe among our brothers and sisters. We hear stories of bereavement, calamity, redemption and salvation.

I have never felt luckier or more appreciative of my life than in this moment. To call the service powerful would be a gross understatement. I actually feel close to God, something I've never really experienced in church before, even though we're only there for the music. Church, when I was a kid and Mom used to make us go once in a while, was a horrible snoozefest. Eventually, she got so tired of fighting us kids on the topic that she stopped trying to force us to go.

Eric and I hardly speak on the ride home. We are too busy beaming with irrepressible joy. There is also an element of mental exhaustion, like the kind of heavy tiredness you feel after spending a day on the beach. Still, I am cognizant enough to know that the more time I spend with Eric, the more I am at risk of completely falling in love with him. I wonder, does he feel the same?

"You wanna see a movie?" he says. I am, of course, enchanted by the kind of easy familiarity that's grown between us. It helps me to forget the distant chasm I sense the rest of the time.

"Sure. But how 'bout we order food and OnDemand—make it a lazy Sunday?"

"Perfect."

I half-walk, half-float into my apartment with Eric right behind me. I rummage in the kitchen for the takeout menu of a great sandwich place nearby and am distracted enough that it takes me a moment to register what Eric is referring to when he says "What's all this?" and holds up a sheaf of loose papers from where they were scattered on the sofa.

Notes for the blog. FUCK.

"Oh, God, don't look at that ..." I say, hoping the panic isn't coming through in my voice. "I'm helping a friend research the different kinds of men that roam the Manhattan streets." I smile and roll my eyes, trying not to look like I'm rushing over to grab the pages from him.

"Hey, is this that blog they were talking about on the news? I'm impressed!"

"Uh ... yeah," I stammer. "Don't tell anyone I know the blogger. I'm sworn to secrecy."

He makes the tick-a-lock gesture of turning an imaginary key against his lips. "Your secret is safe with me," he says, holding up a scribbled note. "Yellow Fever Player? Let me guess: a guy who only dates Asian women?"

"Yes! How'd you know?" I squeal.

"I did live in Asia, remember? I dated a few Asian girls, too. A friend of mine used to joke that I had Yellow Fever."

"Interesting," I purr, happy to have a reason to move closer to him. "And now ... ?"

He leans in close to my face so our lips are almost touching.

"And now it looks like I have Vivi Fever."

Holy shit holy shit holy shit.

I clear my throat gently and gather up the remaining papers. I stretch so the smooth skin of my long neck makes an elegant arch. I am trying to combine seduction and subterfuge to ensure Eric doesn't spend too long looking at my blog notes.

"I could use some help with the iPhony," I say. "You know the type—only communicates via text?"

"Ah, yes, that infamous scoundrel," he says with mock seriousness. "Evidence suggests that it's pretty much over when you get the old 'Wut up?' text. If we haven't called and we send you a random greeting that would be appropriate for our bros, well ... let's just say there are a few things that could be going on, and none of them are good."

"That's what I've been saying!" I grab paper and a pen and begin scribbling furiously as he continues. I dare not pull out the recorder. That would show that my research is way more than casual.

"Well, the first possibility is that he's blasting out

mass texts to groups of girls to see who responds and what his best offer is. That's unusual, but stranger things have happened. The next option is that he's wasted, lonely, can't find anyone else at the late hour, and he really wants to get laid. Third, he doesn't want to call for some specific reason. Maybe he has a girlfriend. Maybe he lives with his parents. Whatever the reason, he can't call you because it'd be a disaster if you called him back. It's the same for dudes who never answer their phones. If he only texts, he's shady. Period."

"Ooo, you know what I love?" I say, ignoring the fact that the Canadian only texts me, "When you have plans with a guy but he doesn't call to confirm until eight or nine P.M. He texts, casually, with a 'u around?', proof positive that this loser is trolling for a hook-up. He's timed his communication so it's too late for dinner and he doesn't actually have to take you anywhere. He thinks he's being charming when he adds a winking emoticon to the 'sup sexy' message he sends as a follow-up."

Eric clearly cannot contain his laughter. "Girls fall for that shit all the time! I've been guilty of it, I can admit it. Some girls just make it easy to treat them like the booty calls they are …"

Is he talking about me? Is that what this is?!

I plaster a smile on my face and pray my inner freak-out doesn't shine through my eyeballs.

"I know, right?" I say. *Pull it together, pull it together!*

"Look," he adds, "if a guy keeps checking his phone and repeating he's sorry he has to do business after ten P.M., he's bullshitting you. If he wanted to be with you, he'd be present mind, body and spirit."

"That's a beautiful thought, Eric. Seriously."

I let the quiet bloom in the moment.

"People should be holding hands, not phones," he says, reaching for my warm palm.

"Cute," I say. I allow him to pull me down next to him on the sofa. But I'm still rattled by the idea that I might be a booty call. Do booty calls get taken to church? Is this a new breed of player? The Spiritually Inclined Poseur, perhaps?

I think of all the "Sup sexy?" texts I've gotten. Usually the sender is an idiot I haven't spoken to in months, even years. These messages always seem to show up right when you have a hot new boyfriend you're completely infatuated with. It's as if past lovers can smell happiness like sharks flocking to chum in the water. "Oh, she's happy and in love. Let me see if I can go ahead and fuck that up for her." I have no problem catching up with old flames who harbor a genuine interest in finding out what I'm up to, but those guys are like Bigfoot—rumored to exist, but there's no empirical proof.

I've made the mistake of answering a random text before. I was headed home one night around eleven when a message came through from a cutie I had a crush on. It was the standard "Hey sexy" text. I went to meet him for a drink. After our second round, he realized I wasn't going home with him. So I can't say I was surprised when I walked to our table from the bathroom just in time to see him zip a quick text to who-knows-what skank he knew he could count on for a late-night lay. Thirty minutes later, *she showed up at the bar.* What a coincidence! They got to chatting, and I got in a cab. Alone. The best part? He still texts me sometimes. I never respond.

"What did we do before cell phones?" I say.

Privately I chastise myself for allowing my mind to wander when the present moment is so luscious.

I flip my hair and smile to hide the fact that my right foot is sliding a piece of paper titled "Our Relationship" under the sofa. My heart is racing. *God, please don't let him see the part about me falling for a guy and really, really wanting him to be my boyfriend. I went to church this morning, remember?*

"Who cares?" he says, his gaze tracing the curve of my collar bones to my décolletage. "Get over here."

I feel two kinds of relief: first, disaster has surely been averted; second, I am back in Eric's arms once again, where I'm suddenly filled with warmth I didn't realize was missing until it floods through me.

He kisses me then hoists me on the kitchen counter, gently lifts my dress and slowly, ever so slowly, peels off my black lace Cosabellas. He uses both hands to spread my legs, and there it is again— the burning fire that rages through every fiber of my body. He kisses my inner ankle, then works his way to the back of my knees, where a nip from his perfect teeth makes an erogenous zone of a seemingly insignificant patch of flesh. His tongue samples my inner thigh. I am dripping wet. His breath is warm and soft.

Like he has nowhere to be for the next three millennia, he licks me from side to side, languishing at my clit. I feel myself contorting and twitching, trying like hell to not fall off the counter, and a throaty moan escapes my lips. He drops to his knees and I lay back, careful for the wine glasses on the counter next to me, and wrap my legs around his neck. He is teasing me right to my edge, and as I feel the moment come I arch my back. His tongue moves in fast circles now as his hands grip my thighs tight. The lights exploding behind my eyes are so bright and so enormous I imagine this is the kind of feeling that drives people to get high. Because that's what I am— high on this moment, this man.

"That was amazing," I say when my breathing slows. He helps me down from the counter and we both collapse, sitting side by side on the cool tile of the kitchen floor. "I've never come so hard in my life."

"Challenge accepted," he says, and before I even have time to make sense of it all, his mouth covers mine and we are climbing to new heights again, right there on the floor. An hour later we are both in need of major nourishment. Unfortunately, the only items in my refrigerator are champagne, a block of parmesan and Pellegrino.

"I'll be right back," he says.

He throws his jeans on and I watch that sexy ass walk out my door. Twenty minutes later he returns with a bag of groceries.

"I am making us a Capellini Arrabiata," he announces.

Angry pasta? Now that's fuckin' hot. But pasta? How many calories in that!

I quickly calculate the calories in my head. *Is he crazy? I can't eat that!* I soothe myself by remembering that after all of that sex, I've earned it. We must have burned at least three hundred calories.

He grabs and caresses me through the chopping and boiling. He's delicious. At this point he could be making Chef Boyardee and I wouldn't care.

He feeds me ever so slowly and seductively.

After a few bites I say I've had enough.

"You've barely had any!" he says deflated.

"No, it's not your cooking, it's that I have to watch what I eat. ALWAYS," I say sheepishly and embarrassed. "I gain weight just watching you cook! It's my heritage. If I'm not careful, I'll end up as fat and round as my old Italian Nonna!"

"Listen, I love your body and frankly you could stand to gain a few more pounds. Besides, I got gelato for dessert. Isn't that diet ice cream for you Italians?" he says poking me in the rib and smiling.

Is this guy kidding me? Is he the perfect man?

I am not sure where the time flies but once we got to the gelato we were back on the kitchen counter. We can't get enough. I ask him to spend the night but he declines. He says he has an early shoot and then another meeting with Dan and Roger. I also have an early meeting. A new pitch from a company that has designed a new app that can detect if a person is lying. This should be interesting. Oh I wish I had that app at this exact moment. He is, seriously, too good to be true.

CHAPTER 12:
ARIANNA GOES LIVE!

For the first time ever, being lazy ended up paying off big time. I've gotten behind on transcribing my notes and recordings into readable prose, so I just typed up Arianna's blog on Gold Diggers. I thought it was good, as is, so it was simple, easy—bing bang blogged.

What I didn't count on was her reaction to seeing her words in print.

As soon as Arianna saw my email telling her that her blog was live, she called and asked, "Darling girl, why didn't you put my name on that blog? Would you? I want people to know I wrote it. I feel very strongly about what I said, and I want credit for it!" Her motherly tone told me that she wasn't being bitchy, but she was definitely serious.

I wasted no time in updating the blog, adding her byline and saying she was my Guest Blogger. I had assumed she'd want to keep her identity secret, like I do, but she was ecstatic and proud and told everyone she knows. And she knows A LOT of people.

She sent out email blasts to her entire contact list and her Facebook friends, some of whom are pretty important. They were all so impressed to see her writing for an up and coming, trendy new blog that they told everyone they know. My stats went through the roof!

I've also been inundated with emails and blog comments from women all over the city, and a few men who want their sides heard, too. But hey, they can get their own blog. It's not like men have any difficulty in having their voices heard. They own the media and there is no shortage of their opinions about women everywhere you look. Feminists may have made huge strides, but it's still a man's world.

One over the top comment, from a particularly angry man, started a heated debate. He took great offense to Arianna's defense of the Gold Digger and crudely shared his opinion that women like her are perfect examples of everything wrong with male/female relations:

> Dear Menhattan Project,
>
> You should tell your guest blogger to take her highfalutin bigotry and shove it up her well-polished and probably bleached asshole. Any woman who can write that sort of thing and still have any pride is nothing but a money-grubbing bitch. (I was going to say "whore" but I have too much class to go there.)
>
> Is it any wonder that no one in New York, or the rest of the country for that matter, can find a decent relationship partner? I can't tell you how many women have dumped me once they found out that I'm not going to be supporting their self-entitled asses for the rest of their lives. Your entire blog is a disgrace to decent men and women everywhere.

Sincerely,
A nice guy with an average income

The responses came in fast and furious:

Dear Dickhead,
How about if "nice guys" like you help change the laws so women can finally make equal pay for equal work?
By the way, "self-entitled" is not a word. Sincerely,
A nice, but broke, gal who makes less than the idiot guy in the office next to her

And:

Dear Mister Nice Guy,
You're not so nice. Your hostile attitude shows me a lot more about why women dump you than your limp wallet ever could.

And, my favorite:

How do these women find out that you don't intend to support them? On the first dinner date when you wait until the check arrives to announce that it's Dutch treat?
Your violent language sounds like you might benefit from a few therapy sessions. Or a boot in the ass. Either way works for me.

Mr. Nice Guy came back for more, in response:

Dear Nice Broke Gal,

You're just upset because you need a man to pay for you to get your asshole bleached and you probably have to shave your vagina because you can't afford to wax it.

By the way, "self-entitled" is too a word. Look it up.

Nice Guy

Her comeback cracked me up:

Dear High School Dropout,

A vagina is an internal organ and doesn't grow hair. You mean "vulva." Look it up.

Bored-with-you Gal

Thank God, some folks tried to be the voice of reason, like this man (who I suspect might be a friend of Arianna's—I don't see a lot of wealthy, mature men reading this blog on their own):

Thank you, Menhattan Project, for giving us this forum to discuss an age-old issue. I'm proud to call myself a feminist, and I'm a man. Yes, unfortunately men usually make more money than women. This blog about Gold Diggers gives voice to women who are willing to carry their own weight in a relationship, even if it's not a financial weight. The writer is obviously an intelligent woman who values her man as much as she values herself. She doesn't come off as a scheming user, but as someone who knows what to bring to a high-powered relationship.

I am a very wealthy man, and I appreciate

being able to afford to have a charming, gorgeous woman on my arm. I know the difference between a woman of refinement and class, and a broke ho. Wealthy men who fall for the latter are just as confused about what makes a relationship work as are the silly girls they date.

But even his reasoned response caught some flak and took the conversation off on a whole different tangent:

Who you calling a broke ho? You think I want to be broke? You think I don't bust my ass, working two jobs just to survive in this city? Is it wrong to want a man I don't have to carry? My ex couldn't hold down a job for more than six months, and now he ain't even paying child support!

And I ain't a ho. I don't sell myself to the highest bidder. But I sure ain't putting out for some loser who can't afford to support me and my kids.

Her words triggered this response:

Shut up, bitch, and make me a sandwich.

Another guy chimed in with:

We want prenup! We want prenup! #burnedbefore

From there, a flame war erupted that was comical

at times, but mostly it was a lot of juvenile tit for tat. This was the first blog to elicit this sort of visceral response, and it was a little scary. I didn't expect people to get this angry. As crazy as it sounds, I never thought about the obvious fact that literally anyone with a computer can read this and that I might attract some nutjobs. I didn't think that far in advance. I had sort of a naïve fantasy that only women like me and my friends would be reading it, and we'd all laugh and dish about what we had in common—men.

I was about to close the comments on this craziness, and change the settings to require my permission before they get posted, but I was pulled off task when I saw that Arianna herself made an appearance and responded:

> Well, I'm glad to see so many people feeling so passionate about what I wrote. Some of you get it, and some not so much. Let me remind everyone that this began as an adult conversation about what it takes to get by in this world.
>
> Some of us are okay with scraping by and living on nothing but love or drama. But many of us are not. We want more out of life. We see nothing wrong with having nice things, and only getting involved with someone who can supply them. But as I stated in my blog, it needs to be an equal exchange. If the man is the one supplying the money, he deserves to have an able partner who won't embarrass him.
>
> I hold up my end of the bargain, and expect the same in return. And lest that sound like I'm selling myself, I assure you that I am not. This isn't just about money, although that is how it

appears on a surface level. This is about respecting one another and honoring what each party brings to the table.

The conversation went on, with both sides making excellent points and the occasional immature troll trying to reignite the flame war. But I was gratified to see an overall intelligent exchange of ideas. This is exactly what I was hoping to accomplish by creating this blog.

It was interesting to hear what the men think about the blogs, but the women! Oh, the women have a lot to say and they're saying it, through blog comments and private emails! So many funny and sad stories, all told by women who just want to be happy. They're not trying to screw guys over; they're not trying to be users or manipulators. They just want a nice guy who has a decent job, with a little responsibility and maturity. Yes, the party life is fun, and one night stands or friends with benefits are great for a while, but eventually everyone with any substance gets tired of that. We're all just trying to find someone to happily spend our lives with.

One email summed it up perfectly:

Dear Menhattan Project,

I hope you don't mind me responding to you privately. I don't want my comment to be publicly posted, but I do want to share it with you.

Not long ago I moved to Manhattan from Ohio and it didn't take long for me to learn that dating here is very different from the Midwest. We, too, have our share of men who are players, and women who give the rest of us a bad name but in NYC it's a whole new ball game. The cost of living is so high, and the pressure to look like you just stepped off the pages of a magazine is crazy. I've never felt so judged about my appearance; at least, not anywhere I've ever lived before.

It seems to me that the problem is the almighty dollar. Many people, both men and women, have forgotten how to be nice to each other and treat their dates the way they would like to be treated. They're too busy scrambling to grab the brass ring except, in New York, the ring is made of platinum.

I tried to live by the Golden Rule, and "do unto others" when I first moved here but discovered that, in the dating world, I was seen as a naïve country bumpkin. I dated my share of Minnows and Poseurs (even though I didn't have your lexicon to sort them at the time) and became quickly jaded. I reluctantly learned that women really do have to pay attention to how much money a man might have and how he handles it. It's not avarice, it's self-preservation!

All I ask for is a man I can share my life with who is also willing to take care of me like we're family. I don't mean just financially because I'm not dead weight, even though I don't make as much as I'd like (I'm a social worker). I'll take care of him in return, like family.

The problem is, if I marry a man who shares my desire to make a difference in the world over making a lot of money, we're going to starve. So I have to look for a man who makes a good living, but the competition for them is stiff. Men know that and they use it to their advantage.

Even though I'm not a Gold Digger like your guest blogger, I can relate to what she's saying. There's nothing wrong with wanting a man who makes a good living, but we women have been made to feel ashamed for saying that out loud.

Sincerely,
Donna from Dayton

I wrote back and asked if I could post what she said if I paraphrased it—I told her that I understood her desire for privacy, writing an anonymous blog and all—and she graciously said that I could. The bonus is that I bet she can't help but tell all of her friends about "my" blog that she wrote. The word continues to spread!

This thing is getting big. I'm so excited!

CHAPTER 13:
TRUSTAFARIANS

The week has flown by, and when I finally stop to catch my breath it's Thursday. I haven't heard from the Detergent King or Mr. Canada. The former is probably waiting for me to touch base—I'm the one who ended our last date so abruptly, after all—and the latter said he would call during the week when he left Sunday night. I'm not the type to check in, especially when I'm in constant danger of blurting out something stupid, like "When can I see you again because I can't stop thinking about the way you rock this body?"

I'm using all my pent-up energy for the blog, learning Twitter and maintaining the blog's Facebook page. The blog topped ten thousand views on Tuesday and I have been pinged, tracked-back, liked, followed, retweeted, hashtagged, shared, pinned and subscribed to in record numbers. I can't believe that it got so viral, so fast! Apparently even on the internet it's all about who you know. The big question is, how long can I stay anonymous? It's a huge challenge.

My readers are clamoring for more, and I know exactly what to give them:

THE TRUSTAFARIAN.

The Trustafarian can be deceiving. Don't be blinded by his glitzy last name or socialite mother; trust fund boys are on a monthly stipend, so the luxe treatment you quickly acclimated to from the first to the fifteenth of every month just as quickly disappears come the sixteenth. "Can you spot me a hundy?" the Trustafarian asks. He keeps his tone casual—because what's a few Benjamins between friends?

Trustafarians are the children of parents smart enough to know that giving a generational fortune to a young gun in his sexual prime is a recipe for disaster. Often, the Trustafarian is expected to foot the bill for his friends—and whatever lovely morsels they've picked up along the way. Of course, all those bottles at Provocateur or Lavo cost a pretty penny—so many pennies, in fact, that brother won't have a dime by mid-month.

The Trustafarian is a rare blend of fifty percent player and fifty percent poseur. There's potential for a prosperous future if you can ride the wave of flush and lean times, but you're either going to have to wait until his stake in the family business ripens or—well—or his parents die unexpectedly. Even then, if he hasn't outgrown his spendthrift ways, that inheritance won't last forever.

Our friend Melissa dated a textbook Trustafarian. He was charming, funny and incredibly well-connected. His parents had a mega-yacht in Sag Harbor and a mansion in

Palm Beach, and he had every toy a rich boy could ever dream of, but it was costing Melissa her own money to date him! The last straw came when his mother turned to her and said, "I can't wait for you to marry my son so I can finally cut him off." Needless to say, they didn't last.

Melissa encounters Trustafarians on a fairly regular basis because of her work at one of New York's most well-known PR firms. Melissa, a Jewban (half Jewish, half Cuban), loves to say her heritage has given her perfect balance: she can pick out stocks and salsa rhythms with equal ease. She's an alpha female who doesn't take shit from anyone. She can pay her own way and is proud of standing on her own two feet.

It's easy to get sucked into Melissa's world. Within it, you'll attend the best parties and exclusive charity events, eat at the hottest restaurants and meet people you've only read about in Page Six. A Trustafarian may not be ambitious, but he finds himself among the elite that have earned rightful places in Melissa's social sphere.

Yes, the Trustafarian balances his time among swanky soirees, lunching with his parents, shopping on Fifth Avenue, hanging out at Nello's, and of course, weekly therapy sessions. He pays handsomely for professional pity: his parents deemed it more important to jet off to the south of France and leave him with the housekeeper/nanny/playmate in his most formative years—how could he not be damaged?

Before they split, Melissa learned about another classic Trustafarian trait: bad manners in group dining scenarios. Her beau would order everything on the menu (which nobody will eat) and rounds of shots (which nobody will drink) with the kind of authority that led everyone to believe he'd foot the bill. Even the waitresses took his alpha-attitude at face value and inevitably brought him the black check presenter at the end of the night. But in true Trustafarian style, Melissa's guy would take one look at the total, throw in a little cash, then say something like "Let's just make it an even split, okay guys?" More than once, Melissa revealed, she had to cover her portion of the cost of his extravagant orders.

Another unpleasant tendency? Drug use. These boys are rich and bored—a dangerous combination. Melissa says she used to find bags of blow ("white espresso") on top of the fridge and a bag of Molly crammed behind the TV. "I guess coping with his really difficult life was just too much," Melissa explains. "Who wouldn't need an escape from the lap of luxury every now and then?"

Long story short: when it comes to Trustafarians, trust me—cut your losses and move on.

After I proof the entry and upload it to the blog, the phone rings. Matthew. *Phew, someone still loves me.*

"Hey."

"Hey, babe. You wanna go to dinner?"

"Sure. Tonight? I can be ready in thirty."

"I'll text you when I'm downstairs."

I catch an image of myself in the mirror as I

make my way to the closet. I'm smiling ear to ear. Clearly I like Matthew. Or is it just the convenience of him that makes me happy? He's my primary distraction between Mr. Canada meetings—but is that all he is to me?

When I hop in the car, I've already rehearsed a little speech about my freak-out during our last date. It's a riff on the old "I've been hurt before and I can't fall too fast" story, but I've embellished just enough detail to make the story feel vulnerable. The truth can do that to a lie.

But when I slide in the front seat and lean over to kiss him, Matthew gives me an easy out.

"Hey, hottie," he says, "I can't stay out too long. I have the kids in the morning."

"No problem," I answer. I hope he can't sense my relief. "So where are we going?"

"This little Mexican dive down on Mulberry Street that has the best roasted corn. It's very *Me-hi-co Chic*," he says, looking at me sideways.

I slap on a smile and say, "Amazing! Sounds great."

This feels a little low-brow, even for Matthew, but a part of me feels like this is a test. I've obviously enjoyed our fine dining experiences, so maybe he wants to see how I do in a less refined, more down-to-earth scenario. *Bring it on, Detergent King.* I silently pat myself on the back for making the right wardrobe choice tonight: jeans and a new H&M sweater anyone would easily mistake for Dior.

Funny, but this is precisely the kind of date I need to get to know this man without being burdened by the dread of post-date sexpectations. As easy as it is to imagine myself getting comfy-cozy in that swank apartment of his, in all of my visions I'm still fully clothed. Does it say more about Matthew or me that tonight is exactly what I need?

We slide into a corner booth with red vinyl seats. I take in his casual attire: jeans and a polo. Matthew has the kind of body that carries its modest extra weight well. His physique says to the world, "I'm here, I'm enjoying life, but I'm not going crazy." It's like his very bone structure communicates the balance of ambition and sensibility.

"Listen," I say before I can stop myself, "I hate to bring this up again, but I really feel the need to apologize for my crazy behavior the other night ..."

"Ahhh, so you're mentally imbalanced? I thought so, but I wasn't going to say anything. I find your shortcomings endearing." His warm smile feels merciful. I didn't realize until this moment how much I would have regretted fucking this up.

"Oh, wait," he continues, "I know what happened. You're so head-over-heels in love with me already that you're terrified of making one wrong move. That's it, right? I should tell you I've always been a little psychic."

"Do you read palms?" I feign a slap to his face, with my palm deliberately extended.

"God, you're violent tonight!" he cries, dodging my hand, "But c'mon," he says, suddenly more somber, "what happened?"

I take a deep breath and let it out. All of my prepared answers seem really insufficient now that the time has come to use them. "I guess ... well, it's like I said. I want to take it slow. I'm figuring out what these feelings are and ... I want to make sure I do this right. For once. Y'know, and all that jazz. If it's just sex …"

"Well, I'd hate to think that you'd consider going to bed with me 'just sex.' I can wait until you decide you simply cannot live without ravishing me."

Again, I feel his light humor wash over me like a warm rain. It feels wonderful, and soon our easy laughter is made even easier by oversized frozen margaritas. Matthew may have brought me to something of a dive, but the man knows how to order a top-shelf drink in any circumstance.

An hour later I've had enough chimichangas to bring down Pancho Villa. Since a purging feather isn't on the dessert menu, I suggest we walk around outside for awhile. I manage to push the thought of the eleven hundred calories I have just consumed—and the fact that I'll have to make up for it by not eating tomorrow—to the back of my brain for later torture.

"I still have a few hours," Matthew says. "I know a great place where we can shoot some pool and down a few brewskies."

"Ummmm, brewskies? Really? What are you, a hundred? Who still says that? "

"It's making a comeback!"

"Okay, old man," I say. "Let's do it. Pool and brewskies."

We walk a few blocks further south until Matthew puts a hand on my lower back and guides me through an unmarked doorway. Inside, I smell the seedy, beer-soaked aromas of my college undergrad years and Texan upbringing. Sadly, it makes me briefly homesick and tired of always trying so hard to be posh, just to fit in here in NYC. The place is on Canal Street, close to Chinatown—not an area known for its refinements.

I have to give him credit, though; the more time I spend with Matthew, the more he surprises me. He can go from swank to swill without missing a beat, and he breaks a mean rack, too. I got my ass handed to me in two rounds of solids and stripes, but Matthew says my consolation prize is another draught.

"Next round is on me, Matt," the bartender says.

Okay, now I'm floored.

"First name basis with the bartender," I say, taking a sip from the pint. "You come here often?"

"Is that a line? I can't believe you think I'd fall for that." I give him a mock head-to-toe appraisal. He laughs then says, "Yeah, I come here to chill and think about my day sometimes."

Over the next hour, several patrons walk up to Matthew and greet him like he's an old friend. None look like the type I'd think Matthew socializes with—they're regular Joes with scuffed shoes and frayed tee-shirts. Still, Matthew shakes each man's hand and asks after girlfriends or families or jobs. Then he introduces me with an easy familiarity. "This is Viv." I smile and wave, and Matthew's friends give him a nod before moving along.

"That's Al, he's the doorman for that building across the way," Matthew says, pointing out a guy at the bar. "He comes in here a lot, if you know what I mean. And that's Jose over there. He's a New York bus driver. Man oh man, does he have some stories."

"You really are an interesting man," I say, and I mean it. I'm beginning to really like him, as a person.

"I'll ignore your surprise and thank you instead," he says with a smile. He leans in to kiss me and I feel myself lift my lips to meet his.

I can't help but ask again, "So what's the real story with your ex-wife?"

He gets a look on his face that I can't quite figure out. Pain? Shame? Anger at me for inquiring? "Why do you care so much?" He looks at me intently for a moment, as if trying to figure out my motive for asking and then decides to trust me. "If you want the truth, she left me."

"Why?"

"She didn't want to work at the marriage anymore. Nothing is perfect and she left."

"Matthew, I don't think you're being honest with me."

"Look, she left me for a woman, okay? Happy now?"

"Oh." Silenced, abashed, I finally say, "I'm sorry, I didn't mean to pry. I just thought … you know … let's get to know each other and all that. I didn't realize it was so …" my voice trails off.

He waves off my apology, "It's okay. I'm sorry I snapped at you. It's just a pretty touchy subject. Now you know why I drink," he says, draining his brewskie. "And, as you can imagine, it took lots of therapy to finally come to terms with the fact that it wasn't because I wasn't man enough to make her happy—it's that I wasn't woman enough. Even so, I really don't like to talk about it."

"I can only imagine. I mean not really, but you know what I mean? I'm sorry."

"It's not your fault but, there, now you know everything."

He looks at his watch.

"Well, time to get you home, Cinderella."

We walk back to the car, holding hands in companionable silence. I really *like* this guy. He has such a big heart and I feel like I don't have to pretend with him. Not having to carry around a false persona—one I wasn't even aware of until now—makes me feel weightless. I float down the sidewalk and feel the electricity growing between us, like a light bulb pulsing with an ever-strengthening current. The shock of it brings me back to myself; I haven't thought of Eric since I opened Matthew's car door so many hours ago.

CHAPTER 14:
SMOKE & MIRRORS

Another weekend has come and gone, and still it's been radio silence from Mr. Canada. Meanwhile, Matthew texts and calls often—not in an overbearing way, just to check in and say "Hi, how's your day going?" I like that. I like being liked.

Canada is on thin ice, as Matthew is solidifying the pond under his own feet. But every time I think of Eric, I'm reminded of his supreme hotness and the raw, animal sex he brings to the table. Plus, maybe he's just slow to open up. He did bring me to *church* with him, didn't he? That's pretty intimate. I remember thinking, when we first met, that I wasn't the type he'd bring to church, but I guess I am ... or was, that once. We do have fun together, *when* we're together. I wonder if he just needs more time.

The suspense is killing me—literally, I might be dying due to a combination of dry mouth, anxiety, and a major heart rate spike whenever my phone vibrates.

To be honest, I don't understand what's happening here. Our last date was off the charts, unless I was hallucinating. I mean, he's not *not* going to call, is he? The more I think about it, the angrier I get. All of my elegant musings eventually give way to a single question: *What the fuck?*

How busy can one man be? Not for nothing, and I don't mean to disparage the noble profession of modeling, but Eric isn't exactly the President of the United States—and even they find the time for some fun under the Oval Office desk. And, there is a well-heeled Detergent King who acts like he can't wait to spend time with me. He's impatiently waiting in the wings, and he won't wait forever.

Before I know it, my anger has boiled over into my fingertips and I am dialing, hitting send, tapping my foot ...

"Hello?"

"Hi!" I say, instantly trying to hide my rage despite the fact that his casual tone makes me want to reach through the phone and strangle him. "How are you? Where've you been?"

Flirty and casual. You're flirty and casual, Viv. Flirty and freakin' casual.

"Yeah, I've been busy. Had to go to Miami for work. How are you?"

"Great, great. Thanks for asking. I hadn't heard from you in a minute, so I thought I'd call and see what you were up to." *A minute—good one, Viv. How 'bout "I haven't heard from you for what feels like eighteen months. Been in prison by any chance? Dropped into the Congo?"*

"Hey, actually, are you around tonight? I'd love to see you and I want to talk to you about something."

My stomach drops and the alarm bells going off in my head come to a sudden silence, almost like the whole world has gone deaf. *Talk about something?* What in the hell does that mean? Fuck. I just fucked this up.

"Yeah, sure," I say, back to "flirty-and-casual" mode.

"See you soon."

My heart sinks as the call ends. I know what's coming.

I've just been played by the old Smoke and Mirrors Guy—a decidedly unsexy kind of S&M.

I kill the time waiting by making some quick, angry notes for a new blog:

> The S&M Guy tells you everything you want to hear to ensure you see him exactly as you want him to be. He's the fulfillment of your unspoken wishes, because somehow—and this is the real magic—he lets you convince yourself that he's actually perfect for you. He showers you with love and affection, says and does all the things you've dreamed of. All the while, he's biding his time until things get too serious or you—God forbid—ask him to commit. Then it's *POOF!*— just like that, he's gone. You've been ghosted.

I'm a savvy New York woman. I write a pretty popular blog about men and their conniving ways. How did I not see this coming?

I sit on my bed and wait for Eduardo to call up. I don't bother scrambling to reapply mascara or change into a perfect oh-I-just-had-this-insanely-adorable-outfit-on ensemble. My mind and heart are racing. I feel my face get hot. Tears are welling in my eyes and just as I think I might have a handle on things, the floodgates open and I am in full-on Oprah "Ugly Cry" mode. *You've only known this guy for a couple weeks!* I tell myself. *Stop it! This is insane!*

That's the trouble with S&M. When it's done right, you never see it coming.

Eduardo calls to say I have a guest. I pinch my cheeks and dry my eyes. I still have to look hot for godsakes.

He knocks.

"Just a minute," I mutter.

I check the peep hole out of habit. The fucker looks like he has a fucking halo over his fucking head. More gorgeous than ever. I feel like punching him. No, kissing him. No, punching him. FUCK.

I open the door and there he is, grinning those perfect rows of white teeth. Grinning is a good sign. I feel my breath leave me for a few seconds. The tingle I've become so addicted to shoots through my body. The rush I get now is a small fix compared to the full-on, body-to-body, direct-vein injection I'm used to.

He steps forward and grabs my face, drawing me into a slow kiss. It's like he hasn't seen me in lifetimes.

This isn't the way a man about to dump a woman treats her, but I don't have time for mixed signals—I only have time to melt into this feeling, his mouth covering mine, my hands across his smooth, broad back.

I am struck by the memory of me, telling myself I'd be okay if I never saw Eric again after that first night. I told myself I'd be okay. I am a fucking liar.

"Let's sit," he says, inviting himself to my sofa.

"Sure." I smile and sit back against the arm rest, facing him.

He holds my hands and looks into my eyes. *Here we go.*

"You know I'm crazy about you," he begins and

my smile freezes on my face. Nothing good ever follows an opening line like that. "I think you're an amazing woman. Sexy, smart, howlingly funny, and you know how much I love hanging out with you."

Hanging out? Is that what we've been doing? I can't help snorting—a sound I'm not proud to hear coming out of my face. "Yeah, but … ?"

"But I can't be in a serious relationship right now. I have a few things to sort out. I can't be what you need at the moment."

Fuck you. What I need is for you to not be an asshole, I think, but say instead, "Okay. That's … fine. I understand. I wasn't pushing. I like hanging out with you the way we've been …" I hear myself using his same casual language and agreeing to be Mr. Canada's fuck-buddy, and I can't seem to stop myself. "For the record," my dignity forces me to say, "I'm kind of a great catch."

I think my efforts at keeping this conversation light are working, and I'm not sure how I feel about that; relieved or pissed as hell that he doesn't care more that he's hurting me. Eric is smiling. He's relieved. I'm not crying—at least not right now. Tears are kryptonite to the Smoke and Mirrors Guy. Fucker.

Just then, there's another knock on my door. I apologize and explain that I'm not expecting anyone, then move to answer it. It could be maintenance or a neighbor or—

"Matthew!"

Holy shit mother of God what is happening?! What is the point of having a doorman if he doesn't actually guard the door?

"Hi, babe, how are you?" he says, moving in for a hug and kiss.

Red alert! Shut it down! Shut! It! Down!

"All good, honey. Actually my friend Eric just stopped by to say hello." I take a quick step backward and introduce the men. The faster I can get this runaway train back on track, the better off I'll be.

"I was just leaving," Eric announces. I can practically smell his relief. Inside, I am a hurricane of emotions—anger and lust and shame and excitement and feelings I can't even name. It makes my head spin.

Eric gives me a peck on the cheek and closes the door behind himself. I don't have a chance to say anything other than "Bye," which sounds incredibly lame to my ear. There wasn't even a flicker of jealousy on Eric's face at Matthew's entrance. The voice inside my head whispers. *Why would he be jealous? You're just another notch on his bedpost.*

On the other hand, Matthew looks devastated. Not only is there another man in my apartment, but a Greek fucking god! "Who was that?" he asks, sharply.

"A friend, just a friend," I say.

"Don't lie to me, Viv. I know something else was going on. You've never been into me one hundred percent. Is he why?"

"Matthew, I—"

"No. Don't keep lying. You know I want to be with you." His voice catches, and he pauses to contain himself. I briefly wonder if he's trying not to cry. I hope not. I haven't seen a man cry in a long time, and I'm over my head with something like that. But I do love his ability to show vulnerability. It's kind of a turn on, in a twisted sort of way.

He rushes on, "I came over here on a whim to tell you I can't get you out of my head. That I'm willing to wait as long as it takes for you to feel comfortable. That I want you more than I've wanted any woman I've ever known, but wanting you and waiting is better than having a fucking parade of other women in my bed. And, for the record, I *could* have other women. I'm kind of a great catch, you know."

"I know that," I say quickly, contrite, struck by the coincidence of hearing him utter the exact same words I just said to Eric, minutes ago. I know he's not saying it to brag—he's saying it for the same reason I did—a vain effort to convince himself that he really is a great catch.

"Well, it looks like I would have been wasting my time telling you all that, since you're clearly hung up on someone else."

I'm momentarily stunned. From the look on his face, I can tell that Matthew is, too. After a few long moments, I manage to speak.

"Matthew, I … I need to think about this. Can we talk tom—"

"There's nothing to fucking think about," he says, his voice filled with angry hurt. He doesn't look at me as he walks to the door and leaves. I hear him press on the door once it's closed to make sure it's secure. Even amid his rage, Matthew is trying to take care of me.

You're a fucking moron, chimes my inner voice. She's in a bitchy mood today. *You want someone to be jealous? You got it. Why can you only feel worthwhile when a douchebag chases you? Why can't you accept kindness from a good man who could—dare I say it?—love you for who you really are?*

I sit down and cry. Then I pour a glass of beautiful pinot noir and cry some more. Screw calories today! My loneliness starts to take shape, like a dark presence in the room. I call Lauren before it can grow hands and throttle me.

"Calm down," she soothes as soon as she hears my garbled hello. "I can't even understand you, girl. Start from the beginning."

So I do. I tell her everything about my predicament, blow by blow. Lauren listens, dutifully interjecting with the occasional "No he di-in't!" or "You shut up, girl!" or "Oh, shit—seriously?"

Her prognosis isn't unexpected: Eric isn't ready for a relationship. Matthew isn't only ready, but ready and waiting for me specifically.

"Matthew, on paper, is really who you should be with, but we've all been in your shoes: the electricity sets you ablaze for the wrong guy. You can tell yourself Eric will come around, and maybe he will."

"Who are we kidding?" I say, exhausted by my tears. "I'm no spring chicken. I don't have time for this shit."

There's a moment of friendly quiet between us. I know this is a tough scenario for any woman. Her friend calls with a love problem, the answer to which is startlingly clear. But if a girl can't see things clearly—if her heart is working overtime to cloud the crap out of her usually practical mentality—there's not a whole lot you can do.

"Tell me about you," I say. "And make it good. How's it going in the land of 'gators?"

"Fuck the 'gators, chil'!" she says in an exaggerated Southern drawl, "They got flying cockroaches here, as big as your hand!"

"Oh dear lord. And you want to stay there?"

"Well, if you must know, I'm in love," she says.

"What the hell?! With who? You've only been

down there a hot minute! And why haven't I heard about this before now?"

"You've been a little ... ahem ... distracted, remember?"

"Oh my God, I'm so sorry! I don't mean for our conversations to be all about me! Let me know next time I'm being a story hog!"

Lauren laughs, "It's okay. Sometimes we need to be the center of attention. But now it's my turn! He's amazing, Viv. He lives down here. Moved from Venezuela ten years ago. I already met his family! A friend down here set us up on a blind date two weeks ago, and we've been inseparable ever since. I didn't want to say anything because I was so smitten and felt so totally ridiculous, but ... but when you know, you know. And I know."

"Lauren, this is incredible. I'm so happy for you I could scream!"

"Finally, right?! He ain't no Triple P like the last one."

We burst out laughing as usual, but the wine and crying have already given me a headache.

"Sounds like you need to get to bed."

"I do, babes. Thanks for listening. Love you."

"Any time. Love you more."

Tired beyond measure, already cried out, I just have enough time to wash my face and turn off all the lights before I sink into the pillows and sleep.

CHAPTER 15:
FLIMFLAMMERS

It is a gray morning as I wake up feeling puffy, groggy and alone. This seems like the perfect moment to hang out with all my cyber friends on the sofa. I put on some green tea, snuggle up in my cashmere blankie and open my iPad to find over a hundred new comments on various blogs on the site, some of which are blog submissions from my readers!

A sudden jolt of validating energy rushes through my body as I start to read the comments. Could there be someone else struggling with a "lust versus love" scenario like me? Say what you will about depravity on the internet—when you're in a bind, it's nice to be able to bring other people's experiences into your living room.

I scroll down and read the first subject line: *OOPS! Sexted the wrong man!* Been there, done that. Next. *Shower me with love.* That's either about a money-hungry gold digger or a fetish for "yellow showers." No thanks. *Watch out for the Flimflammer!* reads the next line. It's rare that I come across a male "type" I haven't heard of—I am writing the blog on the topic after all. Intrigued, I click the post, throw my feet up on the new birchwood ottoman I scored from HauteLook.com, and prepare to enter a whole new world of heartbreak and disaster.

It's time I come clean about a very … *interesting* … man I once dated. Or rather, it's time I warned my fellow single ladies about a predator who takes his hunt to a whole new level. I call him the Flimflammer. You may have encountered his type before, or you might be familiar with the other name for this species: *Piece-o-Shiticus.* Here's what happened:

I was dating this guy who raved incessantly about his car collection—which he kept in Connecticut. I mean, this was near-constant bragging, and he kept begging me to go for a spin in one of his "babies." Finally, I agreed.

I got all decked out: I got a blow out at the blow out bar, lipstick, spiked Brian Atwoods, the works. My doorman called to let me know my guy was downstairs, and I surprised myself with the excitement I felt. Maybe I was finally wrapping my head around the hullabaloo people make over fast cars. Bugatti, Ferrari or Maybach, I wondered?

When I emerged from my building, fully prepared to be dazzled, the first thing I noticed was the paint job: red with black racing stripes. But the next thing I noticed was that my man had showed up in a Smart Car.

I was struck by a flashback to *Scarface*, when Tony picks up Elvira in his leopard-print-seat, beat-up old car and asks her in his heavy Cuban accent, "Wot? Ju don' like dee car?" "That looks like someone's nightmare, Tony," Elvira says.

"So this is part of your fine car collection?" I asked as I gingerly slid into the miniature front seat.

"I'm going green," he said.

"A Smart Car isn't green," I said seriously. "It's just tiny. I think you're thinking of a Prius."

That's when I saw it: the crazy look in his eyes that told me I was trapped in a tin can with a moron.

"I like to drive this in the city," he said. "It's easier to buzz around. And it's fun! Don't you think it's fun?"

Uhhhh, no.

The rest of the night was spent parallel parking in impossibly small spaces and eating dim sum in the East Village—not the five-star evening I had imagined.

I can't help emitting a chuckle despite feeling really bad for this faithful reader. The truth is, her ex's car switch was pretty low on the scale of Flimflammer deceptions, but it will still make an excellent standalone blog. It shouldn't get lost in the comments like this. I post it as a blog, and thank her in the comments with a link to its URL.

I decide to respond with a sad tale from a few years back. My friend Melissa, the publicist, got an up-close and personal view into the treachery of the Flimflammer—also known as "Ponzi scheme founders"—before names like Madoff were household curses.

I begin a new, follow-up blog:

Dear Flimflammer Victim,

Sorry to hear about your tale of auto-deception! Totally lame. You bring up a great point—and one that deserves a little more elaboration. I'd like to introduce you to another breed of Flimflammer—the man I like to call the "In-the-Slammer Flammer".

My friend met a middle-aged divorcé who seemed like an amazing catch. He ran a successful hedge fund, had a marquee family name and properties in all of her favorite places, like Brazil and Mexico.

He was working on a new deal but had most of his money tied up in the fund, so after they'd been together for a respectable amount of time, he asked her family for a significant loan. Her clan is wealthy by way of her maternal grandfather and, in the interest of welcoming her man into the fold, they agreed. Their money would be safe and sound, he promised, and returned to them with interest within a year.

Meanwhile, my friend became pregnant. Plans for a shotgun wedding started to form. What was the harm? They loved each other. Everything was perfect.

That is, until two days before the wedding, when federal agents came knocking on his Tribeca apartment door. Turns out, her man had been running a Ponzi scheme for years. His last name had zero connection to the blueblood family he'd claimed to belong to—it was just a convenient coincidence.

She was devastated. Not only was her wedding to the man she loved cancelled, but he was sent upstate for six-to-ten. The stress of it all caused a miscarriage.

It's a lesson best learned early, ladies: BEWARE THE FLIMFLAMMER. The man who claims to have it all but never seems able to prove it is hiding something—and it's usually something best left swept well under the carpet.

I post the blog and remember my tea when the kettle starts whistling. As I pour the water over the bag, the distraction of the blog fades and I feel last night starting to creep in at me from the shadows. Still not ready to deal. I need to get out of the apartment. I need to laugh too loud and get swept up in someone else's stories. And I know exactly who to call to make it happen.

"Gil! It's Viv."

"Veeee!!!

I love him. He's a real character, and plays the off-the-charts queen role to a T. Though he squeals my name so loudly that I have to hold the phone away from my ear, I can barely hear Gil's voice over the cacophony behind him. I hear good silverware clattering against plates, champagne corks popping, and laughter, laughter, laughter.

"You're at a big, crazy, loud, super-gay brunch, aren't you?" I yell.

"At Elmo's! Come join! It's gettin' cray-cray up in here, girl!"

Music to my ears. Brunch at Elmo's with some fabulous gays sounds like just the thing to get me out of this funk. Besides, this is absolutely the perfect moment to be showered with adulation and compliments from men who genuinely appreciate my style choices.

Keeping with Gil's specific instructions to "dress tramps, girl," I put on my sexiest dress, highest stilettos and my new Chloe shades that I scored from Gilt Groupe. Even for two P.M., I look oddly appropriate.

As I walk up to Elmo's I see Gil holding court with a gaggle of sexy male models. I feel a momentary catty hatred for them. Male models—feh! Then I wonder, in dismay, maybe that's why Eric is the way he is. Maybe I'm just his beard. Thankfully, Gil grabs my hand and escorts me to his table by the DJ booth.

"Someone wants to see you!"

Inside I'm surprised to find Shannanigans in among "the girls"—but there she is, looking trim as ever with the addition of a gorgeous, deep golden tan.

"Where the hell have you been?"

Before I can protest, Shan grabs my arm and a pack of cigarettes from the table and drags me out front where we can hear each other talk. It's clear that Shannon's been taking advantage of the drink specials on this morning's menu. She's even more smiley than usual—and of course, there's that whole smoking thing, even if they are organic and chemical free. She offers me one as she lights her own with a set of matches emblazoned with Elmo's logo. I hesitate for the briefest second.

"Oh, take one, Vivi! It's Sunday!"

I can't help but relent to her giddiness. It's no secret that all drunk New Yorkers turn into smokers—even the most devout Jivamukti devotees. As I take the first drag and feel the nicotine go straight to my head, I remember why this is so fun, as I try not to fall off of my spike heels.

"Have I got a story for you," Shannon says. She lowers her voice conspiratorially, "You know ... *for the blog*." She mouths the last three words and I'm grateful; the last thing I need at this moment is to have my cover blown.

"Let's hear it," I say, leaning closer. I don't have my recorder with me—didn't expect to need it today—so I take a lot of mental notes.

"Well I met this guy a couple weeks ago on P.O.F." She pauses at my puzzled look and explains, "Plenty o' Fish dating website."

"I only know Tinder."

"You should check it out. Anyway, he seemed like a nice guy. Really nice guy. And he actually has more money than I do!"

"Well, that's a first!"

Shannon laughs, "Well, maybe not a first, but certainly a rarity. I was thrilled when he surprised me last weekend with a trip to South Beach. I'm usually the one who foots the bill for weekends like this. He said he had a gorgeous place at the Setai—you've heard of it, that luxury high-rise resort that only millionaires can afford?"

I nod. I certainly have heard of it. It's a pretty famous place.

"He told me that he has a spectacular ocean view and sunrises on tap—not that I'm ever up that early, but I was delighted, as you can imagine. I'm sure I can pull off at least one early morning sunrise meditation, om-ing on his balcony. Anyway, I crammed some smokin' hot ViX bikinis and sarong dresses into a carry-on, plus a few easy silk evening dresses, tied on my favorite espadrilles and was ready to make a dash.

"My first clue that something was amiss was

when he bought me a bargain ticket on Spirit Airlines to Fort Lauderdale. But Viv, I didn't see it as a red flag. I took 'Spirit' to mean something entirely different—a sign from the Universe that we had some sort of soul connection. I was too excited to think otherwise."

"Who wouldn't be?"

"Exactly. Anyway, he had already been down there a couple days, so he picked me up at the airport when I got in. I could hardly contain myself as we pulled up to the Setai valet. The place was gorgeous, dripping with posh. I was practically dying of hunger and of course at that time of evening, we've all got a thirst to quench."

"Amen, sistah."

"Praise, *amirite*?! So we get up to his place and I'm thinking dinner at Mr. Chow, drinks at the W. He can certainly afford it and, if not, I can. But almost as soon as we walked in the door, my guy goes, 'Oh, hey, I went to the grocery store. Would you like some dinner? I've got rotisserie chicken and pita chips.'"

"I didn't want to seem ungrateful, and I guess I thought it was cute that we would just chill at home. I had been traveling all day, so I was okay with staying in. I thought we were going to have an evening of get-to-know-you sexual experimentation or—bare minimum, a little cuddling—but, instead, he made me watch him do a P90X DVD while I picked at a tiny chicken in a plastic box from Publix. After showered, he started working at his computer. That's when I decided to go to bed."

"Sure, of course. Who wouldn't?" This guy is sounding like a real bore, so far.

"The next morning," Shannon continues, "after a

peaceful night's sleep, I might add, where Mr. Fitness didn't get near me with his six-pack abs—he wanted to do another workout. I put my foot down. 'I flew all the way down here,' I told him, 'and I'm going to the pool.' He kissed me on the forehead and said he'd be at the gym.

"It was near three o'clock in the afternoon and still there was no sign of my guy. I'm thinking he's manorexic for all the working out he does, but whatever—a girl's gotta eat. I ordered a veggie wrap at the bar and gave our room number for the charge. It's standard procedure for a place like this. Harmless enough, right? Wrong again. After waiting ten minutes, the waiter informed me that my guy had *banned all room charges*. All fucking room charges, V! Can you believe that?"

"No. Why would he do that?" I'm truly puzzled. The guy's a millionaire but he's made sure that his weekend guest, to whom he's only supplied one half-assed meal in twenty four hours, can't eat. It makes no sense.

"I have no clue. He's a cheapskate I guess, but that didn't change the fact that I was starving. Starving!"

I shook my head with disbelief.

"Wait, it gets worse! The waiter says he's supposed to call this guy if anyone tries to charge anything to his room! I can pay for my own food and was perfectly willing. I offered, but that's against policy and the waiter tells me that my guy is already on his way down. Next thing I know, he's sprinting toward me across the pool deck toting a plastic bag, looking like I just killed his dog. He plunks down in the chair next to me, completely oblivious to the fact that he's a sweaty monstrosity. 'If you're hungry,' he says, 'eat the chicken. We have chicken. Eat the chicken.'

"Suffice it to say, I didn't want the chicken. It had already been dinner *and* breakfast, and there was nothing left on the raggedy carcass but greasy scraps of dark meat. I needed some veggies. Is that so terrible? It wasn't even about the money, by this time. It was the humiliation of being treated like I was some broke ho, trying to scam him! I put up with a lot from the men I date, but this was more than I could bear."

She looks to me for confirmation and I give it to her, "Yes, Shan, no one could ever say that you don't give your men a fighting chance."

"Thank you. Don't make me travel across the country just to be ignored and starved. I can do that at home, so that's where I went. I packed my bags and left on the first flight out. But not before I stopped at Le Sandwicherie on the way to the airport. I wasn't about to make the trip a total bust."

"Love Le Sandwicherie!"

"I know. Saving grace."

"But still, Shan—that's awful."

"Right? The guy had the romance stylings of a fifteen-year-old, which is cute when you're fifteen. But he and I are both twice that age. Why do you think I'm here, drunk as a co-ed in a sea of gays on a Sunday morning?"

"Babe," I say, grabbing another ciggy from the pack, "I know what you mean. This is worthy of a blog. Give me a sec so I can jot down some notes," I tell her as I pull out my ever-present notepad and scribble a quick reminder or two.

The next few hours are spent consuming anything put in front of me: huevos rancheros and truffle fries help a girl forget her troubles. Day two, not counting calories, oh I'm in trouble, now.

But Providence brings me deliverance in the form of one of the models. He and I huddle in a booth, while I half-drunkenly grill him for information. Fortunately, he's got quite a buzz going for himself, so he doesn't notice my sometimes clumsy questions, like my first, "So, what's it like being a male model? Do you, like, get laid all the time?"

He laughs and sparkles his gorgeous eyes at me. I forget for a minute that he's gay and lose myself in those eyes, briefly. He says, "Honey, if I had the time and energy for it, I would. God knows there are plenty of opportunities, but I work hard, and I think you'd be surprised if you knew what it's really like."

Intrigued, wondering if he speaks for Eric, I egg him on. "That's why I'm asking! I know this guy, a model—he's straight though—and he's dating a friend of mine. She is going crazy trying to figure out why he's not willing to commit. She's tired of being his fuck buddy."

"Are you sure he's straight? Maybe he plays for both teams." he winks at me, and continues, "No, I'm kidding. I'm sure that's not it. But your friend has to understand that it's a different life for us. We travel. A lot. Being mobile and not tied down is mandatory if you're going to succeed. We learn to save ourselves from heartbreak, for both us and our lovers, by just keeping a casual dating scenario and being honest from the start and telling them that we will be leaving in a few months. Did he tell her that?"

I try to recall if he's ever said anything like that to me. "No, I don't think he said that to her. Not in those words, anyway. She would have told me. He's not around a lot, but when he is in town, he's amazing and I'm … my friend … is crazy about him."

He doesn't notice my slip up and puts his hand on mine, "Well, tell your friend that he's either not being honest, or … well, maybe he's just not sure yet. Most of the time, when you are honest, and tell a new lover, straight up, that this is what it is, it always works out very well. Nine out of ten times they agree and just come along for a fun time, no hassles or problems."

My face must show that I'm crushed, because he says, "Tell your 'friend' that there is hope. It all really boils down to timing. I know that most of us really do want to settle down someday, but for now, we've gotta grab the work while it's there and while we still have our looks. Plus, we really do need to find someone with the desire for a different kind of life. After having the world at your feet, it's going to be impossible to settle for any less than that."

He sees someone waving at him from across the room, and suddenly he's lost interest in me altogether. He waves back and pecks me on the cheek. "You're gorgeous, darling. Don't give up hope." Then he is gone and I'm left to ponder what he's said.

Has Eric told me these things, indirectly? He certainly did the last time I saw him, but up until then, was he stringing me along, or was I just not paying attention? Was he being vague or was I being clueless? I wish, futilely, that I had recorded all of our conversations so I could play them back and search for answers. If only life had a rewind button.

I see "the girls" disappear into the bathroom in clusters, but what they do in there is none of my business. Their party had started last night and was clearly going to continue for another twenty-four hours at least. By the looks of it—and by "it" I mean dainty rims of white powder being delicately wiped from noses—the fun wouldn't stop for a long time. For me, though, five hours was all I could take. I had partied like a rock star—or at least brunched like one. Good enough for me.

I walk out and look up at the sky. Rain will start to pour in buckets any minute. I sprint home as well as a woman can in her sluttiest heels, but halfway to my building I feel a large wet drop plunk onto my forehead. In typical New York fashion, I'm caught without an umbrella.

And that's when it hits me like a full-on monsoon: men in New York are very much like umbrellas. It takes years to find the perfect one—strong enough to weather the most brutal storm, sensible enough to fit seamlessly into your life, sturdy and broad enough to keep you sheltered when it pours. They're often lost or need replacement. But every once in a while, you find one that sticks. One you can't lose no matter how many times you nearly forget it in a cab or underneath the table at your favorite café. You can't lose it, because it refuses to lose you.

CHAPTER 16:
CROCS AND NOT THE SHOES

I pace back and forth with my cell phone in hand. I have to call Eric. Even if part of my brain knows I should follow Lauren's advice and commit to Matthew, even if my conversation with that other model gave me an insight I never had before, my whole heart won't let me give up on Mr. Canada. And maybe there's another part of me—decidedly south of my brain and heart—that can't say goodbye just yet.

I punch in the digits and feel my hands shaking. *Get a grip!*

"Hey babe, how are you?"

His voice surprises me. He sounds carefree and, besides, I didn't realize I'd actually hit Send.

"Oh, hi." I start to apologize about Matthew showing up but he cuts me off.

"Look, babe, I like you. I want to keep hanging out. But like I said, I can't get into anything serious. I don't care if you see other people."

Wow. What felt carefree and easy a moment ago now trips dangerously toward the cavalier. This is not-so-secret code for "I want to fuck but I don't want to be your boyfriend." The other model was right. I am just another fuck buddy to this guy.

I'm suddenly furious. Is this guy for real? Who

does he think I am? He really must not want to screw up the deal with Prodigy Partners. Is he using me? Then I wonder, why does this hurt so much? I've had fuck buddies in the past and it never felt like this. Why do I feel like I've got to have him?

"Me, too," I say. My mouth has completely divorced from my brain and is seizing independent control of this situation. "I'm totally fine with the way things are." *When did it get so easy for you to lie?*

"Cool. See you later then?"

"Yeah, great. Later."

As quickly as the line goes dead, I am sucked back in.

I don't know what to feel at this moment. I know I should be ashamed that I am willing to take this man—how little or how much of himself he is offering—any way I can get him. Am I pathetic? And if I am, why don't I care?

The moment I set my phone down, it starts to vibrate. Is he calling back? Am I about to experience a torrent of fragmented sentences loosely scripted from a rom-com? Professions of love, lofty promises, proclamations about forever?

"Hello?"

"Is this Vivian Fiori?" a woman's voice asks.

Dammit. So much for that.

"Yes, who is this?" Then, realizing I sound like a total bitch because the woman on the line isn't Prince Charming, I clear my throat and add, "How can I help you?"

"I'm a writer for the *New York Post*. I got your name and number from an anonymous source."

"Yeah?"

"Well, we were told you might know the identity

of the person or persons behind the Menhattan Project blog."

"Who told you that?" I ask, trying to sound as nonchalant as I can, wondering if I gave anything away yesterday—I was pretty buzzed, and talked to a lot of people. Maybe I can channel Eric's casualness and find a silver lining in this situation after all. But my heart is beating so hard I'm afraid this woman can hear it through the line.

"Like I said, an anonymous source," she says, defensively. "Do you know who the blogger is? We want to interview her—or him—or them. We're getting lots of calls, every day. New York wants to know! Hell, *The Today Show* is snapping at our heels."

O. M. G.

"I wish I could help you—and really, I'd love to know myself. When you find her—or, I mean, whoever it is—please let me know. The Menhattan Project blogger is my hero. It's about time someone laid it all out on the line."

"Well, we won't stop until we uncover this person's identity. You understand that, don't you?"

"Of course. I'm … I'm counting on it, just like everyone else."

A zillion thoughts race through my head when the call ends. Who sold me out? I run through the finite list of people who know about my connection to the blog. Who among them would hand over my name and number to the press? Or who, among their friends, told the press? My friends are all sworn to secrecy, but if I even have a hard time keeping it to myself, how can I expect them to do the same? What's that old adage? Three may keep a secret if two of them are dead?

And what about coming clean? Am I ready to put myself out there as the voice of Manhattan singles? If I do, what will happen to my personal relationships? Will it affect my job? My sex life?

I don't have the answers, but I do have a mani-pedi appointment with Publicist Melissa. I wonder if it was her who ratted me out. She is, after all, a publicist. I vow to keep this phone call to myself, for now.

I pull a bottle of "Sure Shot" Essie polish from the shelf and hand it to the diminutive Korean girl who knows how to make a pedicure last for three weeks. I slip my tawny tootsies into the warm water, adjust the settings on my vibrating chair and turn to Mels. "What's up, hockey 'ho?"

Melissa has been seeing a young, sexy Rangers player. She met him at Employees Only a few weeks ago. According to her, she's quite enjoying having her puck shot.

"Very funny," she says drily. "We've been having a good time, but he's so young. I doubt it will go anywhere. Still, I like spending time with him. He never realized women in their thirties are voracious lovers."

I roll my eyes. "What happened to the Ivy?"

"He's still around. I need to break the streak I've had with the Ivies lately."

She tells me her crazy story, and I'm ready, with recorder in hand. I'm going to post this one when I get home. Meantime, sitting at the dryer, admiring my newly polished nails, I consider calling Matthew. I don't feel ready yet, since I can't quite discern how I came to be in this situation to begin with. I didn't realize at the time that one drunken night of boozing and fucking the most gorgeous man I've ever seen would lead to such a quandary.

Instead of dialing Matthew, I call my friend Jonathan to meet me for a walk in Central Park. I've been blowing off exercise lately because I'm too busy, so I'm willing to stuff my newly polished toes into a pair of walking shoes and get moving. Jonathan is one of my walking buddies and the smoothest player I know. Since we've never slept together, I can find him charming. I say goodbye to Melissa and run home to change. I have just enough time to type out and post her blog:

> We all love a smart man. And if you're an Ivy Leaguer, well … chances are you're on Wall Street or have a successful entrepreneurial venture of your own that'll get our engines running. Alumni from Harvard, Wharton, Yale and the others have a certain air of arrogance that women find extremely attractive. I guess it comes from knowing you're part of an elite group of educated, dinner-club-going, yuppy-chic gentlemen who are making it big. The Ivy League hottie will always make sure a woman knows about his academic pedigree within minutes of a first meeting.
>
> There are indeed a few drawbacks to dating such a distinguished fellow. He'll always feel superior to you, and might verge on dismissive when it comes to your views on finance, politics and most random trivia. He'll tell fraternity stories with as much enthusiasm as if the events had just taken place yesterday;

he'll laugh at his own jokes, particularly the ones that aren't funny. He will always ask a woman where she went to school so she'll be forced to reciprocate. And if she happens to have attended an Ivy herself … well, he'll lose interest quickly. His dominance in the relationship is almost exclusively dependent on his sense of academic self-importance.

I dated a Harvard guy for awhile. Brian worked at a hedge fund and was from Connecticut—all pluses in my book. But his alma mater seemed to make an appearance in every conversation. Every. Single. Conversation. It got annoying pretty quickly, but he was so handsome and successful that I just kept dating him. None of my friends wanted to hang out with us—and his friends and their wives didn't want anything to do with me.

He was nerdy, shy and awkward. At first it seemed like my outgoing personality would balance him out, bring him out of his shell a bit. But eventually I grew tired of being corrected almost constantly—about anything and everything. Eight months after we broke up, I ran into him at Whole Foods in Chelsea. He introduced me to his wife! She was a mousy, skinny brunette. They wore matching Harvard shirts—though as they turned to head for the fromagerie and me to the frozen food aisle, I saw her tee was emblazoned with the words "Go Crimson" on the back. Match made in heaven.

"Sometimes alcohol can lead to bad decisions," Jonathan says as we enter the park. "Only on rare occasions can a woman turn a one night stand or a booty call into a real relationship. Period."

"But we went to church! It was electric, I tell you, electric!"

"I'm sure it was. But you need to let it go. You have a nice, stable guy who wants to be with you. Don't fuck it up. Just be thankful you got to wake up next to a demigod for a morning or two, and be double thankful you didn't open your eyes the morning after to find a dawg."

He's right. I know he is, and I think about this for a moment while I am too winded to talk. It really has been way too long since I've walked. I shouldn't be out of breath already. I should get back on track taking care of myself, file Mr. Canada away under "greatest hits" and move on. Jonathan's other point is sound, too—at least I made a good judgment call with my champers-goggles on.

"God," Jonathan continues, walking faster once he sees I've caught my breath, "you could have ended up with a Sandy."

Sandy is a woman Jonathan was seeing for awhile. She is what men refer to as a "Butterface"—everything about her is hot, but-her-face. Cruel but often true, and Sandy was proof. Jonathan liked spending time with her; she cooked him fabulous meals three nights a week, gave the best blow jobs he'd ever had, and rocked his world in bed. She satisfied man's two most prevalent moods: horny and hungry. But Jonathan never took her out to meet his friends.

As he talks, I realize that this is great material for

a blog for men, but my hands are full enough. "Her face ... it just looked like she could have been an extra for *Avatar*," he admits. "So true that beauty is in the eye of the beer holder."

"Asshole," I say, but we're both laughing.

"I once took home a Butterface from the club, and in the morning I woke up to these strange black bugs all over the bed. Of course, they weren't actually bugs—*they were her fake eyelashes*. It was so strange—clumps of artificial lashes all over the bed. Then I saw the chicken cutlets on the floor ... and the back acne," he feigns a gag. "I couldn't get her out of my place fast enough."

"That's all well and good, but aren't you forgetting a certain Butterface who rather got under your skin as I recall?"

"Ahhh, yes. The ugly one that got away. I'll never forget her. She played the game perfectly: never gave too much information, stayed mysterious for months. I fought it as hard as I could, but eventually I just said 'screw it' and started dating her on the up-and-up. My friends thought I was crazy, but we stayed together for six months. She ended up dumping me, and is now married. I still think about her. I got played."

We walk for a long time in silence, the only sound is our shoes hitting the ground. I wonder if Jonathan is thinking what I'm thinking: that for all our sarcasm and flippancy about matters of the heart, the ugly truth is that we are as susceptible to devastation as anyone else. While I may pretend to everyone that I'm just in lust with Eric, I can't pretend to myself anymore. I really have feelings for him, even if I don't understand exactly what they are. How can I feel such a powerful, electrical attraction for someone who doesn't feel about me the way I feel about him?

We finally reach the top of Harlem Hill, the biggest one in the park, and we stop for a brief rest and a couple swallows of water. I look around at the view and feel a deep appreciation for living in the most exciting city in the world, and having access to this glorious park. I'm on the verge of bursting with an emotion that I can't define and I can't help shouting out, "It was electric, damn it! It was electric!"

Jonathan laughs and says, "I know it was, hun, but it was just sex. Let it go. Whaddya think about brunch at Isabella's? I'll buy. But only if you stop fixating on this guy."

"Okay. I'll let you pay for my silence. Let's go."

Fortunately the rest of our power walk is mostly downhill from here, so we finish up with a minimum of sweaty stickiness, but even so we get an outside table so as not to gross out the indoor patrons. As we're being seated, I look over to the end of the bar and spot a rare breed typically seen in more southern climes. His skin is leathery and wrinkled, though he probably oils himself liberally before bed. I gently smack Jonathan on the shoulder and nod toward the lone creature. When Jonathan looks back at me, he's shining that megawatt smile on me again. At the same time, we lean close and say "Croc Player!" I love that even the guys are in on this game. Now *this* is a blog!

After settling in to my chair and ordering some fresh fruit and an iced tea, I pull out my notepad and jot down a "note to self" to write this up and post it, too, tomorrow. We're pretty much talked out, so we eat in comfortable silence, the way only friends can.

Once I get home and shower off the day, I type up the new blog and save it as a draft.

> A Croc Player is an older, single guy, never been married, usually in his late fifties or early sixties. He still works on his tan, hits the gym for three hours a day, roams around trying to find The One. He's often in denial about his age and thinks he can date women you might easily mistake for his daughter. The thing is, the Croc Player is like a Corvette: it was a really big deal in the Eighties, but you wouldn't be caught dead in one today.
>
> Before one of my good friends got married, she was set up with a Croc Player who was clearly over bro-toxed. He was really nice and fun, though, and they enjoyed a great night out together. Then they decided to share a bottle of tequila in his large bath tub. Bad idea. She completely blacked out. She woke up the next morning completely naked, her underwear dangling from a bedpost. She sheepishly collected her things and left, but not before getting an eyeful of the Croc's tired, saggy, reptile-skinned ass hanging out of sheets. The collection of high-octane medications on his vanity didn't help the situation. She never heard from the guy again, but she ran into him a few months later at the Dream Hotel. There he was in all his glory, chatting up a very young, cute blonde at the bar. He didn't give her a second glance, but as she walked by she heard the toddler say, "I only drink Cristal."

> She couldn't help but chuckle. Good
> luck, Croc—this one's gonna cost ya!

My meet-up with Jonathan leaves me with the unsettling realization that Eric was only ever supposed to be a really good, handsome lay. When did I turn into one of *those* girls—the ones who can't let a one night stand fade into the past as it should?

Of course, all of this is complicated by the fact that if I do stand up and take credit for the Menhattan Project, or if I'm outed against my will, it will be clear that all of my anonymous posts about "an impending relationship with a super hottie" are all about him. I might be ready to tell the world who I am, but I'm definitely not ready to tell the world about Eric, especially my office. If they found out I was sleeping with a potential investment partner they would flip out—the fact that neither of us knew who the other was when we met, at least as far as I know—is beside the point. I should have disclosed our "relationship," if you can call it that, immediately. I wonder if I should go back and delete those blogs, or at least edit them a little.

I decide to go ahead and do that, but I hear a knock at my door and quickly close my computer. Has Eduardo completely lost his mind, or does he think I'm totally okay with an endless parade of people being let upstairs? I'm thinking about the call I'm going to make to the building supervisor when I open the door.

I hadn't realized the rain started up again.

But Eric is soaked.

"You're all wet," I say quietly, in an effort to contain my excitement and surprise that he's here. He must care. Right? "I think you need to take your clothes off."

"Yes, I do."

He picks me up and carries me to the bedroom without another word. He lays me down and I watch as he peels off his wet clothes a piece at a time, never breaking eye contact with me. I reach down to pull off my panties but he stops me with a look and proceeds to do it himself, taking his time as the fabric glides down my legs. He works systematically through every article I have on until I am fully exposed, naked for him, because of him.

When he lies down next to me, I fight the urge to take him in my mouth right away, fight the urge to show him how much I missed him. Still I position myself between his long legs, and while I tease his cock with my tongue I run my warm hands along the inside of his legs, touching every inch of him, tickling and caressing him. I feel him shiver. Our eyes lock again and our breathing falls into a single rhythm. I nibble the inside of his thighs as my hands roam his hips, his ass. Finally I take the hard length of him into my mouth. He moans, and after a minute reaches down to slip a finger inside me. I'm soaked already, and he can't wait another second. He pulls me up and onto him. I am on fire.

We make love for two hours, and eventually I fall into a dreamless sleep. That is, until I can hear pans and pots clanking in the kitchen. *What the hell?*

I walk into the kitchen and see Eric chopping and dicing AGAIN!

"Hi, sleepy head. I ran out and got a few things for dinner."

This man is going to make me explode. OMG. How do I

tell him I can't eat like this or I will officially need gastric bypass! Oh fuck it! He's worth it! Or is he?

"I am making a Vietnamese Pho soup. You're going to love it. I learned to make it when I lived there for three months."

"Wow, Eric. That's great. I only need a small bowl, thanks."

"Stop it. Crazy girl, it's all vegetables and healthy and I need to fatten you up." That sounds like he plans to keep me around and I'm ecstatic, even as I think, *little does he know how easy it will be for me to start gaining weight, eating like this..*

"Sure, ok." If eating his food is what it takes to keep him in my life, bring it on! I have a couple pairs of fat pants in my closet. I'm ready for anything!

CHAPTER 17:
DINKS

I pace the room nervously. I seem to be doing that a lot these days. I pick up the phone, spin it over and over in my hands, put it down, and pick it up again. What will I tell Matthew when I finally find the courage to call? How can I say what I know I must without hurting him?

I'll lie.

Yes. A lie is just the thing. It's not him, it's me— doesn't that always work, even ironically? Men use that line on women so often, the whole idea of it has become a joke. Why can't I use it too?

I punch in the numbers and for a brief moment miss the days when phones had real buttons. Dialing was so much more expressive back then. Just as I'm formulating a prayer that this call will go straight to voicemail, he picks up.

"Hello?" he says, though I know his caller ID has shown him my name and number.

"Hi, hun. How are you?"

"I'm okay." He sounds annoyed. "What's up? I haven't heard from you in a few days."

"Right. I know. I'm sorry … I've just … I've been thinking a lot about us. I needed some space to get my head clear." *Lies, lies, lies.* Again I wonder when this became so easy. My mind wanders to a vision of Mr. Canada thrusting into me doggy-style. I feel myself zoning out but snap back to the present and clear my throat.

"And?" he presses.

"And I want you to be happy. Really happy. Only I don't think I'm the woman who can do that for you—make you happy, I mean. I'm just … trying to be honest."

"I appreciate that," he says quietly. "But I think you're going to regret this. I would marry you tomorrow, Vivian Fiori. I would give you everything you ever wanted, and a lot you don't even know you want yet."

"Please don't make this harder than it already is."

"Fine. I'll make it easy for you. Just understand that I won't be around when you come to your senses. "

I know this is man-code for "my feelings are so hurt, I don't know what to do," but still his tone stings. I want to soften the blow, explain that I'm a slave to feelings I can't control, that I know he's the right guy—maybe even the right guy for me—but I can't act on that knowledge because my heart refuses to be ignored. I never get the chance to say any of this. He's already hung up the phone.

I feel horrible. I wonder if Matthew is right, and this really is a huge mistake I'll come to regret. All I know for sure is that I wouldn't be able to live with myself if I didn't see this thing with Eric to its end. He *will* fall in love with me. Things *will* change. I can't tell if these are statements—affirmations of an inevitable future—or prayers.

I finish packing and drive to Margarita

Meredith's on Long Island, where I'm spending the night. When we spoke earlier this week, I could hear in her voice that she needed some one-on-one time, a little rejuvenating girl talk over some really fantastic wine. We'll be quite a pair, she and I. Of course I don't plan to tell her about the love triangle I've embroiled myself in—not when I fear she's going to confess that married life is far from perfect. Being the shoulder another woman cries on always helps me gain some perspective; fingers crossed this weekend is no exception.

I try to wrap my head around what Mer might have to say. My mother always told me never to date a man who has children by a living ex. Supposedly this was the root cause of her second divorce: her husband's ex held so much sway over the children, she managed to ensure that the children never fully accepted her. "Avoid the instant family," she used to tell me. "When all you need to do is add water, whatever crops up is bound to dissolve."

I pull up to the palatial estate and park my ZipCar next to the Mercedes 500 and the convertible Jag. Meredith comes to greet me. She looks exhausted, like she hasn't slept in days.

"Hi, babe!" she says, harnessing energy in her voice from I-don't-know-where.

"Hi!" I lean in for a double-cheek air kiss. "I'm starving."

"Great. I'm making fettuccini Alfredo. How was the drive?"

Holy crap, the calorie trifecta: cheese, butter and heavy cream. I silently vow to only eat a few bites, enough to not hurt her feelings. By the looks of Meredith's sunken demeanor, what she really needs is a healthy salad and some spring water. I've never seen her so pale and puffy.

"It was good. Easy."

The interior of Meredith's home is spectacular. It's the perfect combination of East meets West. I give the obligatory compliments on the Ming-dynasty-era vase on the table Meredith swears she found on discount at Home Goods, then follow her into the pristine kitchen. I'm actually ready to gnaw my arm off—I can't believe how hungry I am. I guess a diet of red wine and marathon sex will really take it out of you.

As we situate ourselves around the marble island, Meredith tells me the boys are with their mother and Joe is on a golf trip with his guys.

"He doesn't want any more babies," she says. "He changed his mind. He said we would have a kid together, and now … now he won't give me one."

I'm caught completely off-guard by this. So much that I can't help but tell Meredith just that. "I thought you were going to tell me he was cheating on you or something. I had no idea!"

"Well, I found out he actually cheated on his first wife," she says. "And this 'golf trip' …"

"Why the air quotes?"

"It's our anniversary!"

"Right." *How did I not realize?* "Geez, sorry Mer. That sucks."

Shit. My hostess gift of top-shelf tequila is now a much needed anniversary gift.

Joe promised Meredith the moon when they first met, but it has become clear that he sold her a bad bill of goods. She still works her poor fingers to the bone to help pay for his kids' private school educations—

and his alimony obligations. I think back to my mother and her warnings. As much as I hate to admit it, she's right: the divorced man with multiple children knows he's not going to score with a hottie in her twenties or early thirties unless he acts like expanding his brood is a number-one priority.

The red flags started flying when Meredith first met the ex-wife, Judy at a family event. She was sweet, Meredith tells me, and so happy that she wasn't married to Joe anymore. All that afternoon, Meredith saw Judy rolling her eyes as Joe told his stupid jokes or launched into boring stories about past glories at the office. Lately, she tells me, she's been catching herself doing the same thing. At one of their more recent encounters, Mer asked Judy why she and Joe got divorced.

"He cheated," she said, point-blank. It didn't seem to bother her. Joe denies it to this day and claims that Judy is delusional. But five years later, Meredith is stuck raising Joe and Judy's two kids while the ex-wife has the house and an alimony payout that supports a healthy shopping addiction at Bergdorf's and a girls' weekend in Cabo three times a year. Judy never worked and now she never will. Meredith has always worked and now will always have to.

Second wives get the short shrift when it comes to pre-nups, and the hefty one Meredith signed basically says that if she chooses to leave the marriage, she'll be entitled to what she came to the table with initially, what she earned during the partnership, and nothing more. She'll never see the kids she's been helping raise, and she won't get any financial assistance as she sets up a new home and gets back on her feet.

"He's stolen my best years," she says, tears leaking out of the corners of her eyes. "I don't know what to do. I'm past my prime. My best years are behind me. I—"

"Hey," I say, covering her hand with mine. "That's not true. Stop talking crazy."

"I'm miserable, Viv."

"What do you want to do?"

"I don't know. I just ... don't know."

The silence stretches between us. This seems to be happening a lot these days.

"I guess being a DINK doesn't sound so bad now, huh?" I say, hoping I can make Mer smile.

"I'd take that any day!" she says, and actually starts to laugh. "Double income, no kids is the wave of the future! Marry for love, Viv. You'll be much happier in the end."

We laugh some more and Mer cries a little. I feel horrible for her, but we all make our own decisions in life. Meredith isn't crying because of the choices she's already made; she's crying because of the choice she knows is coming. She won't leave Joe. She will choose misery over loneliness, over starting again. That's worth crying over.

The next morning as I pull out of the long drive, I call Lauren in Miami. Her voice will distract me from the hangover I'm nursing; three bottles of Silver Oak were worth it, but I'll take entertainment just the same.

"Hey, Lauren!"

"Hiii! What's shakin'?"

"Just left Meredith's. Major problems with Joe."

"Shocker! I mean, not to be harsh, but she forced

his hand. He didn't want to get married. She knew what she was getting into. Besides, he's cheap as hell."

"Right? He always lets me pay for part of dinner! And he's rich! Or so he claims!"

"How's Canada? You still wasting your time on that boy?" Her disapproval has a lighthearted delivery, but I can still hear it loud and clear.

"I can't quit him, Laur," I say, doing my best impression of the *Brokeback Mountain* drawl.

"And the blog?"

"Too good. I got a call from a reporter asking about 'her.' Someone told this chick I know the author. I feel them getting closer and it scares the b'jeezus out of me, honestly. But it can't actually blow up in my face ... can it?"

"I don't know," she says, all seriousness now. "You might need to prepare for a shit storm."

"Ugh. Too much to process in my current state. New topic! How's your Latin luvah?"

"I think I might be getting engaged soon."

"What? No way! Shut it down, that's awesome! You *are* getting up there ... no time to waste."

"Bitch."

"No, seriously, that's great!"

"I know! But it's just moving too fast. There's so much potential here and for once, I want to slow things down, but dayum, Viv, he is so sweet. I really think he might be the one, but how many times have you heard me say that before?"

"I hear you. We all have."

"But you're right. I'm not getting any younger, but I don't want to rush into another bad relationship. I don't want to fuck this one up." Lauren sounds more serious than I've heard her be in a long time.

"Is that you I hear, preaching to the choir?"

"Ha! Yeah, that's me, praise Jesus." I hear her doorbell ringing and she says, "Ooh, girl, gotta go. That's him."

"Love you. Talk soon."

I call Eric.

After the initial pleasantries, I get down to business. "You coming over tonight?"

"Yup, can't wait to see you."

This is our relationship. Can I even call it that? "Relationship". It might not be the norm, but it's the best I can do at the moment.

I pull off my Bluetooth and turn up the radio. Rihanna is on my favorite station, so I turn up the volume in spite of my pounding head and sing at the very top of my lungs. "We found love in a hopeless place ..."

Dayum, Ri-Ri, you better be right.

CHAPTER 18:
MAGIC MIKE

Though Eric and I are keeping it light, we seem to be spending a lot of time together. This week, however, he's on location at a shoot, so it's been a slow seven days. A slow, excruciatingly un-sexed week. I've spent that time carefully blogging about hypothetical relationship partners who cannot or will not commit. I'm very cautious to fictionalize my plight, saying that this is happening to my handily fictional "friend" so I can get feedback from others, and not give myself away. Unfortunately, the feedback hasn't been very helpful. Most of the comments put it very bluntly: tell him goodbye—this is going nowhere, fast.

Consistent with the Sunday morning ritual I've been enacting for years now, I crawl back into bed with the *Post* and a glass of fresh carrot-ginger juice. I scan the headlines, which are the typically sensationalist hyperbole this paper is known for, and start to peruse the opening lines of a few articles. But as I turn the page I see something so horrifying, I nearly spit a mouthful of pulpy juice all over my duvet.

It's me.

Me, staring back at myself from page three of the *New York Post*.

They figured it out. *#HolyShit!*

Next to my face is a screen shot of the blog. And beneath that I see ... *ohmigod* ... pictures of the men I've dated over the past few years from my Facebook page—pics I thought I marked "Friends only" in my privacy settings! The pictures have captions, puzzling out who represents which male "type" from the blog. "Could this be the Grouper?" one tagline asks. "Meet the BBD!" screams another. I see a smattering of *distinguished*-looking gentleman along one side of the page, with a bubble caption that speculates about whether or not I was a gold digger in my reckless youth. I hope someone will notice that these not-so-retired Players are still being photographed with women half their age—who have been conveniently cropped out of these pictures, of course.

I read the article, stomach churning, to see if they say how they found out. And there it is. It was me—I fucked up. Oh my God, it's my own fault. After all this time of being so cautious, so careful and so anal retentive about not leaving a trail of bread crumbs, I stupidly responded to one of the readers' comments while logged into my personal email address, and not the anonymous blog email address.

Fuck me running. I have no one to blame but myself for this one. The paper even included a screen capture of my name, Vivian Fiori, next to my comment saying, "Thanks for your response. It's readers like you that add so much depth to my humble little blog ..."

Like a tidal wave crashing on the shore, suddenly my world is thrown into chaos. My phone starts ringing off the hook. My head is spinning. Somehow I manage to console myself for the briefest second with the idea that all the men pictured in this article are extremely handsome. No Crocs or Butterfaces to be seen, thank my lucky stars.

Another saving grace: Eric is out of the country. He doesn't exactly strike me as the kind of man to read a girly blog about relationships—or the *Post* for that matter—but there's no guarantee someone won't bring this to his attention. He won't be back for a couple weeks yet, so I'll have time to play down this nonsense. At least that's the way this shakes out in my perfect world.

The phone rings again and I pick up without looking at the screen. How can I tear my eyes away from the printed page at this point?

"WHAT?"

"Uhhh … Ms. Fiori? This is Brenda from *The View*. I'm a production assistant. We'd love to have you on the show to talk about your work."

My work? I can't help chuckling, though I know this must seem like a completely inappropriate response from Brenda's point-of-view. The Menhattan Project might just be my life's work. My opus to the penis. My masterpiece to the—

I shake my head to clear it and ask, to buy some time, "You work on Sundays?"

She responds with a chuckle of her own, "You do if you're a PA. Gotta grab those guests before anyone else can. So? What do you think? Will you do me a favor and help make me look good for landing you?"

I hate to admit it, but I'm flattered. "I need some time to consider that. I'll get back to you," I say. My voice is calm and measured, a surprise given the circumstances.

I sit in silence for a few moments, taking it all in. I've been outed. The need to kick myself for revealing my own identity isn't even the first thing on my mind. Other questions bubble up from the deep recesses of my brain, float around my consciousness for awhile, then burst as other questions rise to take its place.

There's a knock at the door. "Seriously, Eduardo," I mutter as I make my way to the foyer, "you have *got* to stop doing this. I don't care if Bradley-fuckin'-Cooper is here, asking for my advice on a new tattoo, or the entire cast of *Magic Mike* needs a choreography consultation—"

"Hello, darling. And might I add, what the hell?"

Arianna is like a mirage in the Sahara, especially since I notice the bottle of champagne and container of orange juice sticking out of a bag swinging from her left hand.

"Thank God," I say, ushering her in. I check the hallway before closing the door, like I'm in some throwaway episode of *Law and Order*. DUH. DUH.

The phone rings twice in the time it takes Arianna to put down her bags, kick off her shoes, and grab two champagne flutes from the cabinet near the sink. "Don't be ridiculous," I say into the phone, giving Arianna an apologetic look. "Of course it's not you. The Minnow could be anyone. Okay. Buh-bye."

When I hang up, three beats pass as Arianna and I exchange a look.

"Rick?" she asks.

"Rick," I confirm.

"Well, at least you didn't use any of *our* real names," she says, forgetting that her name was bylined on the Gold Digger blog, waving a copy of the paper in the air. "I'm assuming you need a mimosa right about now."

"You're an angel. Seriously. No joke."

We are silent as we prepare our drinks and move to the sofa, where I shove my phone deep into the cushions and send up a silent prayer it gets sucked into a vortex under there, never to be seen again. We hunch over a single copy of the article and re-read it for what feels like the billionth time already.

"Great picture there," she says. "Where'd they get that? Patrick McMullan? He always takes such great photos."

"That one, yes, probably from that Charity: Water event. The rest I think are from Facebook."

Another quiet minute passes but I can practically hear the wheels turning in Arianna's head. She gives me a sideways glance and says, "Hear me out …" Already I am on the defensive, but what can I do besides listen? "I think you need to own this. You're the perfect person to represent single ladies everywhere. Beyonce's got nothin' on you—especially now that she's wedded, bedded, and babied. You could be the voice of women all over the country!"

Arianna continues the hard sell for awhile longer, until I start to think she doesn't need to try so hard. It makes sense. What started as a funny, edu-taining blog for my friends has transformed into a modern girl's dating manual.

We toast. "To the Menhattan Project," I say.

"To the Menhattan Project." We each take a long sip and I'm struck by how refreshing this fine cuvee feels against my throat. It's like I'm slowly being filled with tiny bubbles—of happiness, possibility.

"Your life's about to change, my dear. I was thinking next you could develop an app."

"You might be on to something," I say. "We could have a rate-your-date feature ..."

Laughing feels incredible. The potential for this to go places seems infinite. Then, in classic Arianna form, my friend clears her throat and says, "Remember that guy from Del Frisco's I met awhile back?"

"Which one? We met quite a few ... ehem ... *slut* ehem ..."

"Very nice, very nice," she says, playfully hitting my arm. "But I'm talking about the Van der Sohn guy."

"How could I forget?" I lie.

"Well you'd remember if you saw him. The one with the nice business card. I knew he'd be worth pursuing. Thick stock in both his wallet and his pants. Anyway, we've been spending some time together and he's looking very good for my next ex-husband."

Arianna isn't kidding, though she laughs as she delivers this line. She reveals that Van der Sohn is from an incredibly wealthy royal family from some principality only Arianna can pronounce. They're close to the same age, so they have a lot in common. He doesn't want some young girl, he wants a woman to fall in love with. He sounds perfect for her. Great. While she lands her next husband and Lauren is getting engaged, I still have no idea if Eric will ever fall in love with me.

And what happens if he doesn't? What if some Dorothy from the *Post* pulls back the curtain hiding the wizard behind the Menhattan Project to reveal her as a fraud? Is that what I am? Does my "relationship" with Eric make me less of a mouthpiece for single women everywhere, and more a poster child for how *not* to find true love?

"Is there more champagne?" I ask.

Arianna pops a bottle, and I wait for the bubbles to fill me once again.

I hear my phone buzz again. I dig it out from under the sofa cushion and feel a buzz of angst when I see the Caller ID.

"Shit! It's Dan. My boss!"

CHAPTER 19:
FACEBOOK IS THE DEVIL

"Facebook is the devil. I don't care how many trillions of dollars it's worth now. People just can't handle it. At least, people who date or who are in relationships can't handle it. Single women curate their albums like they're working for the Metropolitan. I know married men that block other people from tagging them in pictures or posting on their walls. Why? Because they're shady. They don't want anyone to know they're married—or they don't want their wives knowing what they do when left to their own devices."

Lauren takes another sip of her cham-bull, champagne and Red Bull, and continues.

"Facebook has caused couples to split and marriages to crumble. Seeing pictures of your boyfriend pop up on the internet with random girls— even if they're old pictures—always starts a fight. Exes will always try to screw with fresh meat by posting and tagging photos of the man in question. I say, don't give in to the bullshit. Shut it down."

"Tell me how you really feel, girl," I snicker.

"No, really. It's total bullshit. I got off FB when I got to Miami. It's not worth having your life plastered all over the web. And, what for? So some loser from high school can send you a friend request? I mean, if I didn't want to be your friend then, why the fuck would I want to now?"

"I get you."

Lauren is in town to pick up what's left of her belongings from the storage unit she rented before she left. I have to admit that the timing couldn't have been more perfect. If there's a time when I need my girls to rally, it's now.

We are waiting for Arianna at Catch. Even with the thirty minute cushion we worked in for her, she's still late.

"Oh, and another thing," Lauren continues. "If you're going to stay on Facebook to meet other singles, please refrain from holding a drink in your hand in every picture. And for that matter, not every shot from June to August needs to be a bikini pic. Give the boys something to look forward to. A drunk slut who runs around half naked three months out of the year doesn't leave much to be desired. Hashtag whorrrre …"

I'm so caught off guard by her joke that I spit out my mouthful of champagne.

Lauren doesn't even notice, and continues, "And don't even get me *started* on Instagram and that damn Twitter …"

"Instagram has offended you … how?" I ask, wiping my face.

"We know you weren't born in the fucking Seventies. We also know you're not a pro photog. Filters do not art make!"

"You make a point, sister. But—"

"But there's still value in FB?"

"You can't deny the value of a good 'falking'

session."

"True. It does make passing on a seemingly good thing easier. For instance, the guy with tons of girls in all his pictures?"

"Pass."

"Exactly. He'll have too many bitchy hater friends, or he's just a player. And the guy you met at the club who seems to love city life but whose pictures reveal his propensity for fly fishing and camping?"

"Pass."

"You know it. Good for someone, just not us city slickers."

I signal to the bartender for another round. I need to keep lubricating this tirade—Lauren's dropping gold.

"If he has an account but doesn't have that much activity on his wall, that's a good sign. If he doesn't have an account at all—that's really the ideal 'sitch. He's focused on business and doesn't have time for games."

Lauren can't hide a bit of smug pride as she delivers this last nugget of wisdom: her new boyfriend isn't on Facebook. She finds it refreshing. And after having my identity exposed to the masses, I have to say I respect a man who carefully cultivates his anonymity.

"There was a guy who kept screwing me over— you remember, the one who kept blowing off our plans?" I nod. "Eventually things changed for him and he got all desperate—kept 'poking' me over and over, trying on the daily to re-friend me."

"The Cyber Poseur."

"Exactly! Forget poking. This guy is tweeting and

twatting even the most remote female cyber presences. He's a cyber slut."

"Oooo," coos Arianna as she slides into our booth. "Are we talking about Facebook? I looooove Facebook! How else can everyone be kept apprised of how much fun I'm having? More than once I've been scoped out by 'friends' who just happen to show up where I've just geolocated myself. And by 'friends' I mean 'super gorgeous men,' of course."

"Obvi," Lauren and I say in unison.

I take a deep breath in what I'm sure will only be momentary silence. "I have news," I announce. "I'm going on *The View* to talk about the blog. I've also been asked to be a contributing writer for *Marie Claire*! A kind of hip, Suze Orman meets a younger E. Jean Carroll."

The girls congratulate me with squeals and clinked glasses.

I left my job last week in order to focus on my blog. Now, I'm in the writing business as it seems. Dan and I met shortly after he called me, for what could have been a difficult conversation, but he was more understanding than I expected. He didn't like the way things happened, but he knows that I was stuck between a rock and a hard place, and wasn't being deliberately deceitful or doing anything illegal. I reminded him how I begged off from conversations and decisions about Eric's funding, and he agreed that he probably wouldn't have been able to handle a similar situation any better than I did. But we both agreed that it would be best if we had a parting of the ways.

"Well, I guess now you'll have to trade in your sample sale Jil Sander suits for H&M Hoodies and

Forever 21 sweats," he laughed.

"YES! Going to work in sweats is a dream come true," I gushed, holding the tears back. So much of my life and identity was this job. But, now the universe has bigger plans for me.

When we said goodbye, he gave me the biggest bear hug he could muster. And a gift. I opened the beautiful gold wrapping paper to discover a hardcover book—*He's Just Not That Into You.*

"It feels like just yesterday, our little girl was telling us all about her big blog dreams," Arianna says with mock parental pride. "Now she's all grown up!"

Everything's been happening so fast. I resolved to accept the role I may or may not have known I'd have to assume all along. I guess part of me was always hoping I'd get "caught" as the author of the Menhattan Project. When it finally happened, I decided to go with it. The only person I have left to tell … is Eric. He's coming home tonight, though, and we're supposed to meet up as soon as he lands.

The girls and I devour the chocolate tart we always share at Catch, then I book out of there as soon as I can. I'm dying to see Eric. It's been weeks since we've been together, and the sexual withdrawal alone—not to mention the fact that I genuinely miss our conversations—has me going out of my mind.

As my cab pulls up to my building, he's there waiting for me in the lobby. I see him framed like the perfect specimen he is in the floor-to-ceiling window. It's a perfect moment as his head turns slowly and our eyes meet. The world seems to melt around me and I have tunnel vision: there's just me, this clear path ahead, and Eric waiting for me at the end.

But it gets harder and harder to keep the world at

bay once I traverse the space between us and receive a polite kiss on both cheeks from a standoffish Eric. We make small talk about his flight and his cab ride from the airport as we wait for the elevator and ride up to my unit.

"We need to talk," he says. Has he even put his bags down yet? I turn to the living room and walk toward the sofa to hide the worried crease across my brow.

"Sure. About what?"

"You know 'about what.' Even before the Post article I figured it out. It wasn't hard. It was pretty obvious that you didn't have all of those papers scattered all over your studio just doing research for a friend's hobby."

"Why didn't you say anything then?"

"Because it wasn't that big a deal. If you wanted to keep it to yourself, that wasn't my business. At least, not until I saw how much you were writing about me ... about us. Especially how you really feel about us."

Shit, shit, shit!

"Oh, well, that was just hypothetical," I stammer. "You know, creative license, that kind of thing. Gotta give readers something to dream about, right?"

"Viv, come on."

A heavy silence settles over the room.

"I think you're great," he begins, more quietly this time. "But I can't ignore what's happening here. For one, you put information about our personal, private relationship on the internet. You know, I may not be a household name, but enough people know who I am and I don't need everyone knowing my personal business."

"I only wrote nice things …" I say lamely.

"Maybe. But you wrote them without my permission. And that's not even the worst of it. The worst of it is that you're in love with me. I think you're great, I really do. But I think we need to end things before somebody gets hurt."

"Hurt? Who, me? Don't be ridiculous."

"Viv, I'm leaving again next week. For London. And for good. I found an investor that wants to launch overseas and we need to move fast."

"For good? What does that mean? And London? What's in London?" I'm flabbergasted and upset, and doing a poor job of hiding it. Is London just code for Hoboken, or is he really moving as far away from me as he can get?

"Look, I always knew I was going to leave again. That's why I told you I couldn't give you a serious commitment. And you said you understood, Viv. You made it seem like this is what you wanted. But the truth is, we've never wanted the same thing. The difference between us is that I never lied about it."

"Eric, what the fuck? You may not have lied, but you never said, straight out, that you knew you were going to leave again. You led me to believe that you might stick around."

He pauses for a long second and says, "No, I didn't. And I wasn't talking about me lying to you. You lied to me."

I feel like he just smacked me in the face. "I lied to you? I didn't—you can't—I just …" I feel tears start to sting the back of my eyes and I swallow a deep breath, trying to take in air and dignity at the same time. "I love you, Eric. I can't help it … it wasn't on purpose. Don't you love me?"

I know I sound pathetic. I don't care. I am exactly the woman I have tried never to be: needy, in denial, weak. In love. And I know I can make him fall in love with me, if he just gives me a chance.

Eric's next words have the potential to make it all worthwhile, to instantly transform me into someone strong and persistent who saw the truth of our love even before it was really real. His declaration of love will validate these many months of telling myself he could change—would change—once he realized I was The One.

"I like you a lot. I really do. You're one of my favorite people. We're great pals."

Great pals? Great pals?!? What am I, your fishing buddy? Your Fantasy Football teammate? Listen, mister, I don't fuck my pals.

I'm about to say this to him, but I realize he's still talking, and his words cause a sudden pain in my chest and a brief urge to throw up, "... but I don't love you, Viv. I'm sorry. I'm—no. I'm not sorry. I was honest. I told you from the start. You chose not to hear me and now ..."

He lets the sentence wither like a grape on a vine until the whole moment shrivels up and dies. Before I can decide if I should cry or beg or take off all my clothes, he starts to gather his bags. I realize in a flash of panic that nothing can make him stay. He has to want to, and he doesn't.

He wraps one arm around me, the other holding his bags slightly aloft so they don't knock into me. He knows as well as I do that the slightest breeze could send me reeling right now.

"Please don't go," I whisper. "Stay with me. Stay the night with me."

"I can't."

Without any more explanation or apology, he is gone.

As the door clicks shut a wave of anger crashes over me. I wipe my eyes and run to the door, flinging it open. I step out into the hall but keep my hands on the doorframe to steady myself as I hurl my voice down the corridor.

"You're a heartless asshole, Eric! A heartless fucking asshole! If I never see you again it will be too soon!" I'm so upset that I find myself channeling my mom, as I shriek after him, *"No lo puedo creer, vete al infierno! Arrogante!! Sin corazon! Pedazo de mierda!"*

He doesn't turn to look at me but I see his face crumple in what appears to be genuine sadness. He knows enough Spanish to know that I just called him an arrogant, heartless piece of shit and told him to go to Hell. When the elevator doors open at last, he half-opens his mouth and begins to turn to say something, but before he can so much as inhale I retreat back inside and slam the door. I might not be able to walk away or move to London, but at least I can have this victory.

This empty apartment.

This cold bed.

This broken heart.

This stupid, stupid broken heart.

CHAPTER 20:
LIFE AFTER LUST

So, there it is. I dumped the perfect guy for the perfect lay who, in turn, dumped me for his perfect life. My blog followers and friends all warned me, and I should have listened. I've never felt so stupid in my whole life. Torn between feeling heartbroken, used, gullible and idiotic, I beat myself up, unmercifully and nonstop. Stupid, stupid, stupid! Everything I've done since I met Eric's gorgeous ass has been one mistake after another.

Except for the blog—even if it did play a role in Eric dumping me—it's given me a outlet for a talent that I didn't realize I had until I found how much people enjoy my work. I love the sense of comradery I've developed with my readers, my new circle of cyberfriends.

And fuck him if he doesn't like what I wrote about us! I didn't use his name—I kept my blogs about us as vague as I could. He's the only one, outside of my friends, who could recognize that I was talking about him. Plus, if he had been more upfront with how he felt about me, I wouldn't have written what I wrote!

I'm so upset after he leaves that I write a long, scathing, therapeutic essay, fueled by an entire container of Ben and Jerry's Cherry Garcia and lots of champers. I have no intention of posting it though. I wouldn't give him the satisfaction. I'm saving it as a draft. I don't even care if it's well written. I just have to get it out of my system, and pouring my heart out into a blog has become a healing replacement for not having Lauren living close by.

I begin a new category, not even trying to be clever or poetic. It's plain and simple, because I'm not interested in being cute. I'm more interested in venting about how much I hate Eric:

THE MALE MODEL

Beware the male model, girls. Yes, he's tempting. He's gorgeous, he's exciting, and it's oh, so flattering to be chosen by someone so desirable. He'll flatter you and sweep you off your feet. But what he's actually doing is using you, like a sailor with a girl in every port. You're just a toy to him, something to fuck while he's in town. Check him out.

I find one of my favorite pictures of him online—the Dolce & Gabbana boxers ad—and add a link to it here.

Yep, that's him, at least my personal version of the Male Model. I didn't stand a chance, did I girls? Would you? Isn't he gorgeous? Wouldn't you fall head over heels for this guy, even if he wasn't the most charming, confident and skilled lover to ever fall into your bed?

But I'm giving all you other ladies fair

warning. Don't date him if you have the opportunity. You might think you will be able to just have a one-nighter—one glorious night of sex with the most exquisite male specimen you're likely to ever get your hands on. But with this kind of man, you'll be hooked.

He'll let you think that you're his best girl. He'll tell you how much fun he has when he's with you. You'll be flattered that he shares his favorite pastimes with you and he might even take you to church with him! Yes, he'll take you to visit God which, in my eyes, is more meaningful than taking you home to meet his parents.

You should know, however, that he's only doing his favorite things with you just because he wants someone to hang out with, not because of a desire to share intimacy and get to know one another.

He'll talk about his world travels, and share stories about the exotic places he visits. He'll show off the recipes he's found, and expect you to eat more than you should, just to please him. Heaven forbid you should wound his massive pride by daring to object to all of the calories he's trying to stuff down your throat. After all, *he's* the pretty one and his BMI is the only one that matters.

He'll pop over to your house, unexpected, and you'll be flattered that he thought of you over everyone else in a city this size. He'll get to know your place so well that the doorman lets him up without buzzing first. He'll become familiar with all the local restaurants and grocery stores. But you won't have a clue where he lives or if he even has a roommate.

He invades your day-to-day life so much that you feel like he's become a part of it, and you won't even notice that you know nothing about his. In fact, if you dare call him, he gets all, "We have to talk ..." so you become too afraid to call him and learn to ignore that this is how you communicate—you wait for *him* to call so you don't seem too pushy.

He'll keep you so flustered that you don't give any other men, even good men, a chance to win your heart because you've given it to him in the desperate hope that he wants it.

What he won't do is tell you the truth— that to him you're nothing but a temporary distraction. He'll make vague comments about how much fun you are to hang around with. He'll call you his pal. But because you're so head over heels in love with him—because he's caused you to be—you won't see that he considers you to be merely a friend with benefits.

Maybe it's true that women have a harder time separating sex and love, but it's hard not to fall in love with a man who treats you so well when he's with you. We women tend to bridge the time between one event and the next by thinking about him and anticipating the next time. It's hard to remember, when he's not with you, that he's not thinking about you. You're just something to do when he's bored.

And in the end, if you dare express that you have feelings for the man you've come to see as Prince Charming, he'll turn instantly into a toad and feed you a poisoned apple by saying it's your fault you're hurt. Then he'll disappear so fast that you'll wonder if the whole thing was just a dream, and you're waiting for his kiss to wake you up.

At this point, I'm so upset that I can't write another word. I'm mixing my metaphors and not even making sense anymore. But I got it out and I feel a little better.

There is no more ice cream left. Normally I would kick myself for gorging and falling into that kind of stereotypical and pathetic behavior, but I'm too pissed and hurt to care that I'm acting like a lovelorn teenager. I save the draft, close my laptop, turn on the TV to some mindless reality show and finish off the second bottle of champagne, straight out of the bottle.

Just as I'm dozing off, my phone blasts me back to life. It's Lauren's ringtone and I'll be damned if I can find the phone with my eyes shut, feeling around for it. I have to open my eyes and get up and, when I do, I see that it's morning. Early morning—like just after dawn—but the sun is coming through the window shade. I thought I had just drifted off the sleep, but apparently it was more of a crash.

Fumbling for the phone, I see the evidence of a bad night scattered all over the place—empty Ben and Jerry's container, two dead bottles of champagne, my laptop askew on the table—and I'm not sure which feels worse, the pain in my heart, or the pain in my head from too much sugar and booze.

I finally find the phone and barely have it to my ear before I hear Lauren screaming, "GIRL, WHAT DID YOU DO???"

"Wha … huh? I don't know. What did I do?"

"I can't believe you posted a blog about him!" she shrieks, "I can't believe you added a link to his picture and I can't believe that son of a bitch had the nerve to dump you like that!

"What? I didn't post a blog about him. What are you talking …" I hurry to my laptop and quickly open my blog dashboard. "I did write something last night, but I saved it as a draft." I'm mumbling at this point, desperately hoping that I'm remembering correctly.

Oh, shit. There it is, live as my most recent blog: THE MALE MODEL.

"OH MY GOD!" I scream, "I gotta go! Call you back!" I slam down the phone and immediately unpublish the blog. Oh fuck oh fuck oh fuck oh fuck, I hope he didn't see that. Please God, if you never do anything for me ever again, please God, don't let Eric have seen that blog.

I check my stats next, to see if anyone saw it. Thank God that it's so early and that I posted it so late. It was only up for a couple hours, and the blog only had a couple hits. One of them was Lauren. The odds against any of the other hits being Eric are astronomical.

I call Lauren back, "Thank God you called me! I didn't mean to post that. Holy shit, what would I have done if he saw that?

"I know! What were you thinking?"

"That's the problem. I wasn't thinking," I explain, "I was so upset that I must have posted it by mistake."

"Upset? You sure you weren't also a little drunk? It sure sounded like you were. You're not usually so … man, I don't even know the right word to use …"

"Yeah, I had been drinking. That's gotta be a new rule: no drinking and blogging."

"Well, that goes without saying! So tell, what happened?"

I give Lauren a blow by blow and, like the best friend that she is, she supports me and agrees that he's a rat bastard. In fact, she's such a good friend that she doesn't bother to say what we both know: I should have seen this coming.

In the light of day, and after re-reading what I accidentally—and temporarily—blogged about, I can see that there were signs. I was too blinded by infatuation to see them but, in my defense, he really was more vague than he should have been. He saw, early on, that I was falling for him and even though he half-heartedly tried to warn me, he should have ended it instead of stringing me along.

I vow to chalk it up to experience and leave it behind me, lesson learned. Therefore, in the weeks after he walked out of my life for good, I split my time evenly among writing, time with my girls, promoting the blog, and searching the deepest reaches of my soul for answers.

Okay, maybe my time wasn't split entirely evenly.

As I question and reexamine all that had happened between Eric and me, the truth of that relationship emerges: no matter how far I think I've evolved, part of me will always be the lonely, heavy-set girl with few friends, no romantic prospects, and enough self-loathing to sink the *Titanic*.

I'd be embarrassed by this confession if I hadn't gotten a rousing chorus of "Amen, sister!" from practically every woman I confided in. My friends—and even friends of friends—were ready and waiting to commiserate with me, ready to share the insecurities that they've allowed to define them. Define us.

It helps that one of those friends, Shannon, is always ready, willing and able to dissect relationship issues. I run into her at Whole Foods one evening when I stop in to get some organic veggies and a few healthy frozen dinners for those times when I'm trying to not cave into the craving for something bad for me—comfort food—and we end up leaving our carts in the middle of the aisle and walking across the street to Starbucks to get a much needed cup of caffeine. The irony that I've even learned to love coffee because of not wanting to disappoint Eric does not escape me.

I explain to her what happened, the whole thing, sparing no details and even sharing how some of it could be my own fault. I've finally come to a place where I can see that clearly. But she doesn't care about that. She's more interested in finding out if I have a pattern of certain kinds of relationships. "Didn't you used to do the same thing to other men that Eric did to you? You only dated musicians and artist types that you knew wouldn't want to get attached. Wasn't that a friendly arrangement? How is it different when Eric did the same?"

This pisses me off. "I was always honest with them, and they were honest with me. Everyone involved knew that those were fuck buddy situations. That's not exactly how this went down. I never knew where I stood with him!"

"Maybe so," Shannon continues, looking around at all of the people at their tables with their computers out or phones in hand, to see if they're listening— apparently I was kind of loud—"but didn't your dad dump your mom like this?" she asks.

"Not exactly. They were married for a while and had three kids. He did dump her suddenly, but it was for another woman. Mom was devastated, but the worst part was that he left her after draining their bank accounts and setting everything up in his favor. He planned it all behind her back. That's not anything like what happened between me and Eric."

"Maybe not, but I'm sure you ended up with abandonment issues, and you keep playing out the same pattern, over and over ..."

I roll my eyes and remind her how I feel about mommy and daddy issues. "That's not what I'm talking about," she says, "I mean, didn't you feel the same way when Eric left, like the person you trusted most and devoted all of your attention to, up and left after draining you of everything you put into this relationship?"

I recognize the parallel, but still don't see how it applies to me. "Shan, this wasn't a replay of that whole thing. This was a powerful sexual attraction that blinded me to what he was really like, and I felt like he played me. Then I mostly felt stupid for falling for it."

"Okay, but didn't your mom and dad have a passionate and tumultuous relationship? You've told me about their 'Latin love affair,' a macho Italian man and fiery Mexican woman. Didn't you once tell me about how your mom used to scream at him in

Spanish, like you did to Eric? You're just playing out the same storyline that you learned from your female role model, with a man who fits your father's role—a gorgeous and unattainable player. This is how you expect relationships with men to go down, and so that's what happens. Didn't you dump a perfectly nice, marriageable guy for this schmuck?"

I sneer into my coffee and gulp it down.

"How do you wish your mom had handled it when he left?"

"That's easy," I snort, "she could have had some dignity and not thrown herself at just about every man that came her way, marrying each and every one of them who offered to take care of her. She could have taken care of herself!"

"Is that what you're doing? You said you were in Whole Foods to buy some healthy stuff, but all I saw in your cart was chocolate and wine."

"That wine was organic! And besides, I ran into you before I got to the produce aisle."

"Okay," Shannon says, patting my arm, "let's just pretend you were actually going home with nothing but arugula. Are you getting any exercise? Are you dating anyone else? Or are you sitting at home, pining for the one that got away?"

"Shut up," I snarl, eyeballing the chocolate croissant on the table next to ours—it looks mighty good. "Maybe I was just hoping that I would be Angelina to his Brad."

"Honey, I know how hard it is. Come on. We *all* know how hard it is. But as your friend," she says sternly, "and I *am* your friend, I'm advising you to get off your ass and start taking your power back. You're giving this guy too much power over your head, your heart and your life."

As much as I hate to admit it, she's right. I've been wallowing in self-pity and embarrassment. All of my friends know how crazy I was about him, and it feels like they're all looking at me like I'm an idiot. They all tried to warn me, and I know that it's all Arianna can do to not lecture me about dumping Matthew for Canada. I vow to Shannon, "Starting right now, I'm letting him go. I'm putting him behind me and moving on."

"Well, let's start after an espresso. You deserve it." She goes to the counter and orders two shots. "Here's to one of the most beautiful goddesses I know!" Shannon says, opening two Sugar in the Raw packets and dumping them both into her tiny cup.

"Back atcha, babe!" I sweeten my own espresso, and blow on it to cool before tossing back the shot. I feel it hit my veins instantly and I involuntarily shudder, even if it is really good coffee. The high dose of caffeine and sugar hits fast, reigniting the fire in my soul.

"You know what? You're right about taking care of myself. I think I'll go for a run. Call me later?"

Shannon smiles and says, "Of course! I'm glad you're feeling better."

We air kiss and I head home to change. If I hurry, there will still be enough daylight to get in a decent run along the Hudson.

Running along the river gives me a lot of time to get lost in my thoughts. I really have given my power away. Before I met Eric, I felt great about myself and, since then—killer sex aside—I've been in an almost constant state of panic, wondering how he feels about me and whether I'll see him again. I realize how crazy

I've been. Wow. How did I get so far away from center?

My feet pound in rhythm as they beat the pavement. I'm glad I decided to go for this run. I needed it. I needed some time to think, to clear my head. The riverside is peaceful and other runners nod as they pass me, coming from the other direction. I feel a sense of connectedness with them, other folks who are trying to take care of themselves, who are taking some time out from the stresses of everyday life, like I used to. A bubble of joy works its way up from my heart to my lips and, not even caring if anyone is listening, I declare, "I'm back, baby! Look out Menhattan! Vivian Fiori is back!"

CHAPTER 21:
FRANKLY, MY DEAR ...

I take my sense of self-actualization straight to the blog, where I realize there must be thousands of women in predicaments just like mine, waiting for someone to admit the secret we all share. The response is instantaneous. Women flock to the blog to share their stories, comfort one another, remind each other that none of us is alone. For all our focus on the dangers of bullying in schools and office environments, on the playground and in domestic abuse scenarios, many of us have forgotten that our most serious aggressors are ourselves.

Now there's talk of changing the focus of the blog: *MEhattan: Getting lost and found in the world's greatest city.* It's just something my agent and I are thinking about. Did I not mention that? Yes, Vivian Fiori has representation at last.

I was surprised, during the course of my post-Eric blogging, by what I found when I searched the far reaches of my heart. Because what I discovered was that I missed Matthew. A lot. The problem was that I wasn't any better than Scarlett O'Hara, at long last realizing that she really loved Rhett Butler only after Ashley Wilkes finally told her that he loved Melanie all along. And we all know how that ended. I couldn't bear to call Matthew and lay my heart on the line just to possibly hear him say, "Frankly my dear …"

So what else could I do? I blogged about it. I poured my heart out to my cyberfriends, and got such an avalanche of support in return that I finally began to feel a little better, slowly but surely.

Then one day, after a particularly heartfelt blog about how I realized that I was selling myself short by chasing after an impossible dream, how I might have been using someone so gorgeous to feel better about myself—after all, if I could hook someone so divinely beautiful and exciting, I must be his equal—I saw a three-word comment buried among the paragraphs left for me by all the other women who've been there, done that.

It said, "Call me. M."

My heart actually skipped a beat, at the risk of sounding cliché. He didn't leave any sort of emoticon, or other indication to show why he wanted me to call. Was it because he still loves me? Does he want me to stop writing about him? Does he hate me? Does he want to chew me out some more, in response to what I've written?

Okay, Scarlett, I told myself, *here's your moment. Put on your red gown and go to that party.*

I didn't call. I chickened out and emailed him, "What's up?" I asked, hoping to sound light and breezy.

His email reply was encouraging: "I've been reading your blog. I'm sorry you're feeling so badly, but now you know how I felt. If it helps, I find that I'm still carrying a bit of a torch for you. Shall we discuss this?"

We meet for lunch and brewskies a few days later

at his favorite dive bar. We sit at "our booth" and order what Matthew promises are some really excellent chili dogs. I take a deep breath and do it. I reach out to him and tell him everything. Eric, the blog, how torn I'd felt between two such wonderful men, how I was more sure now—of him—than I've ever been of anything in my whole life.

"How convenient," he says, quietly. "That's me, Convenient Matthew, ready, willing and able to pick up where the better man left off."

"Damn, Matt, that's harsh!" His comment feels like a blow.

He gives me a wide-eyed look of disbelief, as if to say "Who's calling who harsh???" He clears his throat and says, "You know, when my wife left me, I never thought I'd trust a woman again. I know that sounds trite, but I dedicated my life to her and our children. I was in for the long haul, and when she made her big announcement, I was devastated. Truly. Devastated. I swore off marriage forever."

The look in his eyes says that he really means what he's saying. He isn't just being dramatic to get at me. I take his hand and say, meekly, "I'm sorry … I never meant …"

Matthew pulls his hand away and interrupts, "No, hear me out. I just … want you to know what a big risk I took in opening my heart to you. I felt like you were different, like you were real. Like," he pauses, searching for the right words, "like we had a connection beyond the day-to-day bullshit of dating and fucking and all that singles crap. I felt like … like you were the one." His voice trails off and he sits, silent, for a moment.

I try to smile, but it comes out more of a

grimace. I feel horrible.

"And then," he declares, coming back to life, "I come over to your place to surprise you and declare my undying love—the kind of scene you women love in the movies—and find ..." his eyes get big and he gestures with frustration, "*him* ... this perfect male specimen, obviously very at ease in your home, and you, looking so guilty ... well, I just felt like I'd been kicked in the teeth."

I admit that I totally understand how he must have felt and apologize for the umpteenth time. "Look," I say, "I know I would have felt the same way in your situation, and I'm *really* sorry you were hurt. But can't you try to see how you'd feel if you were in my shoes? I had to find out which of you were right for me. I didn't expect you to come over trying to sweep me off my feet."

He rolls his eyes, as I continue, "If I had gone ahead and taken the safe path, with you, I never would have known what could have been with Eric. I would have lain in your arms at night, wishing I was with him, wondering what our life together might have been like."

He looks stunned and hurt by what I'm saying, but hey, it's now or never—time to lay all of our cards on the table. "Think about that. I know it's hard to hear, but wouldn't you rather know that you have all of me, heart and soul, and that I'm not thinking about someone else?"

"Yeah, someone else who dumped you. Where would you be if he hadn't? Not sitting here with me, that's for sure."

Ouch. That hurts. But he has a point. "Maybe. But I don't think I would have been happy, in the long run."

He looks dubious so I add, "Seriously, I've come to realize that what I felt for him was not much more than an intense physical attraction. I rarely felt good about myself when I was with him. I was always second guessing myself. Will he stay or will he go? Am I pretty enough? Am I interesting enough? Why doesn't he call? What's wrong with me???" I wave my hands in the air, dramatically looking up toward heaven.

Matthew tries to laugh, picturing me being so flustered and fucked up.

"And most importantly, I know that I could've never had a conversation like this with him. He wouldn't—or couldn't—connect on anything beyond a surface level. That's why his dumping me took me by surprise, because he was never this honest with me. He thinks he was, but he knew I was starting to fall for him. He gave me light warnings, like 'Hey, I don't wanna get serious'" I mock his casual tone and make my voice sound stupid, "but he should have broken it off with me earlier and entirely, instead of being so casual with my heart."

"As casual as you were with mine," Matthew mutters and looks down at his hands, laying folded there on the table.

"No, that's not true. I gave the idea of a relationship with you careful consideration. I really did. Hey," I say, taking his hands to make him look up at me, "sincerely. I really did. And you were winning. He was giving me one of his let's-be-friends speeches when you walked in and ruined your own chances." I laugh, hoping he'll take the bait to break the tension.

He takes pity on me and laughs, a little. "Okay. So it's my own fault. I guess I need to call first before coming over. So much for standing under your window with a boom box, huh?"

"Yeah, I don't think that would go over very well with my neighbors." I smile and squeeze his hands. "Are we okay?"

"Well, we're better. Not quite okay. I'd love to try again, but I think it's best if we start from scratch."

"I agree. Square one. Total honesty."

"Perfect. By the way, there's this book you might want to read …"

I interrupt him and make a fist. "If you say *He's Just Not That Into You*," I say, through gritted teeth, "I. Will. Flatten. You."

He puts his hands up defensively, "Whoa. Okay. Calm down! So much violence." He shakes his head and tsks at me, "So, I guess you have read it." He looks thoughtful for a moment and rubs his chin, "Huh. Couldn't tell …"

"Alright! That's enough! I was an idiot, okay? Can we drop it and move on?"

He looks me in the eyes, "Can we also make it exclusive this time? You know, I'm kind of a great catch."

He is, indeed. This idea makes me very happy. I beam at him, "Sure, Matthew. We sure can."

CHAPTER 22:
HAPPILY EVER AFTER?

I never thought in a million years he'd take me back, but I was surprised yet again. He only made me sweat it out a little—he easily forgave me and said he knew all along I'd be back. We promised each other to take it slow, but it didn't take long to get right back where we left off. We've been inseparable ever since.

We both like to travel, and I've discovered that Matthew is a bit of a thrill-seeker. He's talked me into accompanying him, albeit reluctantly, on some of his adventures, and only because I feel so safe and secure with him in every other context, I figure I might as well use that to push my boundaries a bit. There was the afternoon spent test-racing Ferraris and an entire weekend of heli-skiing. Today we're skydiving. Matthew booked us into a little B&B for the night, so we'll land in a field close by.

This is just everyday life with Matthew. I mean, not that we do this kind of thing every day, but often enough that it's not unusual. Life with him is adventure and romance, thoughtfulness without smothering, the finer things in life with no pretense. When we finally made love, it was—at the risk of sounding trite—magical. I've never felt so deeply loved. Fireworks, rose petals, violins, all the clichés fit what it feels like when I'm laying in the arms of a man who adores me and wants nothing more than to please and pamper me.

It's almost too good to be true—I'm living my wildest dream. Sometimes I feel guilty because I'm so happy and so many people I care about are having a hard time of it. I feel so blessed and, as Shannon would say, like I've finally found the right karma with my soul mate. I can't believe I thought life with Eric would be more exciting.

We pull up to the launch point and are met by a team of men eager to help us. We're getting the VIP treatment as usual, so we are privately walked through the safety protocols and equipment instruction. I'll be tandem jumping with a burly guy named Phil. After we sign standard release forms that hold the diving company harmless if I splat like ripe fruit thrown off a rooftop, Phil pats me on the back and says, "You'll be fine. Almost no one dies doing this."

Almost. *Gulp.*

Matthew looks a little nervous, which isn't like him. I don't look at him too much since I don't want his anxiety to scare the bejesus out of me, but we hold hands as we're ushered onto a little plane. We keep our fingers intertwined the whole way up.

Once the crew pulls the hatch open, I find that I'm gripping Matthew's hand for dear life. Turning to me, he says, "You know I'll always be here. There's nothing to be afraid of."

"I know, love."

That's all I can squeak out before I have to shut my mouth and swallow hard to keep from vomiting all over Matthew's handsome face which, not for nothing, seems to glow with new confidence. I'm not sure where he found so much gumption—it's been a short flight—but I'm trying to take heart.

"Let's do it!" I say, hoping the enthusiasm in my voice sinks all the way into my bones.

There's a lot of maneuvering, a lot of strapping-in and thumbs-up confirming, and then there is nothing—just me, falling. I don't even realize that I'm screaming bloody murder at the top of my lungs until I look at Matthew and see that not only is he *not* screaming, but he's rooting around in the breast pocket of his jump suit. The crew is in charge of taking pictures, so what the hell is he looking for? If that man answers his BlackBerry ...

But it's not a phone Matthew reaches for. It's a piece of paper. He holds it close to his chest and reads it quickly before gripping it at the edges and turning it to face me. It's comical to watch him fight the wind and hang on to it. I don't think he really thought this out very well.

WILL YOU MARRY ME?

Now my mouth is open, but no sound comes out, just a little bit of slobber that the high wind levels kick out. I slam my mouth shut and hope that Matthew doesn't see. I don't feel like I'm falling at all anymore—just suspended in the air like gravity has stopped working and we're all just floating, weightless and angelic.

The first thought that runs through my head is, *how did I ever think this guy was boring?*

I feel the smile spread across my face like sunshine across the bedspread on a Sunday morning. It warms me even as the wind whips our clothes, struggling to keep us afloat.

I nod. Yes, Matthew—yes, I will be your wife.

I see Phil's thumbs-up in my peripheral vision

but I'm just looking at Matthew now, staring at my husband-to-be, my fiancé.

I press my eyes closed and see my life flash before my eyes. I can't tell if it's the way I'm hurtling toward the earth at what feels like a million miles an hour, or the fact that I have just agreed to get married that's making me feel so alive. Just as I resolve to split the difference, I feel Phil tap my shoulder. We're ready to land.

We slide in softly. A wave of adrenaline hits me as Phil is releasing me from the harness and my legs start to shake. My heart is in my throat as Matthew runs over to me, drops to one knee, and presents me with the most beautiful ring I have ever seen. The center stone must be three carats at least, and it's flanked in diamonds set in the most intricate, brilliant setting I could imagine.

"I love you, Vivian," he says. Both of us are suddenly breathless. "I can't wait to marry you."

"Me, either," I say. *Right? YES! Of course.*

I text the girls as we board a town car that will take us to the inn. Matthew is pressing a champagne flute into my hand. By the time we arrive in our room—filled with fresh flowers, rose petals strewn on every available flat surface—our friends and families have offered their congratulations and I've downed two glasses of champers. I'm heady and giddy and over the moon. In fact, I realize that I finally know what people mean when they say "over the moon." I am celestial, out-of-this-world, lunar.

I'm happy.

"I booked you a massage," Matthew says, nuzzling my neck.

"You think of everything, don't you?"

"Yes. Yes, I do," he deadpans. "Now go. Relax. I'll be right here."

"Matthew, this … I … it's all just so …"

"I know."

"I just can't find the—"

"You don't have to, Viv. You agreed to be my wife. Nothing I could buy you will ever compare to the enormity of that gift."

"I love you."

"See? You found the right words after all."

We share a kiss—a deep, magical, toe-curling kiss that almost makes me wish I weren't about to get a massage. But Matthew gently pushes me toward the door and points me toward the spa. I let this sense of peace and well-being seep into my veins. I feel incredibly blessed. So blessed, in fact, that I step outside for a brief moment so I can take a picture of my ring in full sunlight before texting it to Arianna for approval.

Well done, she writes.

Right?! I text back.

I set my phone down as I change into a robe. There's no way I'm taking off my new ring—they'll have to pry this thing off me once I'm good and dead. My phone vibrates and I know it's Arianna, who's probably already busy making plans for a bachelorette party to end all bachelorette parties.

When I glance at the screen, though, I see that the long message isn't from Arianna. In fact, it's from a number I don't even recognize.

I read your blog the morning after we broke up. You must have taken it down because I can't find it anymore. I don't like what you said, but I have to admit that some of what happened was my fault. I'm sorry. I didn't realize how I was coming off to you and I screwed up big. I can't stop thinking about you and realize now that I love you. I'm coming back for you and I'm not taking no for an answer. —E

O.

M.

G.

My heart lurches in my chest and I feel nauseated. Oh, fuck! Why now? Where was he two days ago, before Matthew and I left on this trip, or two hours ago before I accepted his proposal? Or two months ago, when I was going through heartbreak hell?

Against my will, I feel that old tingle between my legs that takes my breath away. I can't believe it. What is wrong with me? Matthew is like the hero in a romance novel, for God's sake. We're going to get married. I love him. Sex with Matthew is beautiful and romantic and I would be selfish to wish for anything more.

And yet … sex with Eric was electric and earth shattering, and he wasn't even trying. I can only imagine what it would be like if he actually loved me, and my mind is racing with thoughts of what could have been … what still could be.

#VivianFioriYouAreFUCKED.

AUTHOR BIOS

Dating advice and beauty bloggers Victoria Flores and Leslie Wilson are best friends living in New York City, who are both finally married with children on the way. The authors have been featured in the Huffington Post, New York Magazine, Self Magazine, Cosmo Latina, Hamptons Magazine and many others.

Lisa Bonnice is an award-winning, best-selling author and former standup comedienne. Her other books include:

Shape Shifting—reclaiming your perfect body
The Shape Shifter's Daily Diary
Be Careful What You Witch For!
Fear of Our Father

The Menhattan Project
by Victoria Flores & Leslie Wilson
with Lisa Bonnice

Facebook: www.facebook.com/MenhattanProject
Twitter: www.twitter.com/MenhattanBook
Wordpress: menhattanproject.wordpress.com

Lisa Bonnice's home page: www.lisabonnice.com

Cover design by Nilantha Rathnayaka